THE KUMBH CONSPIRACY

THE KUMBH CONSPIRACY

Shubira
Prasad

Vitasta

Published by
Renu Kaul Verma
Vitasta Publishing Pvt Ltd
2/15, Ansari Road, Daryaganj
New Delhi - 110 002
info@vitastapublishing.com

ISBN: 978-93-90961-70-2

First Edition 2023
MRP ₹399

Edited by Shailaja Nair, Wordmeister
Typeset & Cover Design by Somesh Kumar Mishra
Printed by Chaman Enterprises, New Delhi

To

My father, Late Shri Anant Swarup,
from whom I inherited my extreme
love for reading

Contents

Good News	1
The Great Kumbha	25
Kritimukha	39
Vajra	55
Rompo	77
Kabandha	93
Farasi	108
Holiday With The Twins	128
Adheesh Who?	142
Asuri	160
Bhaumastra	177
So Many Children	191
Sarama, The Female Dog	207
Pey And Peymakilir	222

Dahurasuran 234
Fire And Varunastra 254
Another World 273
Alternate World 294

Acknowledgements *313*
About The Author *315*

GOOD NEWS

As usual, Aishani got up early in the morning. Adheesh was still sleeping. She knew that he would also wake up soon and join her for a cup of green tea. That was their sacred time together. But this was her time, her very own time, with only her and her soul together, nothing else. She would sip a glass of water, sit quietly and stare at the vision in front of her and contemplate her life – past, present and future. Or sometimes not think at all. This early morning tryst with herself kept her grounded and tethered to her world and beyond it too. But for the past few days, the mornings were not as pleasant or reviving as they had been earlier. She would wake up with a bitter and nauseous feeling in her mouth which would continue for the next hour or so. Maybe she was coming down with a fever, but her body did not feel warm or feverish. She did not tell Adheesh as she did not want him fussing over her.

This morning, she just sat on her balcony, trying to soothe herself with the twittering and warbling of the birds who were just coming out of their slumber and were now waking their brethren and the young ones. Oh! children were children, any species and anywhere in the world. Suddenly a thought flashed in her mind. She was dazed by her own deliberation. Could it be true? She felt a bit nervous. Well, one thing was sure, she wasn't going to share her feelings with anybody as yet. At least not until she was a hundred per cent sure.

First, she had to come to terms with her own thoughts. She peeped into the bedroom. Adheesh was stirring in his sleep. A wave of sheer tenderness enveloped her. He was her husband, her lover, her guide, her protector and maybe something else too. She blushed. This had not happened in any of their previous births, she was sure of it. She shook her head. She would not go in that direction.

Adheesh had woken up and was now coming out of the bedroom, seeking his morning tea. She went up to him and kissed him. He kissed her back, slightly but pleasantly surprised. They had their tea in comfortable silence. Their life was such that these were indeed very precious moments not to be wasted on any shoptalk or demon-talk or any other inane topic.

Later, they went to the Gurukul. Adheesh went to the library. After that he would go to the meditation hall. This greatly helped him in enhancing his potential and effectiveness. Both of them practiced archery and other martial arts with the senior students, which benefitted both the students and them too. Aishani went to meet Ruby. They met in their favourite place or what once used to be their favourite place. They loved to sit on the rocks half submerged in the stream that ran through the Gurukul. It was just slightly away from the hustle and bustle of the main Gurukul though still comfortably near it.

'It's been such a long time, Ash. Remember how we used to come here daily and spend loads of time on these rocks? What fun we had!' Ruby reminisced. Then she looked at Aishani closely. 'Why so off-colour, Ash? Are you OK?'

Ruby looked perplexed when Aishani did not answer. They were extremely close to each other. Ruby waited silently for Aishani to speak her mind. Aishani seemed to be mulling over something. She finally looked up at Ruby. 'I get nauseous in the morning,' she whispered.

Ruby smiled. 'Oh that's nothing Ash, you must be eating very little or no dinner at night. It is nothing which an extra chapati won't sort out.' She paused for a minute. She looked thunderstruck.

'Don't tell me! Ash! Really?'

'I don't know, Ruby. You are the only one I could turn to. The others would not have been able to hold their excitement. It would have made headlines everywhere. And I'm not even sure myself as yet.'

They talked some more with Ruby asking some pertinent but probing questions. Finally, they arrived at the conclusion that Aishani was indeed pregnant. Ruby hugged Aishani. Her eyes glistened with tears of happiness. 'Does Adheesh know about this,' she asked.

'Not yet.'

'He should be the first person to know. I am honoured that you told me, but I think you should tell him now and face the storm along with him," Ruby said, sounding a bit sad. Aishani noticed her sadncss. "Do you want to tell me now Ruby? Can you muster enough courage to confide in me now?'

Silent tears fell from Ruby's closed eyes.

'That baby is yours.' Aishani didn't ask, she stated. Ruby nodded dully.

'Oh, my dear!' Aishani enveloped Ruby in a hug. 'What tortures you must have gone through, having your baby in front of you and not being able to acknowledge it. May I ask who the father is?' Aishani asked.

Ruby was quiet for some time. Then she whispered, 'Swami Sivananda.'

'Who?' Aishani did not remember any such person. Ruby was silent but her expression was tortured, then the words came tumbling out, as if a torrent broke inside her.

'He had come to visit our ashram with the exchange program students. He was a great teacher and scholar. You know there are many Gurukuls all over the world with exceptionally talented and capable warriors, but our Gurukul stands out because of you and Adheesh. Your combination is blessed by the Gods themselves. Then Guruji is rumoured to be the avatar of Hanumanji himself. He is your Guru too. In such a scenario who wouldn't like to poach both of you!'

'Oh yes! I remember now. He was such an excellent teacher. I learnt many things from him,' Aishani said. Then her eyes narrowed. 'What has that got to do with you? Oh! Don't tell me, you fell for him!'

'Not really then,' Ruby said with a grimace, and then went ahead bravely, 'Guruji guessed Sivananda's plan to spirit away both of you. It is my official duty to protect you, and I am an apsara too.'

Aishani looked shocked. 'So, you had to entice him away from me. Oh Ruby! Why didn't you tell me?'

'It wouldn't have served any purpose except to upset you. I had Guruji's orders too. One thing led to another and then....'

'Oh, Ruby how did you manage the whole thing?'

'Well Ash, I had to confide in my mother. There was no problem there. Ma knows the whole scenario and who I am. Furthermore, Ma is also a protector, albeit the non-operational kind. Ma cooked up a story that we had to go my aunt's place to help in her delivery. We returned with my baby. I don't really know what Ma said. But no eyebrows were raised, and Ma has been raising my baby since then. Ma concocted a story that my aunt died in childbirth, and since there was nobody there to care for the baby, she brought him with us. For this reason, I stay in the Gurukul most of the time.'

Aishani nodded, though she couldn't really come to terms with the whole scenario.

'What about Swami Sivananda? He just left you?'

'When he realized his folly, he was smitten by remorse. He knew that with this one mistake his fate as the head of any Gurukul was sealed. He went to the Himalayas to perform penance and meditate. It might be years before he comes back, if at all.'

'Does he know about the baby?'

'No, he doesn't. He would have never forgiven himself had he known about the baby. Even I got to know about the baby only later. He just left the Gurukul one morning. Ash,

I don't want to talk about this anymore. I've taken the whole thing in my stride,' Ruby smiled tremulously and turned to Aishani. 'Let's talk about you.'

Aishani was still thinking about Ruby and her baby. She had seen the baby once or twice and readily believed the story about him. She had been so busy with her own problems that she didn't even think of probing this angle. But Ruby was not going to have any of it now.

'I'm so happy for you, Ash,' she said, hugging Aishani. 'Tell Adheesh fast or I'll tell him,' she warned. Aishani smiled despite herself. She felt quite excited.

'Yes, Ruby, but I have to be completely sure myself first.'

'What else do you want to confirm? We've calculated and this is it! Oh Ash! I'm so happy for you,' Ruby repeated.

Ash smiled. Dear Ruby, her dearest friend, nobody could have a better friend and protector than her. 'I love you, Ruby. You are a part of my soul. My heart always lights up when I think of you.'

Ruby wiped both of their tears. 'Enough of this, Ash,' she said. Then she giggled. 'Remember the invisible cape which uncle gave you on your birthday?' Aishani nodded.

'Well, now our children will play with it!'

'Oh! Where is it? I had kept it so safely in my cupboard, but after the house burned down, I don't know…'

'Don't worry, Ash. I have it with me. I took it out when the house started burning. Nobody else knew about its existence anyway.'

Aishani sighed with happiness. 'Ruby, you're the best.'

'That I am,' Ruby said with a smile.

They walked in companionable silence towards the Gurukul and then went to their respective practice sessions.

It was a normal day at the Gurukul but there was nothing normal about it for Aishani. She was in a state of flux. After talking to Ruby, she couldn't wait to go home and tell Adheesh. The minutes passed slowly. She could not concentrate on anything.

Finally, Adheesh and she were alone after dinner. During dinner, her mother-in-law had commented on her refusing to eat the two vegetables and her wan complexion. 'Ash beta, you're working too hard. You must eat. You need energy for your kind of strenuous practice.'

'Yes, Ma. I have a slight headache. I'll take an aspirin and I'll be all right in the morning.'

'Ok beta, go and take rest,' Anujaji said. The couple went upstairs. Adheesh went to the medicine cabinet to get some aspirin for her.

'Adhee, come here and sit with me on the balcony,' Aishani said.

'OK,' he answered, walking out with a glass of water. 'Take the aspirin first,' he said, handing her the water and the tablet.

She kept the water and the aspirin on the table and turned towards him. 'Adhee, I have to tell you something.'

Adheesh waited for her to say something. She took his hand and said, 'Adhee, I missed my periods.'

Adheesh looked at her for some time, a bit puzzled, and then understanding dawned on him. 'Ash, you don't say!' He took her in his arms. 'Ash is this really true?' he asked delightedly. She nodded. Tightening his arms around her and asked in a thoughtful manner, 'Ash, did we ever have children?'

'I don't know, Adhee. Maybe we didn't, or we would have remembered something or someone,' she whispered.

'I can't believe it! We are going to become parents! When did we…?'

Aishani laughed and hit him playfully, 'Romeo, you made sure that you had time for things which you wanted, apart from killing demons.'

They hugged again joyfully. 'Are you completely sure?' he asked. She nodded dreamily.

'Let's go to bed now Adhee, it's getting late now. Tomorrow is another long day.'

'Yes, shall we tell everyone tomorrow then?' he asked her.

'We'll have to. Adhee, I feel so shy.'

'Yeah, me too.'

They laughed again and went to bed.

The next morning there was uproar when Adheesh broke the news to his family members. There was much backslapping and yelling of congratulations. Aishani's mother-in-law immediately began to fuss. Adheesh's dietician aunt who was close to them in age immediately wrote a list of do's and don'ts for Aishani to follow. Everyone wanted to add their two pennies' worth of advice. Soon Adheesh and Aishani left for the Gurukul. They sat down under their favourite tree behind the classrooms.

'Whew! That was some awesome reaction. Think what it will be like when the baby is born.' Aishani smiled.

'Adhee, we have to inform some more people.'

'Hmm… like who?'

'Well, for starters, Guruji and my family, not necessarily in that order. Let us go to Guruji first, then you can drop me to Amma's place.'

'Uh Ash, what do we tell Guruji?'

'Nothing. We just go and sit in front of him and stay quiet and let Guruji guess.'

Adheesh nodded. They went and sat in front of Guruji. Guruji's eyes were closed but they knew from experience that his meditation was about to end. They waited patiently. Patience was something that had been inculcated in them over centuries. Finally, Guruji opened his eyes and looked at them. Aishani blushed and Adheesh looked abashed.

Guruji blessed them. This was the usual blessing, not for their news. Guruji looked at them questioningly. When they did not say anything, Guruji also kept quiet. Then suddenly Guruji smiled.

'My children, my old bones have been waiting to hear this news. What did not happen earlier has happened now. My blessings are always there with both of you, now they are there for your progeny too.' Turning to Aishani, Guruji said, 'Beta you can take the full time off for as long as you want. In the meantime, your smaller works will be taken over by other people.'

Aishani looked at Guruji. 'Guruji, now there is all the more reason to destroy the demons. The world has to be a cleaner place for the next generation,' she said vehemently. 'I am fine and totally fit to discharge my duties.' She did not look at Adheesh who was somewhat familiar with her morning sickness.

Guruji looked at them for some time and then said, 'So be it. Still, unless it is of prime importance, you can pick and choose your assignments. Life is very unpredictable, beta, and more shocking and interesting than any story or novel. We just have to accept things as they come and tackle them in the best way we can.'

They nodded, touched Guruji's feet and left for Aishani's home. The Gurukul was looking so beautiful. All the sounds around them – the twittering of the birds, the sighing of the wind through the trees, the stream gurgling in the distance, even the twigs and the small broken branches seemed to be sharing in their happiness. They held hands and crossed the Gurukul towards Aishani's home.

'How I wish Baba was here to share our happiness,' she said.

'Same here, Ash. I miss Panditji very much.'

'Adheesh, why did Guruji say such serious things about life? Did he mean anything or was it just a general sermon?'

'Well, you know Guruji, Ash. He never says anything out of context. Maybe he was telling us about our life in general. Look at us. What do we do? We go about merrily killing demons and feel good about it. Who would believe us? We are living double lives, rather parallel lives. Normal human beings would never be able to comprehend our nature of work. Maybe Guruji meant that.'

'Adhee, do you think Guruji was warning us in some way? Was he warning us about the pregnancy or the baby?'

Adheesh silently mulled over her question. 'I don't think so, Ash. Guruji always speaks straight and plainly to us. This is not the time to mull over such things. Let us be happy and rejoice over our good luck.' Aishani smiled.

Madhuji was overwhelmed when she heard the news. Tejas and Jayant were grinning from ear to ear. Uday was also there. With a big grin, he congratulated Adheesh and Aishani. Uday went inside the library and stood in front of the window. Uday stared at the garden unseeingly. There was a familiar dull ache in his heart of which even he himself was not aware most of the time.

Madhuji fussed around Aishani, wiping the tears that flowed down her cheeks. Everybody knew that the tears were for her husband Pandit Ram Sharan.

'What would you like to eat, beta? What kind of cravings do you have? Pickles or sweets?'

Aishani rolled her eyes. 'Amma, halt!' she said with a laugh. 'I have no cravings. In fact, I don't feel like eating, drinking or even smelling anything.'

'Yes, aunty,' Adheesh chimed in. He had started calling Madhuji aunty. 'Ash has to go for a full check-up and all the tests tomorrow. Pitaji's orders.'

'Of course, beta,' Madhuji said. 'Your father's hospitals have the best facilities, and all precautions have to be taken.'

They stayed at Madhuji's house for some more time and then left for Adheesh's home.

The next day Aishani's pregnancy was officially confirmed. Her other reports came a bit later. Both Adheesh and Aishani were sitting in the gynaecologist's office. She had Aishani's reports before her. Dr. Saroj Mukherjee smiled and said, 'Everything is perfectly fine. You're a very strong woman,

Aishani, and you will sail through your pregnancy with your babies.'

They smiled just a bit perplexed, then looked at the doctor who burst out laughing. 'Congratulations! You are going to have twins.'

'Twins?'

'Yes, twins. It will be a little difficult in the beginning but later it will be a delight when both of them grow up a little. The bond between twins is the strongest of all. They will be their own companions and won't really require too many friends.' Turning towards Adheesh, she said, 'You will have to take extra care of her. Aishani is healthy and strong, but just that extra touch will be required because of the twins.'

'Yes, ma'am,' Adheesh said, still in a daze.

Gathering their wits and reports, they left the hospital, still stunned by the shocking but pleasant and welcome news. They had driven down to the hospital because of Aishani's morning sickness. Once home, she hugged him joyfully. 'Oh Adhee, I'm so scared! How will we look after two babies, what with all our work and all? I don't want to sit at home all the time.'

'Ash, have you any idea how many people will be looking forward to taking care for our babies? I have a strong feeling that Devnath might leave his job and apply to you for a babysitter's job!'

They both laughed at this.

'What will we have?' she mused dreamily. 'Two boys or two girls or one boy and one girl? What do you think, Adhee?'

Adheesh smiled at her innocence. 'It's already been

decided, doll. We don't have a say in that any more than we had earlier. Let us enjoy our life as much as we can for the time being. Who knows what the future will bring? Let's pray for healthy children.'

Aishani sobered up at the thought. 'Yes, Adhee, we must enjoy this pregnancy and then the babies.'

Adheesh took her face in his hands. 'Promise me this, Ash, promise me that you'll take care of yourself when I'm away. I know that you are very reserved and shy, and you will ignore your minor ailments. You know both our families will be at your beck and call.'

'That is what I don't want, Adhee. I am not used to people fussing around me. But if you say so, I will inform them if I feel uncomfortable.'

'That's my girl!' Adheesh kissed her again.

Life went on as usual. And not so usual. There was happiness and there was tension. Everyone in both their families was looking forward to the birth of the babies. These babies would be the first of their generation. Adheesh's uncles Kedar and Kalpesh did not have any children yet, so these children would be the first arrivals.

At last, the day came, and Aishani delivered two healthy babies, a boy and a girl. Both households and even the hospital staff were thrilled and happy. It wasn't every day that the owner's grandchildren were born here. A wave of sheer happiness enveloped all of them. Everyone wanted to see and hold the babies, but there were strict instructions from Dr. Kedar, Adheesh's uncle who was a surgeon and one of the administrators of the hospital.

Aishani was doing very well, albeit very tired. She just wanted Adheesh to be with her. She wanted to share her babies with him. Whenever Adheesh was with her, they would just hold their babies and marvel at what they had created. It seemed to them as if they were the only parents in the world to have performed this feat.

Aishani was discharged from the hospital after three days. Her mother-in-law had made full arrangements for her care and comfort. Their bedroom had been shifted to the ground floor so that everyone could be at Aishani's side at a moment's notice. Aishani did not go to her mother's place, so Madhuji came to stay with her. On the sixth day of the twin's birth was their Chhathi. This was a religious ceremony when the babies were introduced to the rest of the household. A pundit came to perform the prayers in which the deities, the children's ancestors, birds, animals, plants and many more entities were invited to come and bless the babies. It is said that on this day the child's destiny is written by Vidhata or Brahmaji who is a part of the holy trinity. The babies were named Darsh and Divya. Vidyadharji had a large circle of family and friends. All of them were invited to come and bless the babies. It was a huge affair. Adheesh and Aishani were there for the puja after which Aishani retired with the babies while Adheesh mingled with the guests. Tejas was the most excited of all, jumping and prancing around in joy.

Gradually things began to settle down. Aishani was more confident in looking after the twins. Help was available for the asking but she wanted to do everything herself and she delighted in caring for her babies.

When the babies were two months old, Aishani and Adheesh decided to take them to the Gurukul to take Guruji's blessings. They drove to the entrance of the Gurukul and then walked down to Guruji's cottage. Adheesh was holding his daughter while Aishani carried her son. It was a beautiful sunny day with a cool breeze blowing gently through the trees, whispering through the leaves. Small birds were chattering here and there. It was the perfect day for the twins to be in the Gurukul. Adheesh and Aishani smiled at each other tenderly. Guruji's cottage was about half a mile away. The sky was darkening slowly as if it was going to rain. The birds stopped singing and everything was quiet. Suddenly, a murder of crows appeared, flapped their wings noisily and cawing loudly. Aishani almost jumped out of her skin at the loud cawing. Adheesh put his hands across her shoulders to reassure her. Aishani laughed sheepishly. 'Oh! I was startled for a few seconds. I still have to get used to walking with a baby in my arms.'

Adheesh didn't say anything. He merely pressed her shoulders again. 'I think Varun devata is also coming down to bless our babies,' he declared as the first few drops of rain fell on them. They went inside the cottage where Guruji was waiting for them. When they reached for the mats which were kept in a corner, Guruji stopped them. 'Here, take these mats. These have been specially made for the babies.' They smiled. Trust Guruji to surprise them with such a mundane thing as mats. They put the babies on the mats in front of Guruji. The babies were still sleeping soundly. They had slept through their parents' walk without being disturbed even by the crows. Guruji put his hands on their heads, closed his eyes, his lips barely moving as he silently chanted some mantras. They knew that Guruji was blessing the children and putting a Kavach or shield around them, thereby protecting them from all kinds of evil eye, unforeseen dangers, and negative energies. They were confident that after Guruji's blessings, their children would be safe from any negative energy hovering nearby. They noticed that Guruji was chanting more mantras over their son. They looked at each other in puzzlement but kept quiet and waited. Guruji knew best.

Because they were Adheesh and Aishani, they could make out the slight shimmer that began covering their babies as Guruji chanted the mantras. The safety shield would protect the babies for many years after which Guruji would put a stronger protective layer around them. This process would go on till the time the children were able to look after themselves. This initial shimmering layer was white and incorporated other pastel colours. These were soft colours because the babies were too young to endure anything stronger. They did notice with alarm that the glowing beam was not really covering their baby boy. After covering him for a moment it would just glide over and vanish. A normal human being would not have been able to see this anomaly. They would have just seen a mendicant blessing the babies. Aishani looked anxiously at Adheesh who motioned her to be calm.

At last, Guruji was satisfied and both babies were covered with the Raksha Kavach. The parents could see the protective shield surrounding their babies. They heaved a sigh of relief. Something had happened or something was there, they didn't know what, but Guruji had set it right. Guruji spoke to them.

'The almighty has sent both of you to this Earth to alleviate the suffering of the human beings here. The incongruity is that God has given human beings the intelligence to understand suffering and the greed to make mistakes repeatedly. So, they suffer greatly—that is the curse of human beings. Genuine suffering is here on Earth which every human being has to bear, subject to their past and present karmas. You are also human beings, albeit so superior that you are almost on the level of Devis and Devatas. You should always be prepared for suffering even if you have not indulged in any wrongdoing. That is the way of this world. Your ordeals are also harder than what normal human beings have to go through as both of you have more capacity to withstand the onslaught of the demonic forces, thus making our Mother Earth a better place to live in. Well, enough of this sermon, children. Go home safely, God is with you.' They touched Guruji's feet and left.

They were silent on the way back, mulling over what Guruji had said. Was he giving them a general sermon or was he warning them of some unprecedented happening? Was Guruji giving them some warning about their babies? Why did Guruji chant more mantras over Darsh and why did the Raksha Kavach keep slipping from over his small body?

Life went on and Adheesh and Aishani were as happy as they had hoped. The twins were a delight to everyone around them. They were happy children, laughing and crawling everywhere. In between Adheesh and Aishani went about their assignments whenever Guruji gave them a directive. Looking for and caring for the babies was no problem as people were falling over themselves to care for them and play with them.

Aishani and Adheesh loved them with all their hearts and wanted to be with them all the time, but they were seasoned warriors, and when on an exercise, there was no thought in their minds other than that precise engagement. Even their children could never become a disruptor or deterrent. Aishani missed her babies quite a lot during these engagements and tried to make up for the lost time whenever she was at home with them.

Though Divya and Darsh were twins, they were quite different in appearance. Divya was their darling doll, chubby with soft brown curly hair and rosy cheeks. She laughed at the slightest provocation and was friendly with everyone. Everybody was fascinated by her squeals of delight. In contrast, Darsh had dark hair, a long face, and was slimmer and more sober than his twin. The bond between brother and sister was apparent to any close observer. Divya easily had the upper hand in the relationship. She had become Darsh's protector even at such a young age. All her toys were for Darsh first, even their food was for him first. In the beginning, she would grow agitated whenever she heard Darsh crying. Later as they grew up, she would take her brother in her arms whenever he was uncomfortable. Darsh was a happy child, but he more serious and quieter. He liked to play in the garden, especially near the plant beds. Everyone loved to take the children into the garden and watch them play.

Once Madhuji was sitting in the garden with the twins, watching over them when she saw Darsh catch hold of a caterpillar and show it to his sister. Madhuji smiled but was taken aback when she saw Darsh smiling as he slowly crushed the caterpillar. Well, he was a baby and didn't know what he was doing. Madhuji dismissed the incident from her thoughts. However, there was another incident about six months later.

Both the babies had just started walking. It was more like a drunken walk. They were laughing and chasing butterflies. Darsh caught one butterfly and screamed in delight. Divya echoed his delighted scream. Then slowly and deliberately Darsh dismembered the butterfly – first the wings, then the antennae, then the legs and finally the head. Divya began to cry. Darsh tried to console her by catching another butterfly and giving it to her. This time Madhuji could not dismiss the incident. But she did not know how to tell Aishani. She would be heartbroken and so would Adheesh. How did this happen? While fighting the demons had some demon's blood mixed with theirs? There were so many questions in Madhuji's mind. There was so much that she didn't know. She knew that Aishani did not divulge everything to her as it would not be safe, and as she knew her mother would needlessly worry. Madhuji wondered how to let Aishani know in a gentle way her ghastly apprehensions. But she had to tell her. The sooner Darsh's behaviour was noticed and nipped in the bud, the better it would be.

Ultimately, Madhuji did not have to tell Aishani about Darsh's cruelty and to small creatures as Aishani herself noticed it. She had taken the twins to the hospital for one of their routine shots. Both Darsh and Divya were familiar with the hospital and many of the staff members. It was while Divya was being administered her medicine that Darsh noticed a few half-filled tubes of blood on the male nurse's table. Nobody saw Darsh take one of the tubes and drink the blood. Except Aishani. She snatched the tube from her son's hand and threw it away. Darsh was startled and started to cry. Divya moved swiftly towards her brother and began consoling him. The nurse himself was startled. He had meant to keep the tubes in the refrigerator, but Aishani had come in with the children and he became busy with them. Guiltily he looked at Aishani who appeared to be in a daze. Nervously he gave Darsh his shot to Darsh. Aishani took the children home. Devnath was in the car with the driver. He knew immediately that something was wrong, especially when Aishani rang up Adheesh and told him to drop everything and come to her mother's house. Aishani's response was clipped when an alarmed Adheesh asked her what was wrong. The children were playing peacefully, but Aishani was very quiet. Aishani was a sober woman, but Devnath knew that this time it was different. Aishani seemed to be devastated and very scared too. She directed the driver to take them to her mother's home.

A fawning house welcomed them. The house had fallen in love with the twins and couldn't wait to be with them anytime. In turn, the twins instinctively knew about the house. For them, the house was as animate as anyone else. They began playing and talking to the house in their own language. The house understood them perfectly and looked after them tenderly. There was no banging of the windows or unnecessary sighing sounds.

One look at Aishani's face and Madhuji understood. Aishani collapsed in her mother's arms. She cried as if there was no tomorrow. Her sobs turned into hiccups, and she still could not stop herself. Madhuji kept quiet. She didn't know how to console her daughter. In a few minutes Adheesh rushed in. He looked at Devnath who shrugged his shoulders. He went straight to the children. They were cooing and babbling along with the house. He heaved a sigh of relief. At least that part was all right. He then went towards the herb garden where he found the mother and daughter sitting, crying and hugging each other. Aishani ran into Adheesh's arms as soon as she saw him.

'Ash, what's happened, baby?' Aishani didn't answer and just kept on crying. He was getting alarmed. The kids were all right, so what could have upset Aishani so much? He stroked her shoulders, held her, and remained quiet. She would tell him when she stopped crying. But her crying did not stop. It was as if, her world had collapsed. He looked at Madhuji in puzzlement. Her face too wore a sombre look. Finally, he gently drew himself from Aishani and went towards Madhuji. In a low voice, she told him everything. Adheesh listened to her without understanding exactly what she was saying. When comprehension finally dawned, he staggered to a chair and sat down heavily.

'No, this is not possible!' he screamed in his head. He went to the front room where the twins were playing with the house. The house was throwing small soft objects at them, and they were throwing them back, all the time squealing and giggling in delight. Devnath was hovering around the window with a smile on his face. The house was the no-nonsense type. It either liked a person or it did not. Everything was black and white for the house. There was no grey area. They all knew that. Adheesh almost dragged a limp Aishani to the front room.

'See Ash, the house is playing with the babies. Nobody has a sharper sixth sense than the house. It probably has a seventh sense too. If Darsh had even the smallest shadow of a demon in him, the house would have made it clear by now.' In other circumstances, both of them would have laughed at this, but Adheesh was serious, and Aishani was too heartbroken to see the humour. But she did pause when she heard Adheesh's logic. Yes, the house would have definitely told them, if it had noticed anything. Or even Devnath who could smell a negative being from miles away.

Adheesh took her in his arms and said, 'You've been fighting too many demons. You see them everywhere.' Aishani smiled tremulously through her tears, not fully reassured. In their business, they had to rely on their sixth sense and gut instinct and, of course, the supernatural too. They had full faith in the house's and Devnath's instincts, but she still could not allay her doubts. Madhuji had followed them to the front room and heard their conversation, which in any case included her.

She sat down on her cane chair. She was uneasy. The observations though valid still required more explanation. The whole thing was a mixture of tangible and intangible facts. Both she and Aishani had seen Darsh's behaviour, though randomly. Aishani looked at her mother. 'Amma, you are not convinced,' she stated flatly, tears welling up in her eyes again.

'Ash, wait, let us not jump to conclusions too swiftly.' Adheesh took her hands in his. 'We have to discuss this rationally. Let us arrive at our own conclusion first, then we will go to Guruji.'

Aishani was still distraught. She nodded absently.

'I'll make some tea,' Madhuji said. Turning to Aishani she said, 'We will not judge by just a few instances. We have to be completely sure before we take any precautionary measures. Be brave, darling.'

Aishani turned to her mother in alarm, 'What precautionary measures Amma? It's Darsh!'

Adheesh squeezed her hand and gestured to his mother-in-law to go and make tea.

'How could this happen, Adhee? We are the demon killers. Demons are hateful creatures, and we kill them all the time without any mercy or pity. How can this happen to us?' she started crying again hysterically.

'Shh, darling, control yourself. Darsh is not a demon, he is our baby, and he will be a warrior like us. Besides Divya is there too. They are twins. She has not shown any signs. Maybe it is our imagination working overtime.'

'Adheesh, I saw him trying to drink blood and Amma has seen him killing insects with relish. We cannot overlook these happenings. Oh, Adhee! How did this happen?' she wailed.

'I'm wondering too, if at all such is the case.'

They held hands, each consumed with his and her own dark and anxious thoughts. The twins were now playing with each other while Devnath hovered around. They were the sweetest babies in the world, Adheesh thought wistfully. Suddenly a thought struck him. 'Ash, remember Dr. Shambhu's lab? You had to absorb the demon blood kept in the bottles and it was sucked out from your body by the blood-sucking eels. Every drop of demon blood was sucked out from your body and the eels were burnt and buried. Maybe just a trace of the blood was left in your body…' his voice faltered.

Aishani's eyes widened. She pressed his hand, 'Yes… yes, that must be the explanation.'

'But we cannot just assume that that was the case,' Adheesh continued. 'We will have to go to Guruji. Meanwhile, we will have to take Devnath into our confidence. He will protect Darsh with his life.'

The next day they went to Guruji and told him everything. Guruji looked at Aishani and said, 'There was always this possibility, though there is no equal to the doctors and the biologists who undertook this assignment. Many things could have happened, but we cannot speculate on that now. We will have to take great care of the boy. Your children are your legacy to the world. They will relieve Mother Earth of the majority of demons. Both of you have been destroying demons in a straightforward manner. To really destroy the demon species, one has to be a bit of a demon himself. One must be true to one's destiny as well as think like the enemy. Go in peace, children. Your children will do you proud.'

They touched his feet and left. As usual, they were convinced and confused too by Guruji's words. Aishani knew that her children would be safe, but what was their future going to be?

THE GREAT KUMBHA

This was the second Kumbha Mela they would be attending together, this time along with their children. Darsh and Divya were almost three years old. They were a handful. They did exactly what they wanted and were the apple of everyone's eye. They enjoyed life to the fullest. They were loath to go to sleep lest they missed out on anything. Devnath seemed to have forgotten that he was Adheesh's guard. Even he did not know when he became the twins' caretaker. Adheesh and Aishani had disclosed their apprehensions about Darsh to him. They had no choice as there was no parallel to Devnath as far as their children's security was concerned. He loved them as though they were his own. As far as Darsh was concerned, he had discussed the whole matter with Adheesh in his own way. Devnath was not a smooth talker. He could not fully articulate his thoughts.

'Bhaiya, Darshu gets slightly hyper in certain situations, but not dangerously. We know that the minuscule trace of blood which bhabhi may have got from a scratch or something is just not a serious thing. Moreover, it might help him in getting the right amount of cunningness and anger to destroy the demons,' he said, looking at Adheesh in triumph.

Adheesh suppressed a smile. It was quite a speech for Devnath, and well-formulated too. 'Yes, Devnath, but we have to be very careful and repeatedly teach him all about our history and destinies.'

Devnath nodded, 'Don't worry, Bhaiya. Everything will turn out for the better, you just see.'

Adheesh nodded. 'I know, Devnath. With you around the babies, nothing can go wrong.'

There were quite a few people from the Gurukul here in Prayagraj. (Prayagraj was the name given to Allahabad.) Only a skeletal staff remained in the Gurukul for maintenance. Guruji had covered the Gurukul from all the sides with a three-tiered safety net or Kavach. Nobody could either leave the Gurukul or enter it. By the time any demon or negative worked out how to get inside, they would have returned.

There were a number of religious sects known as Akharas that had set up camps on the banks of the Ganges. All in all, there were 13 recognized akharas. If Guruji had wanted he could also have formed an akhara or a camp, there. But Guruji did not want any unwanted attention on the ashram. That is why they had set up their camp a little away from the main gatherings. There were quite a few people from their Gurukul. Such was the belief that if one bathes in the spot where the three holy rivers converge, one could wash away the sins of the past seven births.

Kumbh Mela is one of the greatest religious festivals of Hinduism in India. It is celebrated four times in the course of 12 years in four holy places in India. These places are Haridwar on the river Ganga, Ujjain on the river Shipra, Nashik on the Godavari River and at the confluence of the rivers Ganga, Yamuna and the mythical Saraswati at Prayagraj. These melas or festivals are held according to certain astrological conjunctions of the sun, the moon and Jupiter at these holy places. Of the four, the Kumbh Mela at Prayagraj is the most popular and attracts millions of people from across the world.

The legend of the Kumbh is mentioned in the Puranas too. During Samudra Manthan, the devatas and the demons fought over the pitcher of Amrit or nectar, which came out during the churning of the ocean. Lord Vishnu took the form of the most beautiful enchantress Mohini and tricked the demons into giving her the pitcher of Amrit or the elixir of immortality. As Vishnu was flying with the pitcher towards heaven with the demons in angry pursuit, there was a skirmish between them and a few drops of nectar fell on these four sites of Haridwar, Ujjain, Nashik and Prayagraj. The flight and the skirmish are said to have lasted 12 divine days: each day equal to one human year. Hence the Kumbh Mela is celebrated every 12 years in turn, at these four sites. It is also believed that the waters of the corresponding rivers turn into amrit or elixir of immortality during these times and anyone bathing in these rivers at this time gets rid of all his/her sins of this birth as well as past births.

All of them were instructed to deliberately keep a low profile. Apart from holy people, mendicants and others coming to the Kumbh Mela, there were some unwanted characters, namely demons and others of their ilk. These demons in the guise of human beings would be stalking and conniving all over the place, snatching and kidnapping children and even older people. Child trafficking is known all over the world, but during the Kumbh Mela, it could be a different case altogether. Earlier it was common for children to get lost here and parents and relatives would resign themselves to their sorrowful loss.

There were innumerable children visiting the Kumbh Mela along with their parents. All parents want their children to live a blemish-free, happy and healthy life, and so they bring their children along with them despite the fear of losing them in the crowds. At one time, a favourite trope of the Mumbai film industry was the story of children separated at the Kumbh Mela reuniting many years later. When the kidnappings became more frequent, the government swung into action and stringent measures were put in place. There were helplines and Lost-and-Found police booths were set up all over the place at the Sangam. These strict measures yielded results and things became much better with fewer children being kidnapped or lost.

But things did go wrong still. On the day of the Shahi Snan or the bathing ritual on the first day at the confluence of the holy rivers of Ganga, Yamuna and the mythical Saraswati, the ascetics and protectors of the Hindu dharma were given the moral right to bathe first.

Since women taking part in the Shahi Snan was frowned

upon, only the men of the Gurukul went for the bath. Guruji was in the main group for the Shahi Snan. There was no indulging in feminism and questioning the age-old traditions at the Kumbh Mela. They knew who they were even though their exalted status had to be kept a secret. They, along with other members of the Gurukul, would go for their bath only after the ascetics and mendicants had finished their rituals.

'You take care, Ash,' Adheesh said, hugging Aishani. 'I'll bring the sacred water to sprinkle on all three of you. God knows we all need the blessings of these mother rivers.'

'Don't worry, Adhee. Devnath is here. We'll be safe,' she reassured him. They smiled at each other, and he left to join Guruji and the others. It was early morning and still dark. Darsh and Divya were sleeping. Devnath was outside, guarding them. He would go for the bathing ritual only when Adheesh returned. They were quite far off but could still hear the loud chanting of the pilgrims and devotees as they made their way towards the river. They were staying in tents which had all the modern amenities. The twins woke up a little later. Aishani bathed and fed them. They went outside and looked at the people moving around. Devnath was sitting near the road. Aishani was holding Darsh and Divya's hands. The morning was cool and so serene. At a distance, she could see and hear the devotees moving in lines, singing and chanting. The twins had never seen such a sight. They tried to drag their mother towards the river, but Aishani was firm. 'Babies, we cannot go there, there is too much of a crowd, we'll get lost. Come! We'll stand near that hillock so that we can see them better.'

The twins agreed and they walked towards the raised

ground. It was hardly a hillock, just slightly elevated, more like a pillow covered with sparse moss and grass. It was enough for the twins who were thrilled to climb what to them was a small mountain. Aishani was still holding their hands. They looked at the singing congregation swaying and walking. It was a captivating sight, so many devotees at one place. They stared, fascinated at the whole extravagant phenomenon. But Aishani felt restless. Something was not right. But what? She stared at the long snaking lines. They were as usual, slightly more disciplined than usual. She couldn't pin down her fears. The sky had darkened, and now she could not hear the sound of the singing of the devotees. But why? What was happening? The question again rose in her mind. Was it Adheesh or any of her family members? No, she did not get any forebodings from any of them. But the uneasiness would not go away. Her children were with her, Devnath was also guarding them. She turned to look for Devnath and her breath stopped. Devnath was not there. Squinting her eyes, she searched for him. There he was! Devnath was chasing somebody! Startled, she held tighter to the twins' hands. One hand felt smaller than usual. She looked down. Divya was still staring at the moving crowd, jumping in excitement. Darsh too was jumping. Only it wasn't Darsh. Darsh was not there. Instead, she was holding the hand of a monkey-like creature. She snatched her hand away. The creature looked up. Aishani had never seen such a creature. It did not look like a demon. The creature chittered and ran away. The creature resembled a monkey but was not a monkey. It was larger than a monkey and fleshier too. Their eyes met for a moment. They were intelligent and old eyes. The eyes were black with flecks of yellow that conveyed cruelty and cunningness. All this happened in a flash, but Aishani knew that the devil had stolen her son from right under her nose.

Aishani swayed in shock. From the corner of her eye, she saw Devnath chasing someone or something till they turned round a tent and then she could not see them anymore. She wanted to run after them, but Divya was with her. Quickly she picked up Divya lest the creature kidnaps her too. She could not believe it. They had been so careful in protecting the babies. No, this couldn't be happening. Her baby was gone, and she was unable to do anything about it. Ma Durga, she prayed fervently, please don't let anything happen to my baby, let Devnath bring him back safe and sound.

Divya could sense her mother's uneasiness. 'Where is Darsh, Mamma? Has he gone to bathe with Papa? I also want to go, Mamma,' she demanded.

'Soon, baby. Let Papa come back first, then we'll go,' she assured Divya. Her heart was pounding, her stomach was churning. She tried to divert Divya's attention from Darsh by playing with her. Divya had never been away from Darsh since they were born. Aishani kept praying for Adheesh to come back fast, she prayed for Devnath to come back with her baby. The minutes seemed like hours. She was beside herself with worry and helplessness.

Finally, Adheesh returned. He too had an uneasy feeling, a premonition that things were not all right. The uneasiness did not leave him even when he was having his bath in the river. Somehow, he finished his prayers and rushed back. He was startled when he saw only Aishani and Divya. 'Where is Darsh and where is Devnath?' he asked hoarsely. Aishani mutely pointed in the direction Devnath had run after the kidnapper.

'Stay here,' he barked. 'The others are coming, Guruji will come after some time.' Adheesh ran in the direction Aishani had pointed.

Soon the others came back – Uday, Jayant and Tejas. One look at Aishani and they knew that something was wrong. Aishani told them what had happened. They immediately leapt into action. A telepathic message passed between them, and they fanned out in different directions. Aishani held on to Divya. By now, her mother, Ruby and Ruby's family had also come. Aishani wanted to rush out of their camp and search for her baby, but she dared not hand over Divya to anybody. If somebody could kidnap Darsh from under her nose, then anyone could kidnap Divya too. Ruby went in search of Darsh as well.

Madhuji came and sat beside Aishani and took her hand. She knew that her daughter was fully capable of tackling the kidnapper, but her human side had fully taken over now. She was a mother who desperately wanted her child back. Every minute was a torture for Aishani. She kept picturing Darsh, scared and crying. She was sitting outside the tent when she saw Adheesh returning with Devnath. Devnath was almost unconscious. Adheesh almost carried him to their tent. They put him on a bed. Madhuji made some herbal tea for him. Devnath was almost delirious. The tea calmed him down a bit. He told them that he had seen a man covered in a black shroud running away from them. He was immediately alert. He looked towards Aishani and was shocked when he saw Aishani holding the hand of a small creature. Devnath realized that Aishani was not aware of what had happened. He turned to look at the man in the black shroud. He had gone behind one of the tents. He shouted and then without wasting any time, he ran after the man. The man zigzagged between the tents with Devnath hot on his heels. They must have run for about a mile when something hit him heavily on the head. He passed out. That was how Adheesh found him. He quickly sprinkled some water on Devnath who regained his consciousness and incoherently told Adheesh what had happened.

Meanwhile, the boys had already left the place in the manner that Adheesh had taught them so well. They were so attuned to the dangers around them and were such a cohesive team that they knew exactly what they had to do, which in this case was not much. Aishani, though totally shaken was now behaving more normally. She had to look after Divya who was constantly asking for Darsh.

They waited the whole day and night, but there was no sign of either the boys or Darsh. Aishani was a warrior and a mother. As a warrior she fretted that she could not go out to search for her son. As a mother, she feared for her son. She feared that they might never find him. Late at night, they saw Tejas returning. They rushed to him.

Tejas looked at them helplessly. 'We have not found him as yet. I have reported him at several Lost-and-Found booths. They have promised to help. They are announcing as well as sending scouts all around.' He only stopped for a quick cup of tea and then went out on his search again. He moved from one tent to another, peeping inside each as he went.

The next morning there was still no news of Darsh. The mela was decked with festive decorations and there was a general air of happiness. There were lights everywhere, but in Aishani's tent, there was only anxiety and fear. This trip which was meant to cleanse their souls of past and present sins had given them only grief and despair.

Guruji was supposed to come out of his sadhana only by the next evening. It was now 11 o'clock in the morning. Aishani was sick with worry. Only Guruji could extract them from this bizarre situation. She felt as if a steel claw was squeezing the life out of her heart. At around noon, she noticed some movement in the lane outside her tent. Hope sprung up in her heart, which beat faster as she ran outside. They were all returning, and Adheesh was holding something or someone in his arms. Darsh! It had to be Darsh. Oh God! Let him be alright, healthy, safe and sound. Her legs felt leaden. In a daze and as if in slow motion she saw some people dressed like security guards accompanying them. Everybody was tense. Only Tejas was smiling. He could not stop himself. Ruby and her mother rushed towards them. Adheesh handed over Darsh to Ruby. Darsh appeared to be sleeping. Ruby quickly gave the baby to Aishani. It was only when Darsh came into her arms that she began to breathe again. She held her baby in her arms and began rocking him. Everybody stood at a distance giving mother and son some privacy. By now Darsh had woken up from his sleep and looked at Aishani. 'Mamma!' Just one word assured her that he was alright. Tears came to her eyes. But no, not now.

'Ash,' Adheesh said softly. 'These two people are Mukund

and Ranveerji. They searched for Darsh everywhere and ultimately found him outside a tent, one and a half miles from here. They went out of their way to find Darsh. We are extremely lucky and grateful to have such vigilant officers around us here.'

Aishani handed Darsh to Ruby and folded her hands in gratitude to Mukund and Ranveer. She was incapable of saying anything. They understood. They wished her namaste and said, 'We did not do anything out of the ordinary. We just did our duty. It is quite common for children, and sometimes older people too, to get lost in this melee. Please take utmost care of your children ma'am.' Aishani nodded quietly. There was no need to tell them anything. They wouldn't have understood. It would have created an unnecessary furore.

When everybody had left, Adheesh and Aishani hugged their children tightly. After the initial cuddles and hugs, the twins became restive and squirmed out of their parents' arms. Aishani moved towards Adheesh and put her head on his shoulder. He put his arms around her and kissed her.

'Oh Adhee, how could it happen? I was holding his hand. I have no idea how that devil removed his hand and put his own hand in Darsh's place.' She was crying softly.

'Shh, baby, it's not your fault. These people are on the lookout to kidnap whoever they can find. They are on the lookout for highly intelligent children, whom they can mould according to their whims and fancies. Intelligent people are more at risk.'

'If that was the case then why did they let go of Darsh?' Despite herself, Aishani was intrigued.

'Sometime back, Guruji, in one of our discussions, told me about the scandals behind these kidnappings. These demons and asuras are so intelligent and cunning that they sometimes kidnap someone worthy and clone them.'

Aishani sat up in distress. 'What do you mean, Adhee? What do you mean by someone worthy? How is a small baby like Darsh worthy and why clone him?'

'I don't know, Ash. I am just surmising. It may be just a common kidnapping, or it may not be. But we must examine it from every angle. We cannot leave anything to chance.'

A wild and sudden thought struck Aishani. 'Adhee, could it be because they sensed some demonic blood in him?'

Adheesh understood immediately. 'Baby, in your anxiety you are going off on a tangent. Darsh is our child. How can he ever have demonic blood?'

'I know you too have the same apprehensions, Adhee. You are just not voicing it. We must face it, Adhee. Darsh has behaved peculiarly, earlier too. Maybe a strain of demon blood stayed in my body when I had ingested the demons' blood in my body, even though it was sucked out immediately by the eels. Maybe that strain was transferred to Darsh. Maybe the demons kidnapped him for this, cloned him and then returned him.'

'Why not kidnap him and keep him with themselves?' Adheesh asked, though a shudder went through him at the thought.

'To create more chaos and mayhem, Adhee,' she cried out, despair in her voice. They looked despondently at their playing children.

'This is not possible, even if there is a minuscule chance that it could be so, then we will not let it happen. We are age-old warriors. It is not in our nature to be anxious or depressed or pessimistic. We have won insurmountable battles. We will win this one too. That is, if such a problem exists,' he declared. 'We will go to Guruji tomorrow when he is free.'

But Guruji was not free. In a way they understood it too. Guruji had to accumulate as much of the Amrit or nectar not only by bathing in the confluence of the rivers, but also to proliferate these powers through prayer and meditation. They knew that Guruji was doing this to enhance the powers of his warriors and the Gurukul. This time would come again only after twelve years. They finally had a chance to meet Guruji after two days, and even then, only for a very brief period. Guruji bade them to sit down and came straight to the point. Both of them were aware that Guruji knew, but did he know their fears?

'We cannot understand God's actions and intentions many a time. What we take as a catastrophe can be a blessing in disguise. We just have to wait and watch. Of course, we have to be more alert and continue to do our duties to the best of our abilities.'

Aishani stared aghast at Guruji. So, was Guruji convinced that Darsh had a trace of demon blood in him? Guruji turned to her as if he had read her mind. 'We will always have to give the benefit of doubt to this thought of ours; whether Darsh has been cloned. If not, then why was he kidnapped so cunningly? There are too many questions which only time can answer. As far as Darsh's own behaviour is concerned, he has unlimited powers, acquired from both of you and his own karmas. We just have to gently guide him to make the right choices.'

She nodded teary-eyed. There was no other way. Guruji had said the right thing. He had neither consoled them nor discouraged them. They just had to wait and watch.

KRITIMUKHA

They were sitting on the lawns of Guruji's cottage. Winter was just setting in; the cold just nipping their arms sporadically making them shiver involuntarily despite a benevolent sun shining down on them. It was so pleasant that Guruji had decided to hold the meeting outside his cottage. They laid out their mats on the grass, while Guruji sat crosslegged on a wooden *chowki.*

'There is this ancient Shiva temple in the Northeast. It is broken down through the ravages of time and neglect. The legend surrounding it was that whoever goes there and prays to Mahadev with full faith and belief gets his wish fulfilled. Such was the strength and effectiveness of this temple that people from far and wide went and prayed there. The atmosphere both inside and outside the temple was so pure that trust and conviction automatically built up in an individual and he or she could communicate easily with God and vice versa. But a couple of centuries ago, strange happenings took place around the temple. People still had their wishes fulfilled, people still trekked to the temple, but there was a difference. It happened without fail that whenever one's wish was fulfilled one had to pay a very heavy cost either in the form of loss of fortune or even loss of a life. Slowly people became aware of this phenomenon. A few people reported seeing and hearing ominous sounds and shadows inside the temple. They became scared and gradually the number of visitors to the temple petered down and ultimately almost stopped. A few devotees did go to the temple occasionally, but these people never came back. They were presumed to be either dead or lost.

'With footfalls almost vanishing, the nearby shops also closed down and the whole place became decrepit. The lush well-kept greenery around the temple gradually became a jungle. Barring a few most devout believers of Mahadev, people forgot that there was a temple in this part of the jungle. In fact, they began associating the jungle with cruel supernatural beings and began staying far away from it.

'The existence of the temple became common knowledge when a survey was being conducted on the temples of India and their status and upkeep. A survey party had gone deep into the jungle and discovered the *mandir*. From their experience, they knew that it was an ancient temple and were justifiably excited. Matters came to a head when out of five members only two returned. The other three just disappeared. Not even their bodies were found. A search-and-rescue team was sent to look for the men who had disappeared without a trace. People began to fear the jungle even more when a couple of the members of the search-and-rescue team disappeared too. Now no one dared to go near the jungle. But still somehow people kept disappearing without anybody going into the jungle.

'This is where we come in. The information coming to us is that the protector of the *mandir* has been disabled somehow and dark forces have entered the temple. Your job is to find out who the protector was, how he was disabled, and which dark forces have taken over the *mandir*. Form a team, go to the library, and find out everything about this mandir and its protector,' Guruji instructed everyone.

They nodded their heads in assent, touched Guruji's feet and set off for the library. Everybody from the original team went to the library, though this time the team consisted of only the boys. The girls were there too though, helping with the research. Information was not too difficult to find. After researching for two days, they had quite a lot of information and had reached some conclusion, though its authenticity would be proved only when they went out into the field to execute their plan. They went to Guruji after with their conclusions.

Adheesh spoke first. 'This is a very ancient Shiva temple. There are many stories revolving around the temples of Mahadev. One of them is that one demon, Jallandhar, who was born of Bhagwan Shiva, sent the demon Rahu to convey his love to Shiva's consort Parvati. Bhagwan Shiv already knew about this. So, as soon as Rahu reached Bhagwan's abode, Mount Kailash, Bhagwan created a much bigger and more ferocious demon than Rahu. Rahu got scared. He knew he could not escape, and that this demon would surely eat him. He threw himself at Bhagwan Shiva's feet, imploring him to save him. Bhagwan Shiva took pity on Rahu and saved him. Now the demon, who had been created for the specific purpose of eating other demons had no food. He turned towards Bhagwan Shiva who was drifting into meditation.

'Bhagwan, what do I do now? What will I eat now?' he tearfully asked. In jest, Shiva told him to eat himself. The demon immediately began eating himself. By the time Bhagwan Shiva noticed this, the demon had already eaten his legs, torso and his arms. Only his face was left. Bhagwan Shiva was very impressed by his obedience and stopped him. Shiva blessed him and said, 'From now on, you will be known as Kritimukha, and you will be placed at the entrance of all my temples. No negative being or even a shadow can enter any mandir or place of my worship, where you are present. You will always protect the people who go inside my temples to pray to me.'

'From then onwards, all Shiva temples have a sculpture or portrait of Kritimukha at the entrance, either on top or on both the sides of the entrance. It depicts a grotesque face with two protruding eyes and puffy cheeks. Its teeth are huge with both the eye teeth very sharp and long, giving the impression that it will eat up anyone who dares to cross him. In some pictures it has two horns. All in all, it looks like a cross between a demon and ferocious animal like a tiger or a lion.

'This particular ancient temple in the northeast was also adorned with the sculpture of a Kritimukha. But later the sculpture was found to be missing. We can only surmise that the Kritimukha was either stolen or destroyed as the location of the temple suited the demons and negative and supernatural energies. When this happened, the power and mystique of the temple dwindled and gradually died. It became the hunting and resting place for demons and the like, who pounced on any human being who went there.

'So now we have to find the Kritimukha, exorcise the demons from the temple and reinstate the Kritimukha.'

'All in a day's work,' Uday said with a smile as Adheesh's narrative drew to a close.

'Yeah,' Adheesh said, also with a smile. 'Jayant is going to be the hero of this search. Only he has the special vision to spot the Kritimukha if it has not been destroyed.' He turned towards Jayant, who was concentrating on something. He had been honing his visual skills. He could now see many hidden things within a radius of 5 kilometres.

They presented their strategy to Guruji who gave them some more tips and his blessing.

Since the girls were not going this time, both Ruby and Aishani decided to stay together at Adheesh's parents' place, along with their children. Aishani's sisters-in-law would be there too. They all thought that it would be a good time for bonding.

The next day, the boys said goodbye to their families and left. Adheesh kissed his children who were sleeping fitfully. He looked a bit worried. Aishani put her hands on his shoulders. 'Don't worry, Adheesh, I am fully prepared for any contingency and so is Devnath. We know that this area is out of bounds to demons, and they are not in any danger here,' she said softly.

'I know, baby,' he said tenderly.

'Then go without any fear and stay focused on your mission. Mahadev will take care of all of us.'

'So be it,' he whispered as he kissed her gently and left.

They took a train to Bhubaneswar and checked into a hotel. The next day, all of them reached the village on the edge of the jungle where the Shiva temple was situated. The villagers were simple and welcoming people. They were offered tea and a wide variety of sweetmeats. Adheesh told the villagers that they were researchers and were compiling a list of the Shiva temples in Odisha. This would be sent to the Ministry of Tourism, which would publish a list of temples, and this would increase the inflow of tourists to Odisha, he added.

'We have heard that there are a couple of Shiva temples here too. If you can guide us to them, it will become easier for us and save us time too,' Adheesh said. They were sitting with a group of villagers, who nodded their heads in assent.

'We will take you to one temple which is here itself,' said a man called Bijoy. 'However, there is one other temple here where nobody goes. I don't think you all should go there.'

'Why?' Uday asked. This was where they wanted to go, this was why they had come here in the first place. 'A temple is the holiest place, we should not neglect any temple of God.'

Bijoy and the other villagers looked uncomfortable and disturbed. 'Oh, we care for our Gods,' he said. He appeared to be thinking it over, and then added, 'A long time ago, this temple had the power to grant boons, and people from far and wide came to pay their homage to Mahadev. Suddenly something happened, which offended Mahadev so much that he abandoned the temple. Despite entreaties and havans to placate Mahadev, he never returned. In fact, whoever goes there never comes back. There is this belief that whoever goes to the temple and comes back, will be taken as a sign that the dark forces have left the temple and people can again go freely to the temple. But this has not happened so far since nobody can gather enough courage to go there.'

'Bijoy, we have to take a census of every Shiva temple here. Why don't you just show us the general direction? We'll find the temple ourselves,' Adheesh said.

Bijoy reluctantly agreed. Presumably, the remark of neglecting a Mahadev temple had touched a raw nerve in the villagers. Bijoy and two more villagers took them to the eastern outskirts of their village and left them there.

'Be careful, bhaiya,' Bijoy whispered, as if someone was listening to their conversation. To cut the tall grass and shrubs, the villagers had given them long scythes called talwars.

'Don't worry, Bijoy, nothing will happen. We'll come back either this evening or latest by tomorrow,' Adheesh said.

'What?' Bijoy and the other two villagers appeared shocked. 'You intend to stay the night? Bhaiya, it's not safe!'

'That is just in case we do not complete our work,' Adheesh said, patting his rucksack. 'We are fully prepared.'

Bijoy and the other two villagers reluctantly left them. Adheesh and his group began walking into the jungle. Tejas quickly climbed on a tree and reached the top. From there, he began vaulting from one tree to another. He was given a dressing down by every member of his team, after the accident in which, he had been cut into two pieces and died. Hence, he was a bit more careful now. Plus, he knew that Uday was watching him like a hawk. He knew that everybody loved him, there were no doubts on that score.

There were no dirt tracks in the jungle as people did not go there. The more they ventured deep into the jungle, the more they became aware of the silence around them. They did not encounter any animals. Nor did they hear any birds. It was now becoming difficult to move because of the thick undergrowth. They began using their talwars and hacked at the thick and thorny grass and shrubs. A rough trail was made. It was getting cooler, but this cooling was ominous and dark. They knew that they were going in the right direction. In reality, only two people were using the talwars, Adheesh and Uday. Tejas was looking across the treetops and Jayant was groping and looking into all the hidden places.

'Bhaiya,' Tejas called out from the top of a tree. 'There is a pond half a mile from here. It's dark green in colour and covered with hyacinth and lichen. It's more a swamp than a pond.'

'Ok!' Uday gave him a thumbs up. They continued on their journey.

'Adheesh, there are many hidden things in the pond. In fact, there is a huge demon residing inside waiting to catch unsuspecting individuals. I think this is the Kritimukha that Guruji was talking about. I think one of the reasons that people do not return could be the Kritimukha too,' Jayant said.

'Yes, Jayant, Kritimukha is after all a demon. It may be eating the people trying to cross it. Remember Bhagwan Shiva created it to eat demons. It may have lost its reasoning ability to differentiate between humans and demons.'

'If you have been living in a swamp for ages, you are bound to lose your ability to reason,' Uday muttered good naturedly. They smiled and forged ahead.

'We will have to first confirm whether this thing in the pond is really the demon Kritimukha. It might eat us first. It won't let anybody touch it. If it is indeed the Kritimukha, then we must retrieve it from the pond, exorcise the demons from the temple and reinstate the Kritimukha at the temple's entrance,' Adheesh informed them.

'We will have to distract it in a rather clever and cunning manner. Let's hope it is not intellectually sharp. But how do we fish it out? Jayant, can you make out the negative energies in the temple now?' Adheesh asked.

'Umm, let me check.' Jayant concentrated and tried to see inside the temple. 'There is total darkness there.'

'Hmm, a sure sign that there are dark forces there,' Adheesh commented. Uday nodded. His skills would come to the fore when they would be inside the temple fighting the dark forces or the army of the demon Rahu.

Adheesh thought hard. 'We have to cross the Kritimukha first. In the ancient books, in the senior's library, it was written that only once the Kritimukhas have been overpowered, and even then not all, only a few of them, that too in rare circumstances.'

'How? The only purpose of any Kritimukha's existence is to guard his lord and master's temple, that is Bhagwan Shiva's temples. How could he be dislodged from any temple? He is the protector of Shiva's temples. In turn, he gets the blessings of Bhagwan Shiva and is protected by the Lord himself,' Uday queried.

'Either the books were not absolutely clear, or we did not have enough time to find out. Either way, we are on our own now. That means we find a way of getting the Kritimukha from the water and do it in such a clever manner that it does not harm us first,' Adheesh answered.

'We have to find out why it became so weak in the first place. The first thing which comes to my mind is that it must be praying to Bhagwan Shiva. So great must his concentration be to the exclusion of everything else that the darker demons could manage to dislodge him and enter the temple. I think that if we sit in front of it, of course at an arm's length, and pray to Bhagwan Shiva, he may acknowledge our prayers. Praying to Bhagwan Shiva is what pleases him the most. Maybe this time too he will be captivated and pleased by our prayers, thus allowing one of us to go inside the temple and destroy the demons and the dark forces,' Adheesh said.

'What if it doesn't work? Do we have a backup plan?' Jayant asked.

'At the moment, it is either this or the whole shebang of fighting it out. One advantage is that whenever a Kritimukha has been overpowered, he was invariably thrown into a body of water, from where it could not come out,' Adheesh replied.

'Why?'

'I had read a postscript in the ancient texts which said that whenever the Kritimukha was vanquished, it was thrown into water where its lower parts turn female. This is so humiliating for him that he does not come out of the water but becomes more ferocious and doesn't let anybody cross it.'

'Why does it turn into a female? And what is wrong with becoming a female?' Tejas asked as he floated down from the treetops.

'I don't know, Tejas,' Adheesh replied. 'I don't think it is particularly important at the moment. We can research it when we return to the ashram. Right now, we have to overpower it before we go inside the temple. I will sit near the pond and chant Bhagwan Shiva's mantras while Uday goes inside the temple to ward off the evil spirits. This is on the presumption that the Kritimukha will listen to the chanting of the Shiva mantras. Jayant and Tejas, both of you will keep a sharp lookout for any untoward movement. God willing, if all goes well, I will handle the Kritimukha and both of you will join Uday in destroying the demons inside the temple.'

They all nodded in agreement. Tejas went back to the trees. Jayant began walking carefully around the area, combing it with his see-all eyes, while Uday stayed with Adheesh, who cleared an area near the pond that was neither too close nor too far from it. The Kritimukha had to be made aware that someone was meditating on his creator. It might stop him from searching for food for some time. Adheesh took out a mat from his backpack, sat down and then took out a trident, one of Shiva's most recognized weapons, and set it vertically in the ground. Taking a Rudraksha mala in his right hand, he began chanting Shiva's mantra. He chanted for ten minutes. Nothing happened. If anything, it became colder, quieter, and darker, as if the energies had stopped listening to this dreaded or adored sound, depending on their inclination. Not deterred by all this, Adheesh continued to chant.

Uday, who was hovering around Adheesh, began noticing a slight change. It was too early to say whether it was positive or negative. Uday's hand was already on his weapon, the Pash. His senses were fully alert. After about one hour of chanting, a creature shot out of the water, but only partially.

'Who are you? Why are you here?' It asked in a deep guttural watery sound, more like water dripping.

Adheesh kept the Rudraksha in his hand and did not look directly at the creature. Instead, he folded his hands and talked to the trident.

'I am Adheesh, and this is my colleague Uday. We have come from the ashram of Swami Ramanuj, and we have been sent by him to salvage and restore Bhagwan Shiva's temple and reinstate you to your former glory.'

There was silence for some time. To them, it seemed that the fallen Kritimukha was mulling over his statement.

'How do I know I can believe you?'

'I do not have anything to prove my identity. However, if you look at Bhagwan Shiva's Trishul closely, you will find the answer,' Adheesh answered respectfully.

The Kritimukha's eyes, large protruding eyes, were above the water. They turned towards the trident. The trident flashed its light towards the Kritimukha. For a moment, the Kritimukha shone in all its glory. This was enough for him. He started blabbering. The momentary light was so strong that Jayant and Tejas panicked. They rushed towards Adheesh, but Uday stopped them. Adheesh and the Kritimukha were speaking in an alien language that they could not understand.

It sounded like an audio tape on fast forward, and it seemed to be a positive exchange. Soon, Adheesh waded into the pond with his bag. Tejas wanted to go after him, but Uday stopped him. They stood there, alert and quivering with anticipation and apprehension. Adheesh folded his hands, then opened the mouth of his bag. There was a flurry of movement and the sound of water. They did not see anything, but they knew that the Kritimukha had gone inside the bag of his own accord. Then Adheesh turned towards them. Without saying a word, he nodded to them. Only Jayant could see the Kritimukha. He had never seen such a grotesque figure in his life, but the feeling he got was that the Kritimukha was going to fight and demolish the dark forces along with them.

'The Kritimukha will fight along with us. It has been hungry for a very long time. It was created to eat demons and negative energies, which got the better of him by an unfortunate coincidence. Not anymore. He is raring to have a rather big swipe at them.'

'Looks like we won't have too much work to do,' Uday said drily.

'Seems so,' Adheesh said with a smile. 'Sometimes there are alternative methods which produce the same result.'

Adheesh went into a trance. Surprised, the other three waited for him to come out of it. This was hardly the time to go into a trance. Soon Adheesh snapped out of it.

'The Kritimukha was communicating with me,' he explained. 'It seems he wants to be hung or rather left dangling in the air inside the temple. It does not want to be hung outside on the doorway as yet.'

Uday nodded. 'Yes, it should be. The demons are inside the temple, so he will annihilate them there itself. He won't be able to catch them if he is hanging outside the temple.'

'That makes our mission easier. Tejas, you take your position as usual on top of the trees and keep a sharp eye on any demons who escape. Jayant, you will tell us about the hidden locations of the demons in the temple, and outside in the nearby jungle too.'

They nodded in agreement and swiftly took their positions. They were ready with their weapons. Uday's hand was on his Pash. Adheesh's khukhri was in the sheath tied to his leg. He still had to take the Kritimukha inside the temple. All the time he was chanting Shiva's mantra. Though the mantra was the same frequently recited, when it came out of Adheesh's mouth, it took on a different form altogether. It was the purest form of the mantra and had been chanted millions of times through the ages. In other words, it was fully charged and activated. They rushed inside. Adheesh took out the Kritimukha from his bag and propelled it in the air like a kite. In a split second, he had two khukhris in his hands. The atmosphere inside the temple had already begun to lighten with the loud sound of the pure mantras. The Kritimukha with its round grotesque body, bulging eyes, and huge sharp teeth, was like a dervish swirling around everywhere, biting, swallowing, chewing and devouring the demons inside with total recklessness. Uday and Adheesh were the other two dervishes, slashing and killing countless demons. Of course, the main antagonist was the Kritimukha who was taking revenge and satisfying his gluttonous appetite too. Jayant was giving a running commentary on the hideouts of the demons and of the presence of the invisible ones too. The few who had managed to run away were espied by Tejas, who immediately raised an alarm. These were chased, slashed, and cut up by Uday.

The whole operation was over in half an hour. Most of the demons just turned into black ash after being killed, and many of them were eaten up by the Kritimukha. The air was gradually coming back to normal, sweet and fresh. But there was still a lot of work to be done. The temple had to be cleaned of all the debris of the demons, dirt and rotting vegetation. They began cleaning up the Shivling as well. Adheesh washed the Kritimukha with Gangajal which he always carried in his bag. They hung the Kritimukha at the entrance of the temple. They then folded their hands in obeisance to it. The Kritimukha seemed to be smiling and looking benevolently at them. There was again a dialogue between the Kritimukha and Adheesh. The others surmised that the Kritimukha was thanking them. Soon they left for the village. They had paved the way. The villagers would do the rest.

They went straight to the village where Bijoy and a few villagers were sipping tea and talking. Their eyes widened when they saw Adheesh and his party. They rushed towards them.

'I cannot believe this! You've come back! What did you do there? What did you see there? Did you fight with anybody or anything?' They were all agog with curiosity. Adheesh gave a tired smile and gestured to Jayant. 'No Bijoy, we just reached the temple and took photographs. It took a long time because there was too much overgrown grass and weeds. We cut as much as we could, then we just waded through the tall grass.

The temple is in real bad shape. We cleaned as much as we could. You will have to take volunteers to clear the trail to the temple and you will have to take a couple of pandits for the sanctification of the shrine and its deities again. Gods leave when devotees do not visit them and pray to them. The gods will have to be invoked again.'

Bijoy turned towards Adheesh. He had tears in his eyes. 'We will certainly do whatever you tell us to do. For decades we have been very uneasy about our Shiva temple. Things will be normal now.' He looked at his companions who were happily nodding their heads.

'We will have to leave now,' Adheesh said.

'Bhaiya, will you show us the photographs of the temple?' one of the villagers asked hesitantly.

'Of course, but it will take a couple of days. We will have to go to our studio and develop the negatives. Give us your address and we will courier them to you,' Adheesh replied. Uday took their address, then as an afterthought, he added, 'Before you go inside the temple, make sure you pay homage to the Kritimukha which is hanging at the entrance.'

'Oh yes, definitely, we know all about that.'

Uday looked at the others; they looked back at him, pleasantly surprised. Uday shrugged. The world was full of surprises, there was never a dull moment.

VAJRA

'The existing drought conditions in the country are not natural. They are manmade or we can say that they are demon made. To be more specific, they are being propagated by the demon Vrutrasur.'

These warriors were not in too much of a reading mood today, even though they were sitting in the library. Vashishtji seized this opportunity and sat at their table and regaled them with stories from the epics.

'How?' It seemed Tejas was the only one asking pertinent questions. The others took Vrutrasur and everything else in their stride. They were not surprised by anything anymore. One could surmise that they had become jaded.

Not when they went into action, thought Vashishtji, the head librarian, wryly. These people not only followed the ancient warfare methods and weapons, but they also incorporated new methods and weapons. That is why our Gurukul and our pupils are the best, he thought proudly.

There was widespread drought in the country. The monsoons had failed miserably, and the government was fighting a losing battle to restore a semblance of normalcy. Guruji was not available. He had gone to attend a conference of the heads of the various Gurukuls from all over the world to discuss the levels of degradation seeping into the society, and what extra measures could be taken to prevent and stop it. Today Vashishtji was sitting with several students in the library. He was regaling them with the valour of the gurus and the students of their Gurukul. Of course, these were only the stories that he knew. He was very much aware that there were many happenings and events that went on without his knowledge. It was the rule in the Gurukul that warriors would be told about their operations on a need-to-know basis. So, Vashishtji did not actually know much. Today was an exception, however. He had been directed by Guruji to familiarize some of the warriors with the story of the demon Vrutrasur. As far as ancient stories were concerned nobody knew more than Vashishtji. The students enjoyed listening to these stories. Vashishtji's storytelling was legendary. He brought life to even the most insipid stories, spicing them in the most shocking and hilarious ways.

'It has been written in the ancient books that once upon a time,' Vashishtji stopped to clear his throat. He was clearly enjoying himself. The students settled down for a very entertaining and stimulating storytelling session.

'There was a great king and sage known as Tvasta. He had a son called Vishwarupa. He had three heads which blessed him with prodigious spirituality and mental strength. Vishwarupa was a very saintly person. He was very pious and honourable. On seeing his immeasurable powers, Indra Devata, the ruler of heaven, became jealous. Indra killed Vishwarupa on a frivolous charge. When Tvasta came to know about this he performed a massive yagna. From the fires of the yagna was produced a child, whom Tvasta named Vrutrasur. Tvasta taught this younger son that he was born to avenge the death of his elder brother Vishwarupa. The only way his brother's death could be avenged would be to kill Indra.

'Vrutrasur underwent severe penance and meditated for an exceptionally long time. His prayers were heard, and Bhagwan Brahma came down and blessed him, and told him to ask for a boon. Vrutrasur asked that no weapon should be able to kill him; he would not die of anything made of metal or wood or anything which was wet or dry. Another aspect of the boon was that his powers would keep on increasing whenever he fought a battle with anybody. Armed with these boons, Vrutrasur waged and won the war against Indra and the other devatas and threw them out of heaven.'

Vashishtji paused dramatically and looked triumphantly at the students and warriors assembled there. He did not get many chances to showcase his theatrical skills, and made the most of it whenever he got the chance.

'How was he defeated, Guruji?'

'Yes, now we come to another part of the story. Vrutrasur had become so strong that he could be overpowered only by something more powerful than him. The devatas went to the trinity of Gods, Brahma, Vishnu and Mahesh, and beseeched them for help. Bhagwan Vishnu told them that Vrutrasur could be conquered if he was attacked with a weapon made from the bones of any learned and powerful sage. The devatas then appealed to many sages, but naturally, all of them refused. At the end after much cajoling and coaxing, Maharishi Dadichi agreed. Maharishi Dadichi took Samadhi, and his soul left his body to join the Supreme. The devatas then handed over his bones to Brahma, who along with the celestial architect Vishwakarma, crafted a large number of weapons. The main weapons were Sarang, Pinak, Vajra and Gandeev. The Vajra or the divine thunderbolt was crafted out of the spinal bones of sage Dadichi. This was given to the devatas to defeat Vrutrasur with.'

'But Guruji, what about his boons, which were granted to him by Brahmaji?' one of the students asked.

'I am coming to that,' Vashishtji answered.

'Armed with the Vajra, the devatas again went to Bhagwan Vishnu, who advised them to befriend Vrutrasur and pray to Ma Durga also to give them additional strength. The devatas then prayed to Maa Durga, who promised to come to their aid in their hour of need. Indra befriended Vrutrasur so that he could kill him when he was off guard.'

'Indra then approached Vrutrasur on some pretext and they became exceptionally good friends. They spent quite a lot of time on the seashore. Indra always carried the Vajra with him. He kept it hidden. He regularly prayed to Maa Durga too. Once Vrutrasur fell asleep on the seashore, Indra collected the foam of the sea, and fervently prayed so that Maa Durga's power would permeate the foam. Indra then wrapped the foam around the Vajra. This way it was neither wet nor dry, made of neither wood nor metal and the foam was certainly not a weapon but was fortified with the strength of Maa Durga. Indra then killed Vrutrasur, thus ending years of tyranny and torture. The devatas hailed Indra and he became the king of heaven again.'

The students and warriors clapped their hands in appreciation. It was always a pleasure to hear Vashishtji tell a story. They thanked him and went off on their individual pursuits. Except for Adheesh and Aishani. They were thinking and appeared quite serious. They went and sat at one of the corner tables in the library, where they would not be disturbed.

'Adheesh, Guruji had indirectly instructed Vashishtji to tell us the story of Vrutrasur. We can guess that Guruji wanted us to be mentally prepared for another demon that is coming out of hibernation. Either that or his descendants are becoming stronger and have now to be exterminated.'

Adheesh nodded. 'Yes, Ash, except that we don't know who this demon is, and how will we go about destroying it.'

'We have to read between the lines here, Adhee. Guruji is not here. We have not come across anything even resembling the Vajra.'

'Nevertheless, we will prepare ourselves in readiness for Guruji's instructions. I will increase my physical exercise regimen.'

'And I will increase my meditation of Maa Durga. And we wait for Guruji. This waiting is going to be the worst part.'

'Hmm,' Adheesh was non-committal.

Guruji came back after a week. He immediately summoned Adheesh and Aishani, who were waiting for this call. They touched his feet. Guruji blessed them, and came directly to the point. 'I see that both of you have sensed the danger that is looming over us and are prepared for it too. I'm afraid that the matter is much more serious than we had thought. This Gurukul and both of you and the others have been fighting with legions of demons throughout your lives. But this is slightly different. This person, albeit a demon, has all the qualities of a demon as well as a human being.' Guruji looked at them. They were listening to him intently. Guruji knew that they could comprehend every word spoken by him. Guruji was unattached to any human emotion, but whenever he looked at these two, there was invariably a warm glow in his heart, a feeling that these two would sort things out in the most decisive and precise manner.

'This person's name is Viraj. He is one of the most learned scholars in the country. He has achieved greatness. On top of that, he is one of the richest men in the world,' Guruji said.

'On top of that he is a demon,' Adheesh added. Guruji smiled at him.

'Yes, a fact which is of course very well hidden. There is panic in our part of the world. We can control our fears; but if this reaches the rest of the world there will be so much chaos and mayhem that people will destroy each other. His plan is to destroy the world bit by bit. There is a fire raging in his heart. He wants to take revenge, on anybody and anything. So great are his powers that he is planning to deprive the earth of one of the most essential reasons for its being, water. If that unforeseen disaster happens, then all living beings on earth will die of thirst and hunger.

'A great wrong was committed centuries ago, and retaliation is in his blood. He obviously cannot kill Indra in this age, so he will destroy anybody who comes in the way of his ambition. He has no friends, and he doesn't trust anybody. Most probably he feels that having a friend may dilute his hatred and strong motivation for revenge. He doesn't have anybody around him. Nobody really knows about him personally, but he is known for his ruthlessness and sharp business acumen.'

'And he has to be removed,' Adheesh almost read Guruji's thoughts.

'Yes, Adheesh, and not by normal methods. The boons granted to his ancestor Vrutrasur are there in his bloodstream too. Hence, he must be killed in the same way. There is no other alternative.'

'We know, Guruji,' Aishani replied.

Guruji looked at her benignly. 'Only the two of you have the power to do this job, and it is a tough job. It will require some time too. You will have to gain his confidence first and then work your way to his destruction.'

'Yes, Guruji,' Adheesh said grimly.

'We will perform the Vajra puja, the same Vajra which was made from Maharishi Dadichi's spinal cord bones. Once you master that, you will have to go to Viraj, and work on gaining his trust and confidence. And Aishani, you will have to invoke Maa Durga's Shakti in such a manner that it can be arranged to cover the Vajra, to give it exceptional strength.'

'Yes, Guruji,' she replied. They touched his feet. Guruji blessed them and they left.

They left the Gurukul and went home, both immersed in their own thoughts. Adheesh was thinking of how soon he would be able to invoke the powers of the Vajra. Aishani was thinking of their twins. Worrying about Darsh had become second nature to both of them. At least her mother, Ruby and Devnath knew about this. She was reassured that the twins would be totally safe, though Darsh had not shown any unusual behaviour after the Kumbha mela incident. They could be away for a couple of months, and then maybe the exercise could take more than six months too. Also, they would be away from each other.

'Adheesh, we will have to pick up Amma and Ruby from their homes and bring them here. The babies will be safer here. Amma's place is a bit remote. Jayant is barely at home and Amma won't be able to look after the kids on her own. There are so many people here. I know Ruby will insist on staying here and Devnath will not leave them for a minute even.'

'Yes, Ash, there is only one minus point,' Adheesh said.

Aishani was immediately alarmed. 'What? What can go wrong?' Her heart had started to beat faster.

'Whoa! Wait! Don't jump to conclusions,' he said with a laugh. 'What I meant was that with so many people, indulging their every whim and fancy, they are apt to be spoilt. We are going to face another huge problem when we return.'

'Oh! Don't you scare me like that ever again,' Aishani said in mock indignation. She laughed weakly.

The next day, after handing over the babies to their family, they left for the Gurukul. The twins were quite used to their parents going away and didn't mind it at all. Adheesh and Aishani felt that their people were secretly happy that they left the children behind so that they could have Darsh and Divya to themselves. The twins were like a breath of fresh air in this household of adults. Adheesh's uncles and aunts did not have children as yet. The twins were like two cute toys in this huge joint family, though now they did have Ruby's son for company.

They reached the Gurukul. Adheesh dropped Aishani at their secret tree, which was behind Guruji's cottage and was invisible to the rest of the denizens of the Gurukul. Not that anybody went there, but the kind of meditation Aishani was going into required total concentration without any disturbances. They looked at each other; their eyes spoke to each other.

Then Adheesh went inside Guruji's cottage. Guruji took him to another part of the museum where he had not been to before. In fact, he was not even aware of the existence of this room. It was again a spartan room with only a table and a glass box with a weapon inside it. Adheesh knew that it was the Vajra. The Vajra is said to possess the properties of a diamond, indestructibility, and a thunderbolt which symbolizes gigantic force. It looked like a club with a ribbed spherical head. The ribs met in a ball-shaped top. Adheesh knew that it also represented firmness of spirit and spiritual power. It was one of the most powerful weapons in the universe.

He knew that he had to pray to the Vajra intensely and vigorously for it to recognize him and concede to be used by him. On the first day, Guruji sat with him familiarizing him with the basic and advanced concepts of Vajra meditation. Adheesh was familiar with many of the rituals, but a few of them were totally new to him. He knew that praying to the Vajra in the right manner and in the stipulated time would give him manifold results, such as protection from famine, drought, sicknesses, war, poor harvest, bad omens, and evil spirits. There would be prosperity all around. It also enhanced one's willpower.

Adheesh went through many Vajra-invoking mantras with Guruji. He knew about these mantras, though he did not recite them regularly. One of the mantras which he recited on special occasions went like this, 'Om sahasrayanetraaya vidmahe vajraastraaya dhiimahi tanno indrah prachodaayat.'

Guruji left him after one hour. He was on his own now. It took Adheesh three days to master all the rituals and the Vajra mantras. From the seventh day, he was well-versed with the mantras. On the eighth day, he went to Guruji and touched his feet. Guruji blessed him, 'I have designated one person from our intelligence to be with you. He will be in touch with us, and he will be at your service all the time. He is, in your parlance, a computer geek.' Adheesh smiled.

So, saying, Guruji called to someone to come in. A tall, slim man walked in. He was casually dressed with a lock of hair falling over his left eyebrow. He had a prominent jaw-line and a protruding Adam's apple. He looked like a computer nerd, which he was. He had sharp eyes and wore thick glasses. He did a reverent Namaste to Adheesh., who folded his hands in response.

'Adheesh, this is Satish. He will give you all the information that you want. He has been working and collecting information on Viraj Singh, the billionaire tycoon. Satish, this is Adheesh. You will be with him as long as he requires you. You will assist him in everything,' Guruji said.

'I have heard so much about you, Adheesh bhai. It will be my privilege and honour to work with you,' Satish said, sincerity apparent in his voice.

'Call me Adheesh,' he said with a smile. Then turning towards Guruji, he said, 'We will take your leave now, Guruji. On the way, I will discuss what I need with Satish.'

Guruji blessed them and they left. They climbed up one of the hillocks around the ashram, adding to the Gurukul's breath-taking verdant landscape. These hillocks served as lookouts as well as spaces for the members to sit and talk privately.

'Tell me everything about this Viraj Singh,' Adheesh said.

'Well, he is one of the richest men in the world as you know, unmarried and a womanizer. He is very fond of the good things in life, and plays golf and snooker whenever he has the time. Despite all this, his steely hardness comes to the fore in his business dealings and people are wary and sometimes scared of him.'

'Where is he at the moment?'

'He is not in India. He is on a tour of the Southeast Asian countries, to expand his business.'

'When will he return?'

'He will return after a week, stay in his hotel for a few days to straighten out a few things, and from there he will go to

Goa, where again he has a couple of business matters to attend to. In Goa, he generally combines business with pleasure. He often stays in South Goa as he likes the privacy of some of the less-visited beaches.'

'Hmm, it is here that I'll have to make my move.'

'I agree. How many tickets should I book?'

Adheesh looked at him in surprise. Nobody had done this type of work for him earlier. Well, there was always a first time, he mused.

Aishani was with them when they reached Goa. They checked into a hotel in South Goa and hired a taxi with a local guide to visit the beaches. They zeroed in on two beaches. Both were rocky beaches and the waves constantly washed over them leaving minute algae or deposits from the sea behind. The constant flow of the water along with the small particles, resulted in foam, not too much but more than enough for their purpose.

According to Satish, Viraj Singh would be in Goa after a week, which gave Adheesh and Aishani some time to familiarize themselves with the two beaches and set the stage. They would get up in the morning, complete their Surya namaskar and then walk hand-in-hand along the beaches to get a feel of things. There were no mountains or even hillocks but there were huge rocks on both the beaches. The waves crashed on these rocks forming bubbles of foam.

To a curious onlooker, it seemed as if they were a couple on their honeymoon, who wanted privacy and wanted to be only with each other. With their slim well-toned bodies, they looked much younger than their age. There were very few people on these beaches, probably because of the huge rocks scattered all over.

'Adhee, it's so beautiful and cathartic. I wish we were here for a real holiday,' Aishani said with a sigh of longing.

'I too wish we had come here for a better reason.'

'Now whenever we come to this place we will be reminded of this operation. It'll be difficult to enjoy then.' She sighed again.

'Yes, but the satisfaction of saving the world cannot be compared to any regret whatsoever.'

'I know, Adhee. We have to do what is right to save our world and we have to be ruthless about it, without any mercy.'

'That's my girl!' Adheesh kissed her hand. Aishani became all business-like now. 'Adheesh, I will stay here and charge my powers. You go to that hotel in Bambolim where he stays. It's good that you play snooker.'

'Yes, this hobby of mine is going to pay dividends now. I'll leave Satish with you.'

'No need. You'll need day-to-day information from Satish more than me. I just have to strengthen myself. Baba's training is truly going to help us now.'

Adheesh looked at her.

'Baba had taught us to be faster than the fastest. He also taught us intuition amongst so many other vidyas. I must be extremely fast so that I can be on both the beaches almost at the same time depending on which beach Viraj Singh decides to go to. I have to make sure that my powers do not dissipate if I have to fly from one beach to another. So, you see, Adhee, I have a lot of work and practice to do. In fact, I may even run out of time. You go, Adhee, you have an uphill task ahead of you, you have to make friends with your enemy.'

'Okay, Ash, so I'll go now. Take care, baby.' He kissed her and then left with Satish.

Aishani felt lonely, but only for a moment. She waded straight into the water to clear her head. She swam for some time, then came out, dried herself and walked towards one of the rocks where the maximum amount of sea foam had collected. She collected some of the sea foam in her hands. It was quite fluffy and dense. Denseness was what she and Adheesh wanted so that it would hide the Vajra that Adheesh would hold in his hand. She turned towards the sun with the foam in her hands. The foam reflected the colours of the sun. She turned back and looked at the small hillock that had sea foam along one of the huge rocks there. It was glittering like thousands of multi-coloured crystals. Aishani caught her breath at the beauty of the glittering foam. It seemed as if all the rainbows of the galaxy had collected there and were showing themselves off through the foam. And it would be used to kill a monster! The foam changed shape as soon as a wave crashed into it and took another shape. The shining rainbows remained as long as they faced the sun. Aishani sat down on the side of the rock and began her meditation. She would need all her concentration to transfer her energy and strength to the already powerful weapon – the Vajra.

Adheesh and Satish checked into the five-star hotel where Viraj Singh was also going to stay after a couple of days. Adheesh spent the two days familiarizing himself with the hotel and all its amenities. He polished his snooker game and indulged in some gambling in one of the casinos.

As Satish had informed him, Viraj Singh came after two days. It was obvious that he was one of the most valued customers of the hotel. The manager was almost fawning over him. Viraj Singh did not pay any attention. He was most respectfully escorted to his suite. Adheesh and Satish were sitting in the foyer observing everything. Satish told Adheesh where Viraj Singh's suite was. He also knew that the first thing Viraj would do was to go for a swim in the hotel's swimming pool. To say that Adheesh was surprised by Viraj's appearance was an understatement. He had the most pleasant-looking face, which though, not smiling was not frowning either. He was neither very tall nor very slim. As expected, he was impeccably dressed. He was fair and had dark hair and a square face. There was nothing remarkable in his personality, but his eyes revealed almost everything to anybody searching for signs. His eyes burned like fire or turned to ice on occasion. Today they were neither fiery nor icy. His aura was such that a lesser person would have been singed just by a stare from him. Adheesh knew that Viraj was relaxed, as he had just clinched a hydropower project deal, and had come to Goa to unwind. Was he closer to his goal, Adheesh wondered. By seizing these water-based projects he might be nearing his goal of revenge. Adheesh shook his head. Maybe or maybe not, but his orders were clear. This was a demon that had been killing and torturing humans for centuries just to fulfil his desire for revenge. It wasn't as if he wasn't caught and punished for his crimes. He had been caught earlier, but the whole point was that he couldn't be killed by traditional methods.

When Viraj came to the pool, Adheesh was already there, swimming. Viraj paused for a moment. A deferential waiter brought a glass of cold beer. Viraj took a long swig of the beer and surveyed the swimming pool. There were two more swimmers. But it was Adheesh who caught his eye. Seemingly unaware of anything, Adheesh was effortlessly swimming laps in freestyle. There was such beauty and power in Adheesh's swimming style that it immediately caught Viraj's eye. One thing that Viraj did not have was faith in any person, whether demon or human. There was a fire burning in his heart that had to be avenged. Something about Adheesh caught his eye and affected his heart. In the present era, Viraj Singh was finding it even more difficult to take revenge on anybody. Human beings had become as dangerous, wicked and cunning as demons. He wanted to take revenge on all the so-called good people because they were the ones who had so viciously destroyed his ancestors. This time, he wanted to destroy them en masse so that nothing remained. Nobody could destroy him because of the boon from Lord Brahma. He would not succumb to anything made of metal or wood or anything which was wet or dry. Another aspect of the boon was that his powers would keep on increasing, whenever he fought with anybody.

There was a niggling thought in his mind, however. Despite the boons, the treacherous devatas had managed to kill Vrutrasur through cunning and nefarious means. He would not allow such a thing to happen this time, in this Kaliyuga. The moment Viraj laid his eyes on Adheesh, something clicked in his mind. A long-lost memory was becoming active. He tried to capture the memory, but it eluded him. He sat down on a chair and concentrated. He covertly followed Adheesh from the corner of his eye. A rage began building up in him. He thought he would explode. He was positive now that it was people like Adheesh who had killed his powerful ancestor. He took deep breaths and controlled himself. He was not going to play into the hands of this human. Rather, this time he would find out how his ancestor Vrutrasur was destroyed.

He watched as Adheesh came out of the pool and went towards the shower cubicles. Viraj also swam a bit in the pool, but only to clear his head. His heart was not in it. To unwind, he went to the snooker room. To his surprise, Adheesh was there too. He was seemingly unaware of anybody else in the room. Despite himself, Viraj was impressed. There was so much grace and expertise in the way Adheesh played, it was a sheer pleasure to watch him. This heightened his desire for revenge. It was clever people like Adheesh, who had so cunningly destroyed his ancestor. It reinforced his determination to wipe them off the face of the earth.

Adheesh, on the other hand, was on tenterhooks. He wanted to catch Viraj's attention. Viraj would be gone from Goa in a few days. In this short period, he had to get acquainted with Viraj Singh and become his friend. Quite a tall order. So engrossed was Adheesh in chalking out his own mission, that he did not see the interest in Viraj Singh's eyes. Every moment, Viraj's misguided hatred for Adheesh was increasing, but he was cunning enough to hide it. There was no doubt in his mind that he was going to kill Adheesh. In the present day, he would be called a psychopath and his feelings were well hidden. As he was so successful, people around him tended to overlook his idiosyncrasies. Adheesh needn't have worried too much. He turned to walk to the other side of the snooker table and Viraj was standing there. They looked at each other, and Viraj said, 'That's quite a game.'

Adheesh acknowledged gracefully. His smile burnt into Viraj's heart and mind. You smiling swine, he thought, you will not escape me this time. This time I will kill you and get rid of your soul for eternity.

'May I?' he politely asked Adheesh. Adheesh tilted his head, but he was mystified. It seemed as if Viraj was seeking his friendship. From the corner of his eye, he saw a startled expression on Satish's face. This was not in their script at all. Their reports were that Viraj Singh was not a friendly person and here he was making overtures to Adheesh. Keeping this thought at the back of his mind, Adheesh played along. Both were keen sportspersons.

'Tell you what Adheesh, why don't we go to a beach tomorrow? I know of a couple of beaches here that are comparatively free of tourists mainly because of their rocky terrain,' Viraj said.

They were sitting near the swimming pool, a cool beer each in their hands. Adheesh was vary of this friendship. Both of them wanted to become friends for their own ulterior motives. So be it.

'Okay, speaking of a quiet beach, I have heard of a good one. It's about an hour's drive from Panjim. Why don't we go there?'

'Okay,' Viraj agreed. Adheesh had a hunch that Viraj was also laying a trap for him. Maybe Viraj was too confident of the boons which his ancestor had received from Brahma, and which blessed him too. He could feel the Vajra in his bag. Nowadays he always carried the Vajra with him. It was becoming a cat-and-mouse game. Now there was no need for Adheesh to try and win his favour. Viraj himself was making overtures towards him. Adheesh's intuition was telling him that Viraj harboured malevolence towards him.

The next day, they went to the beach that Adheesh had suggested. It took them one-and-a-half hours to reach there. Satish had already left the previous night to apprise Aishani of the whole situation. It was one of the most beautiful beaches in the world, made even more beautiful by the absence of tourists. A few stragglers were there but they did not mar the beauty of the place. A couple of honeymooners were strolling but they too went off after some time. Adheesh eyed the sea foam which had collected so beautifully around some of the larger rocks. Two of Viraj's men were there, carrying all the necessary stuff. They placed chairs for them and a table to hold their drinks and snacks and a chess set. They also placed scuba diving gear near them. The men retreated after this. Adheesh and Viraj were left alone. Adheesh could now feel the malice and hatred in Viraj.

'Shall we play chess?' Viraj asked politely, opening a bottle of beer. Adheesh agreed. They began to play.

'Why don't you take off your jacket? You'll be more comfortable. It's quite warm under the sun,' Viraj said.

'I'm fine,' Adheesh said, feeling the Vajra beneath his jacket. He tried to concentrate on the game, but he was too distracted. He could play chess reasonably well, but he was losing badly.

'You see this beautiful beach, Adheesh?'

'Yes, it's one of the most beautiful beaches in Goa, the water is a clearest blue,' Adheesh concurred.

'It won't be there anymore,' Viraj said with a laugh.

'What do you mean, Viraj?'

Viraj looked at him speculatively. 'Don't think that I don't know about you. You and your ilk cunningly killed my ancestor out of jealousy and spite. We have to avenge his death. Since the pusillanimous devatas have so dastardly left the people of the earth to their own plight, it is left to us to destroy the earth and its inhabitants. I shall first dry out all the water of the world, then if anyone or anything is left, I will kill them too,' he said, with a cackle of loud laughter.

Adheesh sat back. There was no need to pretend anymore. Both knew that they were each other's enemy.

'Not while I am alive, you won't,' Adheesh declared.

'We'll see,' Viraj said with a sneer. 'Maybe you're not aware of the fact that the boon which Brahma had granted to Vrutrasur has passed on to me. I'm practically invincible you know.'

Adheesh paused for a moment. He did not want Viraj to suspect that he had a weapon to circumvent the boon.

'That may be the case, but no way can the earth be allowed to be destroyed, not while I am alive,' he stated calmly.

Viraj scoffed at him. 'Then let's begin by killing you. Just how do you intend to stop me?'

They both got up from the table. Adheesh folded his hands in supplication to Viraj. They started walking towards the rock.

'Viraj, what happened was ages ago. Your ancestors and the devatas, both are not here anymore. Only we are here – weak human beings, weak in comparison to demons and devatas. We cannot fight their battles. What happened eons ago is gone, forgotten. Let us forget it and carry on with our lives. Our earth is so beautiful, let us work towards making it better and more beautiful,' he implored.

Viraj pooh-poohed his entreaty. He was fuming and smarting with anger at the humiliation that his species had undergone ages ago.

They were nearing the rocks where the sea foam gathered. It was almost dusk now. The rocks cast shadows here and there. They were on the edge of the sea foam now. Adheesh stood in front of Viraj barring his way, not allowing him to walk further.

'Get out of my way!' Viraj bellowed, striking at Adheesh forcefully. 'I will kill you.' He took a gun from his belt, cocked it and aimed it at Adheesh. Adheesh had fallen on the foam. In a flash he took out his Vajra and covered it with the foam so that Viraj could not see the weapon. Aishani's strength and power had already entered the sea foam enhancing the power of the Vajra. Swift as a cheetah, Adheesh jumped up and struck Viraj a strong blow with the Vajra. The breath left Viraj's body and he fell down heavily. The gun fell from his hands on the sea foam and immediately disappeared. He gave a diabolical laugh, secure in the knowledge that he was invincible. He swiftly jumped up and hit Adheesh, who staggered from the blow. He was a strong warrior, but Viraj was the descendent of one of the greatest demons. He was not going to go down easily. He thrust his hands towards Adheesh's stomach, but Adheesh struck him on his forehead. He wobbled and fell down, but he pulled at Adheesh's leg. Adheesh slipped and fell. Now they were both on the ground below the rocks. The sea foam enveloped them, but it was not so thick that it could cover both. If this fight went on, then Viraj would sooner or later see the Vajra, which was still covered with the sea foam. The foam which covered their bodies had the strength of Maa Durga. It was now or never. Adheesh swung the Vajra and hit Viraj on his shoulder. He yelled and quickly jumped before Adheesh could land him a second blow. Adheesh jumped up and hit him on the temple, almost crushing his head. Viraj slid to the ground, vanquished.

Adheesh stood there, panting over Viraj's body. Adrenaline was still coursing through his veins. From a distance, he could dimly see Aishani and Satish running towards him. Though Aishani was there, her powers were in the foam. As soon as she physically reached there, her powers came out from the foam and went back inside her. She and Satish helped Adheesh get up and together they walked away from the demon.

ROMPO

'It feeds on human flesh!' Jayant said, with a shudder.

'So, what's new? Most of the demons that we encounter eat not only human but all kinds of flesh. You haven't come out with any profound discovery, you know,' ridiculed Tejas.

'Okay, maybe not, but here is the difference.'

'What?'

'These eat dead flesh, no, they eat rotting flesh. If the flesh is not decayed, then they wait for it to rot and then they eat it. They enjoy eating this so much that they sing while eating the rotting flesh.'

'Yechh!'

'Ya, Yechh, but that's the way it is.'

'What is it called?'

'It's known as Rompo.'

'Oh, probably because it romps over the dead bodies.'

'Ha-ha, very funny! The name is not derived from the word 'romp.' It is very much an Indian creature, even if we don't know the origin of the name,' Jayant said.

'So why are you telling me this, even if we are told to destroy these creatures? I'll be on top of the trees, spying on them from the treetops.... no smell too, just a bird's eye view,' Tejas said in a teasing voice. Then, on a serious note, he asked, 'Jayant, in some circumstances, it must be good too, as it also feeds on unclaimed carcasses of any species.'

'Yes, I agree, but Uday would not have come up with it, if such creatures have been doing such a good job. There has to be more than that. Uday never talks only for the sake of talking.'

Tejas nodded. 'Uday bhaiya was sounding us off. Maybe this time he will give this work to us independently,' he said, getting excited by his own inference.

'Do you really think so?' Jayant too warmed up to the idea. They were the youngest in the core group of warriors, and hence had not been given any independent charge as yet. It had not really bothered them, but now the idea was growing in their minds, and they were thrilled.

'It may not be so. Let us proceed cautiously. We can impress them if we show them that we have enough information about this creature.'

'Yes, we should be able to find the information in the library. I remember a teacher telling us about such a creature in one of the classes. I wish I had paid more attention.'

'We'll go to this particular teacher, if we don't find such information in the library. Let us keep our research a secret for the time being. We may be fishing in the air for all you know.'

'Ok,' Tejas said with a grin. 'See you in the library in a few minutes.' So saying, he jumped on to a tree and vanished. Jayant smiled and followed on foot on the ground.

They met in the library. Hurriedly they went through the archives and zeroed in on a few books. They took these books to a corner table and began reading. They did intensive research, egged on by the idea that they might be given charge of this mission.

The core group of warriors held a meeting every week, presided over by Adheesh or in his absence, Uday. At today's meeting, the others realised that Jayant and Tejas had something important to tell them. Both of them were very excited and wanted to tell them about the strange creature or demon called Rompo.

'Bhaiya, I know about these creatures. They are a hybrid of many creatures. They have the head of a hare, ears like humans, their front arms are of a badger, and rear legs resemble that of a bear. They have a skeletal body and can change colour like a chameleon.'

'Yes, Bhaiya,' Tejas piped up. 'They are nocturnal, and they love to eat dead humans. They like dead human flesh so much that they often sing while eating.'

'Very good research, Jayant and Tejas,' Adheesh praised them. Tejas looked proud of himself. He could see half smiles on their faces.

Adheesh continued, 'These creatures had disappeared

a long time ago. They had been useful in their own way by getting rid of dumped decaying flesh and unclaimed corpses. But later, they began enjoying their food habits so much that they began killing people and hiding them in lonely places and eating the rotting flesh later on. People must have heaved a sigh of relief when they disappeared. Their favourite food was decayed human flesh though they ate the corpses of animals too. These creatures were known as Rompo in ancient times, were used by the royal armies to get rid of unwanted and unclaimed bodies of prisoners.

'Unfortunately, they have chosen to resurface. They take the shape of human beings, but they don't mingle for fear of getting caught. All of you are aware that our population has skyrocketed in the last century and is consistently going up. The Rompo has very wisely chosen this time to come out. There is so much food to eat. Because they can take the shape of human beings, they just mingle in a crowd and bide their time. When the time is right, they kill a person or in the case of a child, lure it away and kill it. After this, they hide the body and wait for it to decay. And then there is an orgy.

'But generally, they steal body parts from the crematorium or graveyards, which is easier but not as appetizing. They now prefer to procure their own kill, keeping it in a safe place till the time they need it. There is this small hamlet near the jungle. The villagers are poor, simple and uneducated. Fed up with this endless cycle of poverty, many young people have left the village in search of fortunes. The elders of the village have stoically accepted this. Hence there is no great hue and cry when someone goes missing. It's taken for granted that the person has left the village. This is just the right environment for these Rompo in the guise of humans. Our intelligence has reported that some people have left the village, but that's a very small number, as compared to the people who have actually disappeared. Two animals resembling Rompos have been sighted at the village crematorium and the graveyard too. They could be the same ones or there may be more. In the human form, they are diminutive, but one small bite from them kills a person and, their influence is such that when a dead thing is near them, it begins decaying at a much faster rate.'

Jayant added, 'Another trait – their constitution is such that, it does not allow them to eat bones, so they eat only the flesh of their victims. Earlier they would leave the bones at the site but now for the fear of being caught, they bury them. Hence, finding a huge stack of bones will also reveal their whereabouts.'

'Bhaiya,' Tejas began tentatively. 'I think Jayant and I are experienced enough to take on the work, independently.' If Jayant was a bit surprised at Tejas' words, he did not show it.

'Hmm,' Adheesh mulled over Tejas' words. 'That is so. I will have to talk to Guruji about this. I think it'll be better, if Devnath goes with both of you, as he knows about the negative energies in crematoriums. But before I go to Guruji you will have to chalk out your strategy and let me know.'

Tejas and Jayant almost squealed in excitement. Jayant was more mature than Tejas, but even he was delighted at the idea of being given independent charge. It would mean that they were on the way to becoming full-fledged warriors. The next couple of days were spent by Tejas and Jayant in fevered and hectic planning and strategizing. They did not mind including Devnath in their plans. In fact, they were rather relieved that he was going to be with them. They did not know much about Devnath's background, but they did know that he was indubitably familiar with crematoriums and knew quite a lot about dead and even undead people. They trusted him and knew that he would curb their enthusiasm, if required.

A few days later, all three of them were in the crematorium. They had received Guruji's permission and blessings. It was just after midnight. There was no sound or light. The only light was from the smouldering ashes of the fire. It was very quiet and eerie. They positioned themselves. Tejas was sitting on one of the trees on the crematorium's grounds. Jayant and Devnath were slowly walking around. Devnath could see and hear all sorts of creatures and the sounds they made. Jayant, with his additional vision, could see many ghostly shapes but none of which mattered to them at the moment. They knew that the Rompos were eaters of raw and rotting flesh, they wouldn't really be fond of burnt flesh, but a couple of them had been sighted here. Devnath knew that they had been sent here so that they could be initiated to work independently. It was expected that the Rompo here would not be particularly strong, because of lack of proper food.

They waited. But they were now getting the feeling that hunger may have driven away the Rompo.

Suddenly, Tejas uttered something in a soft, guttural voice. He was perched on one of the highest branches of a nearby tree. It was not a human sound, but they understood that somebody was there. Both Jayant and Devnath looked around. Suddenly they saw a man walking towards the burning platforms. He was small and thin. It was strange for a man to come to the crematorium so late in the night, but Devnath knew that sometimes bereft and grieving people did come to the place, to be with the last remains of their loved ones. Nevertheless, he was alert for any signs of malevolent and creepy behaviour. So was Jayant. He was trying to focus. This was one time when his power of seeing things was bouncing back on him. He could see so many lost souls walking around. Some of them knew that they had died, some did not. They were restlessly searching for their bodies. A great wave of pity and empathy passed through his body. God knows how long they will take to adjust to their new state.

There was again a call from Tejas. This time it was an agitated and alarmed cry. Jayant broke out from his reverie. Immediately alert, they looked up at Tejas. He was frantically pointing at the man who had just come. They looked at the man. Nothing seemed to be amiss though he was slightly hidden from view. They walked ahead silently. Now they could see the man clearly. He did not look like a man at all. It was slowly transforming into the creature they had researched in the library.

'Careful,' whispered Devnath. 'A whiff of his breath and we will go into a coma-induced sleep and our bodies will begin to decay.'

Jayant nodded. This fact had been dinned into them by their elders. A slight touch or a smell of the Rompo's breath could be fatal for any of them. It was so risky that Ruby and Aishani were not ready to allow them to come here on their own. The two women had conceded after much cajoling and coaxing.

They watched in fascination as the man slowly turned into a beast. It was not too huge, just the size of a big dog, though an emaciated one. Its head looked like that of a large hare, but with huge, sharp, dirty, yellow teeth. Its neck was surprisingly slender. Its hands and legs turned into paws and claws of a different animal. Its front legs were longer than its hind legs, and they had sharp claws like an eagle. Its hind legs were shorter, and the paws were long and padded. It had a thin long tail, bunched into a ball at the end, probably to beat and stun its victims. From its head to half of its back, it began sprouting long, rough hair, like a lion. Its eyes were dark yellow, ringed with a darker yellow. It had upright ears like those of a pedigreed dog. It was changing colour from brown to muddy green. For a moment, they thought they heard something, as if someone was singing. They realised that it was the creature, which was crooning to itself. Suddenly the crooning stopped. It seemed as if the creature was sifting through the burning corpse to find a piece of unburnt flesh. The wordless singing had stopped because it could not find rotting flesh. It shuffled around aimlessly, searching for a piece of decayed flesh.

Suddenly the Rompo looked directly at Jayant and Devnath. For a moment all three of them stood still, too shocked. They came to their senses immediately. Squealing, the Rompo turned and ran towards the open gates of the crematorium. Jayant and Devnath were very fast, but the Rompo was faster. In a flash it had disappeared from view and the place returned to its unnatural quietness, filled with departed souls. They were disappointed and frustrated.

'It may not come here again. It must have changed into its human form again. Could you make out its human form?' Devnath asked Jayant.

'Only that it was small and slim,' Jayant answered, disappointment clear in his voice.

'Hey! He went that way,' Tejas, said. He had come down from the trees.

Sighing with relief, they ran in the direction that Tejas had pointed. But no luck. Either the Rompo was too fast for them or – or what?

'Jayant,' Devnath said urgently, 'This creature may or may not be as fast as us. Maybe it's just hiding somewhere here itself. If it has the power to take the shape of a small human being, then maybe it can make itself smaller or invisible and hide. You look for it with your vision. I will come back in a minute.' Devnath ran back towards the crematorium. Jayant began inspecting everything minutely. Tejas was with them all the time, perched on the top of a building. Devnath rejoined them in a few minutes. Tejas noticed that his bag was bulging a bit more. They continued to comb the area.

'There he is!' Jayant pointed towards a concrete pillar. The Rompo was hiding almost inside the pillar. It growled when it saw them, transformed into its original form, and ran. Its gait was ambling, even though it was very fast. But the boys and Devnath were prepared now. Nobody and nothing could outrun Tejas. He ran after the Rompo and caught up with it. But he had to slow down for the others to catch up with him. He did not have to wait long, but it did give him enough time to see Jayant and Devnath brandishing swords. Only they were not swords. Both of them were holding burning tibia bones in their hands. Devnath had covered the outer edge of the bones with oil-soaked cloth and set fire to it. They knew that the Rompo ate only decaying flesh, but not the bones. Bones were left just like that. The two things that it was scared of were bones and fire. The boys had both. Even Tejas had small bones covered with flammable cloth. He hadn't ignited them. He was waiting for a signal from the other two.

The Rompo ran. By now everyone had got their second wind and they could have caught the creature had they wanted to, but they pretended that they were unable to catch up with it. What they actually wanted was that the Rompo should think that it was being chased and thus try to outrun them. This way they could reach its lair or wherever it lived. Pretty soon the atmosphere began to change. It began to get brighter, and it became cooler too. The whole operation had taken place silently till now, but now it became even quieter. The dawn should have been pleasant, but that was not the case. The cool air brought along with it a very nasty smell, that of rotting raw flesh and bones. Jayant gagged at the stench. Even Devnath was finding it difficult to breathe. Tejas was too far up but even he could smell the poison.

They finally reached the lair of the Rompo. It was hardly a lair. It was a modest two-room house on the outskirts of the city. There was only one house of its kind there. They now knew that nobody came here because of the unpleasant smell. The creature they had been chasing was still in its original form and when it reached its home, it just rushed inside and banged the door. They did not go inside even though they had the appropriate weapons. There could be more than one Rompo inside the house. The other reason was that they had to be at a distance from its influence lest it contaminated them and triggered the decaying of their bodies. Gingerly they went towards the back of the house. They gagged at the sight which confronted them. There was a mountain of bones in the backyard, presumably of human beings. But they were not sure. Some of the bones could have been of animals too. Most of the bones had been chewed bare of flesh, though a few bones still had bits of flesh sticking to them. The flesh had probably been left to rot in order to make it tastier.

'We don't know how many of them are there, but we have to get them out without us going inside. We cannot risk our lives senselessly,' Devnath whispered.

Jayant nodded. 'I can see inside,' he whispered back. 'There are only two of them. They are like huge mole rats, but uglier, hairier, and more ferocious. There are rotting corpses of humans as well as animals there. It seems that they have killed a few living beings and dragged them here to rot.'

'That's quite a lot of food, enough to last them a couple of months. In the meantime, they'll continue to kill people and stash them here,' Devnath observed. 'We have to dispose of them before they kill more people.'

Tejas had come down to the ground now.

'I have an idea,' he said eagerly. 'There are so many trees around here, I'll climb to the top and throw these firebombs on this house. The house will catch fire. We know that these creatures are afraid of fire. There are only two doors, the front, and the back. You guard one door each and kill them as soon as they come out. They may both come out of the same door or run out of opposite doors.'

'Very well,' the others agreed, obviously impressed with the idea. Jayant patted Tejas on the shoulder, conveying his appreciation. There was no time for anything more. Tejas adjusted his bag and flew up to the top of a tree.

'Jayant, you stand near the front door, and I'll guard the back door,' Devnath said.

'Okay,' Jayant said. He knew why Devnath had chosen the back door. It was because he himself would have baulked at standing near the pile of rotting flesh and bones. With his crematorium experience, Devnath could also use the bones as weapons in double-quick time. They ran towards the front and the back doors. Tejas, from his vantage point, lit a few of the bone bombs and threw them at the four corners of the house. He then flew to another tree and again threw four more bony fire missiles. For some time, nothing happened. No sound, no movement. This was expected. Initially, the enemy would stand still during an unexpected attack. Then it would try to pinpoint the danger, gauge the extent of risk, and then respond to the situation. The Rompo was an animal after all. It would first try to escape, then if cornered, it would fight back. The warriors' weapons may have been simple, but they were more than deadly for the two Rompos. All animals were afraid of fire, but a blazing bone is cataclysmic.

Sure enough, after the initial shock and silence, there was a great scuffle inside the house. Then suddenly the front door opened and both the Rompos shot out. Jayant was waiting for them with his ignited bones. Shouting loudly, he brandished the bones in front of them. One of them squealed and fell down in front of him. The other one, trying to escape, collided with him. It was trying to dodge the bone bombs thrown by Tejas from the treetop. Jayant fell down but not before fatally wounding the creature. Devnath heard the commotion. In a flash, he was in front of the house. Taking in the scene, he immediately impaled the fallen Rompos with the large fiery bones in both his hands. This was to ensure that they had actually died. Tejas came down to the ground, smiling.

'Get back,' Devnath shouted hoarsely. Tejas jumped then looked at Jayant. His left arm seemed to be paralyzed.

'Oh God, no! Has the Rompo bitten him?' Tejas asked.

Jayant looked at them with half-closed eyes. He was slowly slipping into a coma. His left arm was turning grey. Devnath was very calm.

'Tejas, stay here with Jayant. I'll be back in a minute,' he said urgently.

Tejas nodded. Devnath was the most experienced of the three. He saw Devnath run towards the tallest of the trees and begin to climb it. Jayant was very quiet and obviously wanted to sleep. Tejas saw Devnath climb to the tallest branch and cry out in a strange voice. It was a mixture of the sound of a bird as well as the sound of a few animals. Tejas could not decipher the language. In a minute, he thought he heard another cry similar to the one that Devnath had let out. But it sounded far off and very faint. Tejas did not pay much attention to it. Jayant's arm was becoming greyer by the minute. Suddenly the air was rent with similar sounds. Devnath was talking back to them. Devnath came down after some time. Within minutes, a few people came with a vehicle. It was not an ambulance, but Tejas knew that it belonged to the Gurukul. The attendants had a stretcher with them. They were covered from top to toe with some protective clothing. Quickly they injected something into Jayant and then lifted him onto the stretcher, placed it in the ambulance and sped away. Only one person remained with Tejas and Devnath. Slowly he took off his mask. Tejas gasped, 'Adheesh bhaiya! What are you doing here? I thought you were at the Gurukul.'

Devnath was smiling from ear to ear.

'Tejas, we always keep a standby ready for such contingencies,' Adheesh said. 'We always support our people during an operation. We don't interfere unless there is an emergency. Your mission, though not very difficult, was nevertheless dangerous. All of you have done a wonderful job. There's only one thing left, which I have to do. Walk away, both of you, as far as you can, and don't look back. I'll follow in a minute.'

They immediately began to run away. Suddenly they heard a loud explosion and a roar of fire. They were very careful not to look back. Adheesh followed them after a few minutes.

There was another large van waiting for them at the corner of the road. This too was from the Gurukul. They could not recognise the driver as he was fully covered. The van itself was divided into three parts. One was for sick people or for people like them. The next was for doctors and caretakers and, the third was for medicines and medical paraphernalia. A nurse stopped them from going into the van. They were thoroughly sprayed with a watery substance from a machine. Soon they were completely soaked. A doctor directed them to wait outside till they were completely dry. This did not take long. Obviously, it was some kind of sanitizer. Once inside the van Tejas could not stop himself.

'Adheesh bhaiya, where have they taken Jayant? Please, nothing should happen to him. This was our first independent venture and we have failed miserably. He is my best friend,' Tejas was teary-eyed with guilt and remorse.

Adheesh and Devnath looked at each other and a message passed between them. Devnath said, 'Both of you have not only passed, but passed brilliantly. Had it not been for Jayant's ingenious sight and your sighting of the Rompos from the treetops, we wouldn't have been able to reach their lair. The credit goes to both of you.'

Tejas stopped crying. There was no surprise in the fact that Devnath was assessing their merits in this operation. Even though Devnath was Adheesh's bodyguard, his position as a bona fide warrior had been accepted by all.

'Yes,' said Adheesh, 'Both of you worked efficiently as a team.'

'It was not a very difficult operation,' Tejas said, sounding unconvinced. 'It was just a feral animal which had to be killed and we botched it up.'

'No Tejas, they were not only feral animals, but they were also shape-changing demons. You couldn't have done more than you did. What both of you can learn, however, is to take lightning quick decisions with equally swift action.'

By this time, they had reached the outskirts of the

Gurukul. Tejas was not familiar with any of the routes that their van had taken. Though he was not paying any attention to the routes, his subconscious mind did notice that they were speeding through unfamiliar woods. There was no password entry at the Gurukul gates. The van-cum-ambulance sped through the gates of the Gurukul, and they were in front of the infirmary. Uday and Guruji were already there, along with Aishani and Ruby. He knew that he could not touch anybody till he was meticulously cleaned up and sanitised. He looked questioningly at Uday.

Uday understood and said, 'Jayant is in quarantine. We are not allowed to meet him. But Vaidyaji said that he is going to be alright.'

Tejas heaved a sigh of relief. Then he turned and looked at Adheesh. 'Both you and Jayant come to me after three weeks for advanced training,' Adheesh said, giving Tejas a smile of appreciation and congratulation.

KABANDHA

'You know we have been destroying demons from the time we were born and even before that if our memories or subconscious are to be relied upon,' Aishani was musing.

Aishani and Adheesh were sitting with Madhuji on the veranda in her home. Adheesh had come to drop Aishani and the kids at their Nani's place. Good for Madhuji, but their paternal grandparents were going to miss them. This was an age-old tussle between their two grandparents. There is an Indian saying, 'Mool se zyada pyara, sood hota hai' meaning 'Interest is preferred to the principal.' The grandchildren had become more important to the grandparents than their own children. More so in the case of Madhuji as her husband was not there to share her love for Darsh and Divya. Also, she had more knowledge about her grandchildren's innate superpowers. There was another entity totally in love with the children, that was the house itself. It would hoard sweets and chocolates and shower the twins with them when they arrived. The twins would squeal with delight at the treats, while the house would smile, expressing its love by gently banging the doors and the windows. Adheesh left them after having a cup of tea with Madhuji and others.

The next day, the children woke up as usual. Both the twins were playing in the shrubbery in the jungle behind Aishani's house. Aishani was sitting under her favourite tree with a book. Her mother had given them a picnic basket. She felt nostalgic. It was all so familiar. It seemed that only yesterday all of them had been playing here, when Tejas had got stuck in the snake's burrow. So much water had flowed under the bridge since then. Where they used to play now her children were playing. She sighed. Everything was just a bit different from the earlier generation. When they had come here as kids, there was no supervision. But the twins were never without somebody to guard them. Today it was Devnath who was guarding them and she herself was there, of course. It was a lazy afternoon. Aishani yawned and closed her eyes. Lunch had been delicious and now she was feeling sleepy. Her mother had made moong dal koftas, paneer sandwiches and salad with tomatoes, avocado with pine nuts, all dressed in – olive oil and honey. Aishani did not want her mother to make two kinds of food, one bland for the twins and one spicy for her. So, the picnic basket was the same for everybody, though Madhuji had packed extra spiced chutney for her and Devnath. Her mother had packed a separate food packet for

Devnath as he would never dream of eating with them. For dessert, there was chocolate barfi.

Devnath was always alert. He was Adheesh's bodyguard but now Adheesh was in that part of the Gurukul where others were not allowed. So, Devnath was with Aishani. He loved the children as much as he loved Adheesh. With Aishani it was different. Once he got to know about her, especially when they were in the Himalayas, he began to revere her. She was like a goddess to him, an incarnation of Goddess Durga.

Aishani relaxed in the garden, content. She could hear the children screaming delightedly. 'Kabi! Kabi, Kabi!' Divya was calling out.

I wonder who Kabi is, Aishani said to herself. She was amused by the names given by the twins to anyone or anything they played with. Suddenly there was silence. Before Aishani could panic, the laughing and screaming resumed.

Devnath smiled to himself. They were a handful, these two. Never staying in one place, always laughing, and running around. Both of them were hand in glove in any mischief. They were almost three years old now. Aishani could understand them very well; the others took some time to understand their language. At the moment, they were sitting under a tree and playing with their toys. And mud too. Apparently, Divya was making mud dolls and Darsh was destroying them. They would wait for each other to repeat the cycle of making and destroying the dolls. Devnath looked at them and then looked all around. These were precious babies. They had to be protected at all costs. They would have the powers of both their father and mother once they grew up. Maybe even now they had some powers. He looked at them, his heart full of love and pride. They were still making and destroying dolls. They had made up a story around the mud dolls. They had made a small mud house and were trying to put the dolls inside. The dolls were of absurd shapes. The twins were too young to make a proper shape. While putting the dolls inside the hut, the soft mud would crumble and fall apart. Darsh would groan and briefly scream, after which their giggling and laughing would begin again. The twins did not need any other company, though they did play with Ruby's son once in a while. Devnath watched them, absentmindedly touching the small bones and knife which he always kept with him in his bag.

He saw that whenever any doll broke, some sort of a liquid oozed out. He didn't pay much attention to it, thinking it was wet mud dripping from the dolls. Suddenly he looked more closely. The dripping mud was actually dark-coloured blood, and the dolls were real living things! They cried when they broke, and Divya was putting them together again. Thunderstruck, he ran up to the twins, grabbed them in his arms, dusted the mud from their clothes, and ran towards Aishani.

'Bhabhi!' he shouted hoarsely. Aishani was up in a flash. Her maternal instincts were always working overtime. Their lifework was so dangerous that they were always exposed to hazardous situations. Devnath almost threw the babies at her. "You go, bhabhi, I'll deal with the situation here.' Aishani did not ask any questions. She gathered the children in her arms and ran home.

Left alone and filled with dread and panic, Devnath ran towards the place where Darsh and Divya had been playing. The mud dolls were small grotesque creatures. Some were lying on the ground, and some were trying to run away. Only they couldn't. They had very small legs, their face and torso almost merged, but they had long arms. They started screaming, the moment they saw Devnath.

Devnath was confused. These small dolls were too harmless to do any real damage. Their bodies were like headless torsos. The head and thighs were inside their stomach, and one large eye and huge teeth protruded from it. As if to make up for these anomalies, the creatures had quite large arms. To top it all off, they seemed to be saying something. He cupped his ears to hear what they were saying but could not make out anything. They could be dangerous he knew, and the twins had been playing with them for such a long time. Were the creatures screaming, or was it their way of laughing? Had they been dangerous, they would have definitely harmed the twins.

'So, what do I do?' Devnath wondered. He looked at the creatures again. They were fading away and before he could do anything, they completely disappeared from view. Devnath searched for them and waited for them to show up again. Nothing happened. He waited for some more time and then went towards Aishani's house.

Meanwhile, Aishani was desperately looking for anything or any signs that the twins might have encountered anything dangerous in the shrubbery. Were there snakes? Could Dakini or Shakini have been there? No, they wouldn't dare, not with Aishani around. She bathed the twins and asked them about their pretend game. But even she could not understand what they were saying. They were telling her everything in a high sing-song voice, but their words were unintelligible. The conclusion she derived from their excited conversation was that Darsh was pulling off the arms of the mud dolls and Divya was joining the arms again. The dolls too had joined in the revelry and they were also laughing and crying along with the twins. She waited for Devnath impatiently. Devnath came after some time. He was also puzzled. What was more puzzling was that Devnath's description of the small creatures matched the description given by the twins. She was disappointed but intrigued too when Devnath told her that the creatures had disappeared.

The next day, Adheesh and the others had to come back to the main Gurukul, after winding up their exercise and teaching stint. After settling the twins with her mother-in-law, Aishani went to the Gurukul. She and Adheesh met at their usual place under the banyan tree. The others too joined them after some time. Aishani told them about the adventure with the twins the previous day.

'I remember reading about one such demon in one of my earlier classes. I don't remember much, but it was a demon with huge arms who wanted to be killed so that it could liberate itself from a curse,' Adheesh said, as he tried to remember.

'Yes, I too remember such a story,' Jayant said.

Adheesh and Aishani looked at each other. During their training, they were so engrossed in learning martial skills and mantras and meditations that they had not paid much attention to these stories. They were flabbergasted at the idea that Darsh was breaking the monsters and Divya was remaking them. Destruction was possible anywhere and anytime, but how was Divya putting them together again? How could this be even possible? Did Divya have some special power? In their world, anything was possible, but this? Was she capable of repairing a living being, no matter how small it was or how basic? And Darsh was breaking them! Aishani shook her head.

'I will go to the library with you,' she said and stood up to go with them. They were surprised. Aishani had her own private itinerary. Adheesh, however, understood. Both of them were worried about the children. The twins had started showing signs of their powers too early. As parents, they felt that it was their duty to maintain as much normalcy in their children's lives as possible. This is what their parents had also done. Both Adheesh and Aishani had become aware of their powers only after they joined the Gurukul. Their kids were even more exposed to the Gurukul. Adheesh and Aishani often took them to the Gurukul so that they could play and enjoy the salubrious environment.

All of them started walking towards the library. But Aishani's heart was heavy.

Suddenly she stopped. 'I'll come after some time,' she said. They looked at her in surprise. Then they looked at Adheesh. They all understood the parents' worry and anxiety. Aishani walked away. Adheesh looked at the others, shrugged his shoulders, and then followed Aishani. He took her hands in his, trying to reassure her.

'Where are we going, baby?'

'Let's go to Guruji. Adheesh, I'm so anxious about the

babies. We have to give them a normal life. Later they can decide what to do. But it seems they can't help themselves.'

He pressed her shoulder to comfort her. 'Okay, let's go to Guruji. He will have an answer for us.'

Guruji was in meditation. They waited outside and looked around. How beautiful it all was! Manoharji was not here anymore, but there were other people who looked after Guruji's cottage both inside and outside, though Guruji didn't encourage it. This was their home, their Janmabhoomi and their Karmabhoomi. They had no desire to be anywhere else. Just sitting there, outside Guruji's cottage calmed their anxieties and fears. Guruji called them in soon after. They went inside, touched his feet, and sat quietly on the mats before Guruji. Guruji blessed them and sprinkled holy water on them.

After some time, Guruji spoke. 'Your children are an extension of both of you. Both of them have your qualities in different measures. They are a mixture of your qualities and powers. While Divya may have your powers of forgiveness and healing, Darsh may have the focused toughness from both of you, which may sometimes border on cruelty. Your children are destined to be greater than you. They will shine like no other in this Kaliyuga. But their paths as well as yours are ridden with strife and insurmountable difficulties. Life is not easy. And especially your life. In the present context, it is your twins who have led you to the descendants of the demon Kabandha. Find out about them and help them attain moksha. Often, your children will lead you to negative energies and the demons, which both of you will have to destroy. You are indeed blessed to have the twins. Look after them and guide them gently, but firmly.'

They were nonplussed. Guruji waited for them to absorb it all. He waited for them to speak but there was nothing to say or ask. Guruji had summed up everything in these words. Aishani was relieved and so was Adheesh. They touched Guruji's feet and left.

The others were just coming out of the library.

'Oh, we've found out so many things about these demons,' Tejas was the first one to speak. Aishani smiled at him. Guruji's words had soothed and calmed her. She found she could breathe easily now.

'Okay Tejas, let's go and sit near the stream. Then you can tell us everything,' she said with a smile. Adheesh heaved a sigh of relief. They all went and sat down by the side of the stream. Each of them had a designated place near the stream. They looked at Tejas expectantly. He wouldn't have let anyone talk anyway. 'As you might have guessed, this story too goes back to the time of Ramayan and beyond. There was a Gandharva, a celestial musician, Vishvavasu. He prayed for years to the creator of the universe and performed hard penance. Since it was Satyug when prayers alone brought forth the desired results, Vishvavasu managed to win the boon of immortality from Brahma. As is the case with such boons, the benefactor in trying to test the power of the boon or to show off his power to lesser mortals, becomes arrogant and cruel. This is what happened to Vishvavasu. Drunk with the power his immortality, he attacked Indra. Since Vishvavasu did have the boon of immortality, Indra could not kill him. But he struck him with his Vajra. Now we all know that the

Vajra is the strongest weapon ever built. It was crafted out of the bones of Sage Dadichi. The Vajra was so strong, that it drove Vishvavasu's upper torso and his legs and thighs up his stomach. All that remained was a thick torso with the rest of the body inside it. Vishvavasu had bitten off more than he could chew. By the time he realized his mistake, it was too late. He begged and entreated Indra for forgiveness. Taking pity on him Indra gave him a mouth and two very long arms so that he could eat. On more pleading, Indra said that Vishvavasu would return to his former body and regain his lost prestige when Ram and his brother Laxman would kill and burn him.'

Adheesh and Aishani looked at each other. They had used the Vajra in the very recent past when both their powers had fused together to destroy the demon Vrutrasur. Oblivious of all this, Tejas continued. But he was getting fidgety. He had sat in one place for a long time. Ruby understood and gave him a bottle of water. Gratefully Tejas took a long swig of the water and was more relaxed.

'Tejas, that was a very good narration of the research,' Uday said. 'Why don't you stretch your legs, while we decide what is to be done now?'

Tejas accepted the suggestion with alacrity. He jumped up and walked towards a tree. The others smiled and continued their discussion.

'Jayant, you can take up the story from here,' Uday suggested.

'Okay,' Jayant said and turned to the others. 'Somehow in the course of time, Vishvavasu came to be called Kabandha, meaning 'Headless Torso.' Kabandha stayed in the dense jungle near a sage's cottage and began torturing his disciples. It was around this time that Ram and Laxman came to this part of the forest. Kabandha caught the brothers in each of his long arms. But when he heard that they were Ram and Laxman, he released them and implored them to kill him.'

'And?' Ruby interjected.

'So, as usual, some trace of Kabandha was left over. Apparently, these traces become minuscule monsters sometimes and become huge monsters at other times. Through the ages, they seem to have lost their demoniac qualities, but one memory has remained with them, that is, to attain moksha. And for this, they have to be killed by God or somebody(s) with godlike qualities or at least blessed by God.'

Devnath was sitting at a little distance from them. He never sat with them, no matter how much they insisted. He couldn't stop smiling when he heard Jayant's story. For him, Adheesh bhaiya and Aishani bhabhi were gods, and now their children were too. The miniature Kabandhas came to Darsh and Divya because they could sense some higher power in them.

Adheesh looked at Aishani and then announced. 'Now is the time to go to Guruji. He will decide what is to be done.' They all agreed and walked towards Guruji's cottage.

Guruji assigned Adheesh and Aishani to do away with the remnants of the demon Kabandha. The calculations were done, and a day set to slay him.

Adheesh and Aishani were somewhere in the Swamimalai forest near Bangalore in Karnataka. The demon Kabandha was to be found here. The original name of this forest during the time of the Ramayan was Kraunch. Over the course of time, it had been developed by various rulers and was now called Swamimalai. They had reached here a day earlier. The next night was Purnima, a full moon. The Kabandha would attain nirvana if it died on Purnima.

'Not all demons are bad, Adhee,' Aishani said. 'Kabandha just wants to die so that it can become a Gandharva singer and regain its former glory. We hardly have anything to do here, just give it a gentle push to begin a fresh life.'

'Ash, you always see the good in others. Remember, nobody becomes a demon just like that. He has to do cruel misdeeds and think depraved thoughts for long periods to become a demon. Then, when he is punished, he begins to repent. But you have to endure the punishment for an equally long period before you are forgiven, if at all.'

'You're right, Adhee, I tend to forget sometimes,' she said with a sigh.

They waited silently. In the light of the full moon, they could see things quite clearly. The whole forest was bathed in silvery moonlight. Aishani could even make out the colours of some large leaves and flowers, albeit of a darker shade. Even at its quietest, the jungle was never really quiet. They were quite used to that. They were wearing long boots and coats. Mosquitoes were a menace here and they had taken all precautions. They had covered themselves with anti-mosquito gel. They spent the next one hour cutting and collecting dry wood, made a mound of it, and then sat down near it. There was no need to camouflage themselves, as the demon or the traces of demons left behind, came here on every full moon night. They held hands and sat on a tree stump, absorbing the beauty of the moonlit night and waiting. They had their weapons ready. Both of them had khukhris. They did not bring any other weapons with them. Though it required a killing, this operation was more of a spiritual exercise than destroying a villain. Here, the creature desired death. Adheesh and Aishani were certainly not gods, but they did have godliness in them. That would have to do for Kabandha.

After an interminable wait, they heard a different sound, as if a huge ball with stubs was rolling through the undergrowth. They stood up in anticipation. Soon they saw it. They knew what to expect, but it still took their breath away. It was a huge headless torso with a huge stomach that bore two large eyes and a big mouth from which two long sharp teeth jutted out. It was hairy all over and had stumps for legs. As if this ugliness was not enough, it had two very elongated powerful arms. The arms stretched for more than a mile on each side, a sight to behold. Its breath was loud and painful, and its mammoth single eye seemed to be searching for something or someone.

'He comes here every Purnima, waiting for God's emissary to kill him,' Adheesh explained.

Aishani was looking at the creature in awe. There was so much pain, so much despair in it that it was difficult for her to think of anything else. She just wanted to hold him in her arms and pat his head and console him. She stood there, not knowing what to do. Suddenly Kabandha saw them. Screeching, he bounded towards them, tears falling from his eyes. He caught them with his long arms. He knew instinctively that God had sent his emissaries to rid him of his misery.

'Please,' he whispered hoarsely, 'Please, kill me.'

It was such a simple but painful entreaty. Aishani looked at Adheesh. He nodded. Then as if in a slow-motion rhapsody, they took out their khukhris and cut off his arms and sliced his torso in two, killing him immediately. They then burnt the demon with the wood they had collected.

A beautiful and handsome man rose from the burning pyre and touched their feet. He folded his hands and thanked them, 'I am eternally indebted to you. You have freed me from a fate that was worse than hell, and I had to live the horror of that life every moment I was in that body. I don't know how I can repay this debt, but if I can help you in any way, any time, or anywhere, please let me know. I will be most happy to come to your aid.'

Adheesh and Aishani too folded their hands in acknowledgment and gracefully accepted his gratitude.

Aishani spoke, 'There is one favour we have to ask of you.'

'Yes, of course, anything in my power,' the descendant of Vishvavasu spoke. His voice was as sweet as milk, honey, and melted gold. After all, he was a Gandharva, a celestial singer.

'You know about our lives and what we do on this earth. We would entreat you to guide us whenever we are in a tricky situation and…,' she stopped.

'That I will always do,' the Gandharva said with a smile. 'But I think you want to ask for something else.'

Aishani was hesitant. She looked at Adheesh who gave an imperceptible nod.

'Our children are quite young. They have powers of which they are not aware. Sometimes they unknowingly use their powers. Hence, they might harm themselves or others near them. We would request you not to allow any more of your ilk to go near the children for their own good and the safety of the children too,' Aishani blurted out.

The Gandharva became serious for a moment. 'It's good that you have told me this. Now I will warn similarly cursed beings not to approach your children. It might backfire on them.'

Aishani and Adheesh bowed their heads in gratitude. The celestial musician vanished, leaving them alone in the forest.

FARASI

'We don't know for sure how many human beings are trapped in the netherworlds. They are there in the hollow spaces under the earth, below the seabed, and innumerable other places of which we are not even aware, and which are invisible to us. We do not know in what condition these people are, whether they are alive or not. What we do know is that we have got to bring them back no matter what,' said Guruji.

'How, Guruji?' Adheesh asked.

'These human prisoners have not been kept in one place. They have been scattered like grains of sand all over the so-called "hells" that are in the hollows under the earth, under the ocean bed and god knows where else. The first task is to find out where these clusters of humans are beneath the water.

We understand that these places are not visible to the naked eye, hence the failure of the rescue operations. Secondly, these places are so scattered that even if a few people have been rescued from one cluster, it is impossible to reach the other places on time. The demons get to know about the rescue and immediately change the location of other clusters. So far, it has been a losing battle.

'Adheesh, you will be in command. Gather as much information as you can, plan a strategy with your team and inform me.'

Everyone agreed, touched Guruji's feet and left.

Two weeks passed. They had learnt so much about Pataal and the places where humans had been captured and kept, for consumption, for experiments, or merely to be tortured. In their reconnaissance missions, along with Jayant and others, they had discovered the invisible hideouts of the demons, which were inside the earth. But try as they might, they could not find out the sections of the Pataal or hell under the ocean's surface. Adheesh, Uday, Aishani and Jayant went to Guruji and apprised him of their challenges.

'This is no small matter, and it has to be dealt with very delicately, and with great focus.' Guruji emphasised on the word focus.

All three of them were surprised. They knew that Guruji was aware of their total and complete absorption and focus on whatever job they were entrusted with. But if Guruji was telling them to be focused, it meant that some more inner power was required of them.

'Go to the northwest side of the ashram and wait for me

there. It is two miles from here,' Guruji added.

If they were surprised, they didn't show it. So many things that Guruji said or did would not make sense to them initially, but everything was clear later. They had complete faith in Guruji.

They did not have to wait too long. Guruji appeared soon after they reached the northwest side of the Gurukul. Nodding to them, Guruji walked ahead. They followed. Guruji disappeared after a few minutes. They kept on walking and suddenly found themselves in a clearing. They stood and stared in surprise. They had not seen this part of the Gurukul. Their Gurukul was beautiful and full of various kinds of flora and fauna. They had not imagined any place more beautiful than their Gurukul. But this place was even more beautiful, so different and enchanting. The flora and fauna were quite different from what they were used to seeing.

Guruji said, 'You will be coming here quite often now. We need this place, and we have to take the help of some of the animals here to take us to the different Pataals.'

They quietly followed Guruji, awed by this new place. The Gurukul often jolted them out of their complacency. This was one such moment. Guruji beckoned them towards a horse; except that it only appeared to be a horse, it was not a real horse. To begin with, its colour was emerald, and green. Its height and length were that of a normal horse. Its hind quarters were coiled and scaly like a fish. It was nervous in their presence, but not scared. Guruji gently rubbed the horse's back. It whinnied, welcoming the touch.

'These are magical, green, water horses. We have only

two of them here with us. The original water horses are called Farasi Bahari. Their habitat is the bottom of the Indian Ocean. Among animals, they have the greatest endurance as far as galloping and running are concerned. This could be attributed to their not having lungs, which are not required underwater.'

Aishani gushed, 'They are so beautiful, Guruji. But if their habitat is at the bottom of the Indian Ocean, how are they here?'

'These two are crossbreeds, Aishani. The purebred Farasi Baharis cannot survive on land. But on certain days of the year, they swim up to the coast and graze. They are so sensitive and fearful of man that even the scent of a human being drives them away. So, people leave their horses on the coast in the hope that the Farasi Bahari will mate with them, which makes them hybrids. We too have a couple of these crossbreeds. They have retained the qualities of both their parents. One parent is earthbound; hence they are not scared of human beings. The other parent does not have lungs and can run at breakneck speed giving them eternal endurance.'

Guruji paused for a minute, allowing them time to assimilate the information, and then resumed, 'All these Pataals are invisible to the human eye. Jayant will find out the location of these Pataals with his see-through vision. The intelligence team of the Gurukul will give you the true coordinates of these hells, here on the ground and below the seabed too. You will have to do the rest yourself. As far as going to the seabed is concerned, I will be fortifying you with some powers that will take you there without encountering too many obstacles. Work out your teams and strategy and let me know.'

'Yes, Guruji, but once we reach these places where our fellow human beings are kept, how do we get rid of the demons when we are underwater? After releasing the victims, we will be able to come up, but how will the released prisoners follow? They will not be able to withstand the pressure of the water and reach up to the shore,' Adheesh said.

'There is a difference between the prisoners inside the earth and beneath the water,' Guruji said. 'While most of the prisoners inside the earth are in their physical form, the ones under the sea are without their bodies. Their souls have been imprisoned. Once released, they will go straight to their maker. Keep in mind that speed is of the essence here. Do not think of destroying more than your mission. Swarga and Narak will always coexist in one form or the other.'

They touched Guruji's feet and prepared to leave. Adheesh looked at Aishani. He knew that she wanted to spend some more time marvelling at the myriad trees, flowers, and animals. She and the others too were piqued by this alternate world. Were there more such worlds in the Gurukul? But now was not the time to explore. Maybe sometime later they would take Guruji's permission and come here to explore.

Back in their regular Gurukul, they sat as usual under the Banyan tree behind the classrooms and made their plans. They then went to Guruji and divulged their strategy to him. It took them another week to prepare themselves for the mission.

They were astride the two Farasi Bahari horses and had entered the Indian Ocean from the southernmost tip of India. Adheesh and Jayant were on one horse while Aishani was on the other horse. Jayant was not very proficient in horse riding. His total focus was on looking through the floor of the ocean and finding the places where the poor human souls were captured and kept. The others from their team could not come as there were only two Farasi Baharis.

They were astounded by the speed and intelligence of these hybrid horses. It was as if they instinctively understood the requirements of their riders. They were almost at the bottom of the ocean bed in about half an hour. They were not aware whether the horses had gills or not, but they were swimming and going down at a very fast pace. Though they had the exact coordinates of the Pataal under the ocean bed, they did not want to take any chances.

The colour of the water near the coast was green and it began changing to light blue and then into dark blue and finally to indigo as they went deeper into the ocean depths. They encountered many kinds of fishes and sea creatures on their way, but luckily, none were of the predatory kind. For the horses, it was like a homecoming. Even though they had been born and bred on land, swimming toward the ocean bed was like second nature to them.

They had undergone a whole gamut of training and activities, before embarking on this exercise. To begin with, Jayant had been put on a strict regime of specific meditation to increase his visionary powers, after which he had to report to Guruji, who slowly empowered him to see in the dark waters of the ocean, and to withstand the pressure of the water.

Aishani and Adheesh were old hands. Nothing fazed them. Aishani's mornings were spent praying and paying obeisance to the sun. Guruji had handed over a divine weapon to her.

It was the Tejprabha astra, and it belonged to Surya Devata. Once activated, it had the power to disintegrate any being into its constituent atoms. It was a solar missile meant to annihilate the demons residing below the seabed. Guruji had chosen the most appropriate weapon. The rest of the time was spent on various methods to propitiate and activate the astra, which would come into being only after the necessary rituals were executed perfectly.

Guruji had given Adheesh a free hand. Adheesh was a mature and responsible warrior. Guruji knew that he would choose the perfect weapon and train himself with it. Guruji had to keep an eye on both Jayant and Aishani, as Jayant was less experienced, and Aishani had so much power that she had to be restrained from time to time before her powers went beyond her control. Adheesh had chosen a long sword, thin with sharp edges on both sides. It was light but deadly. A heavy sword would have been difficult to manage in the strong pressure of the water as there would have been too much drag. A thin long sword would also be tough to manage but he would have to face only the surviving demons after Aishani had fired the Tejprabha astra. Probably they would not be in a condition to fight back. Guruji had no doubts about the valour, strength, and commitment of his warriors.

It took almost a week to activate and master the Tejprabha astra. This astra would demolish the enemy by burning him to cinders or melting into a liquid form, depending on the nature and strength of the opponent. It took a few more days for the horses to accept them and become one with them.

Jayant's visionary eyesight began to work as they neared

the ocean beds.

'Adheesh, I can see the Pataal. It's not one Pataal, rather it's like a cluster of many small Pataals, each with its own kind of demons and prisoners.'

'Keep looking, Jayant. We have to find the souls who have been imprisoned here.' Adheesh looked sideways at Aishani. She was holding the Tejprabha astra and looking all around. It was as if they were on land, mounted on normal steeds and looking around for an adventure. Which wasn't very far from the truth, he thought wryly. Though their purpose was to search and rescue, they had all agreed that their life was more than just an adventure. It was a different world altogether, almost a parallel world with living beings, flora, fauna, and everything so different. There was not too much current, but they could feel the strong pressure of the water. They felt as light as when they were on land. But try as they might they could not find the prisoners. They kept on egging the horses to take them to different places, but no luck. Jayant could not see anything.

'Adheesh, we cannot go on like this,' Jayant said. 'I will have to go to my highest level of meditation. It will take some time, but we have no other option.'

Adheesh nodded. He caught Aishani's eye and beckoned her. He could make out that she was fully charged, her chest heaving, and eyes dilated. It was a missed opportunity but there was no other recourse. Quickly he explained everything to her. Aishani looked at her brother Jayant and smiled. She knew that he was not a great one for meditation. Now, especially in these conditions, it was going to be quite difficult.

But there was no other alternative. The human souls as well as their kidnappers were there. They just could not abort their mission. She nodded in agreement. Adheesh patted the Farasi Bahari. The green horse understood and swam to a secluded, hidden spot. It was a small opening, camouflaged with huge corals. Jayant dismounted and went inside the opening. He sat down in the lotus position and immediately went into a meditative trance. Aishani and Adheesh swam outside, guarding the opening. Had they not been so tense, they would have been utterly enchanted by the beauty of the ocean. Shoals of colourful fishes swam past. Sea horses also came in groups, curious about human beings. There were innumerable varieties of coral. But they did not see anything, they had to remain focused on their mission.

After almost an hour, Jayant came out. He gave them a reassuring look and mounted the horse behind Adheesh.

'Can you see anything now?' Adheesh enquired.

'I think so. Wait! I see two huge snakes to our right. They are about a kilometre long. My god! Their fangs! In fact, they don't have any heads, only fangs. Can you see them, Aishani?'

'No, Jayant, I cannot see them, they are probably a couple of demons, invisible to our eyes.'

Jayant nodded. He could now see a bewildering array of sea creatures. Many of them seemed to be harmless. Sometimes he thought he saw alluring human females, giving him come-hither looks. He shook his head. He knew what they were. He would have to give a running commentary to Adheesh and Aishani, who would seek out these creatures and destroy the demons. But first, they would have to find the imprisoned souls. He could detect at least two places where they were. Maybe the demons had not expected anybody to reach so far down in the ocean depths. These prisons were not as impregnable as they had thought.

'Can you make out those long flowing corals on your left?' he asked.

They turned to the left and squinted. There was a whole jungle of corals on their left, waving and dancing in the water. Aishani was ready with her Tejprabha astra. Adheesh too was ready. They were at least half a kilometre away from the coral reef. They had to be this far away for the astra to reach the demons and not overshoot them. Adheesh would have to be nearer to annihilate the surviving demons, if any.

'The prisoners are behind the corals. They are imprisoned in catacomb-like structures. Strong enough to imprison the human souls, but not enough to keep us out,' Jayant said with a grin. 'I can now see more than two places where the kidnapped souls are held, but the good thing is that they are mostly together. You can destroy all of them with your astra. The only thing is that the entire beautiful flora and the corals will also be destroyed, not to mention a few sea creatures.'

Aishani was in destruction mode now, and focused on the mission, to hear anything.

'Ash is the last person to hurt innocent beings. Fortunately, the Tejprabha astra follows the orders of the mind. The whole creation is alive because of Surya Devata. His weapon can never destroy his own creations,' Adheesh said.

Jayant nodded. Subconsciously, he also knew that this was the case. They became busy plotting their trajectory. Before pulling her bow and arrow, Aishani respectively prayed to them, then pulled the arrow back on string of the bow. It was like an explosion underwater. They did not hear its sound, but they could feel it. There was a bright light at the place where the corals were swinging. It was like the brightest afternoon. The light went on shining for such a long time that they thought that they had been miraculously thrown on the land. The huge snakes and the beautiful creatures which had followed and surrounded them, had vanished. The places where the Tejprabha astra had been aimed and where the weapon had blossomed, so to speak, did not show any signs of destruction. They waited. They had absolute faith in the astra. But they could not see anything. Gradually as the bright light of the weapon dissipated, they began to see millions of dust-like particles floating in the water. Realisation dawned, and they all gasped simultaneously. The Tejprabha astra had demolished the sea demons into minute molecules. A few huge and nasty-looking eel-like snakes were too far away to be fully destroyed, but they were broken. They were the guard demons who tried to escape. Adheesh pursued them and demolished them with his double-sided sword.

In the meantime, Aishani and Jayant saw an exodus of the trapped souls who had been released. They were flying up but not before each of them folded their hands in obeisance to them.

After that, it was just a matter of time before they came up to the surface. The Farasi Bahari swam with them to land safely on the shore.

A week later, they were in Guruji's cottage. He had acknowledged the success of their mission, but they could see that he was worried.

'Only half these demons have been demolished, the water-borne ones. The imprisoned human beings inside the earth are still to be rescued. The numbers are increasing every day.'

Adheesh, Uday and Jayant were sitting in front of Guruji. It would take Aishani another two weeks to recoup from the exercise of operating a divine weapon. Human beings are incapable of using divine weapons, simply because they are a much inferior species to the gods and the devatas. Since Aishani and Adheesh were blessed by the gods and goddesses, they could, under extreme concentration, use the divine weapons. But there was always a heavy price to pay. During the use of the divine weapons, their bodies and brains were granted permission to use the weapon of any deity, whom they invoked. But later, they would revert to their normal human form, which was a very painful process that took a long time depending on the power and strength of the particular divine weapon.

Adheesh said, 'Guruji, I will go home and explain the emergency of the situation to Aishani. At the moment, she is unable to get up from the bed. It will take her some time to recoup her strength even to go to the hospital. I will see that her regeneration process is done at a faster pace.'

'No, Adheesh, don't do that,' Guruji exclaimed sharply. 'These things are best left alone for nature to take its course. If she does not convalesce properly, the weakness will remain in her body throughout her life and that will just not do.'

Adheesh stood there undecided. Guruji was right. It wouldn't be right to disturb Ash at this juncture. They waited.

Guruji mulled over his thoughts and then came to a decision.

'There is no option but to bestow the powers of a divine astra on you, Adheesh.'

Adheesh was surprised. Aishani was the chosen one, even though he was fully capable of using any divine weapon. He had used a couple of divine weapons when he was with Aishani, and when the demons were too strong and vicious to be handled by one person. He folded his hands and waited for Guruji's instructions.

'These demons are the vilest of the lot. Demons also have some principles, though convoluted most of the time. But these are the worst of the lot. They are cunning, liars and turncoats, with all the attributes and characteristics of demons. They can change their shape, lie convincingly, drink human blood, and imprison human souls. In short, they are the worst kind of lowly demons. They kidnap humans and take them deep inside the earth, torturing them and keeping them imprisoned. There is no escape. Most of their souls have already been extracted from them. In fact, the trapped humans give their souls in exchange for a short temporary respite. After this, they are just soulless bodies made to execute the most atrocious deeds. The relatives of these human beings have no idea where their sons, daughters and friends have disappeared to. They search for them without any success.'

'Where exactly under the earth are they, Guruji?' Uday asked.

'In the centre of the earth, Uday. You will get the coordinates very soon. In the meanwhile, go and practice using your weapons. Jayant, go and increase the depth of your meditation. You will have to sift through all the disguises that these demons will use. I will also direct Ruby and Tejas to do as much research as they can on this subject. Before both of you go for your respective exercises, go to the Farasi Bahari horses, and give them this.' Guruji gave them something in a bag.

It was dark-coloured semi-solid-liquid stuff. It looked like jaggery. But they knew it was not jaggery. They looked at Guruji questioningly.

'These horses are the fastest in the world, but they stay in the coastal areas or sometimes in the sea where the temperature is mild and cool. The centre of the earth is understandably too hot. The Farasi Baharis will wilt within a few minutes. Give them this to eat, give them just a little water in the first hour so that they fully assimilate this elixir into their bodies. Leave them with their grooms after that. They know how to care for the horses after this treatment.'

'Yes, Guruji,' Uday said, inclining his head. They touched Guruji's feet and left. If Uday was happy with Guruji's decision, he did not show it. He was a warrior and always wanted to be with his leaders, Adheesh, and Aishani. Only Guruji noticed the slight bounce in his step. Uday knew that he was going to use more than one weapon; one would be his own Pash and the other would be Einar's Gram, which Einar had gifted him before he left this world.

Adheesh stayed behind with Guruji.

'Adheesh, you will pray to Chandra Dev to bestow the Shishir astra on you. This astra will turn your enemies into ice after which you just have to destroy the ice sculptures. You may not have enough time to destroy these demons as you will be busy rescuing the prisoners. Uday will hold the fort. Jayant will be there to point out the hidden spots. Now let us go and meditate on Chandra Dev and the Shishir astra.'

Adheesh followed Guruji to the Gurukul's museum. He stayed in a corner room of the museum for seven days. It was a bare room with a low table in the centre. This table was covered with a white and silver satin tablecloth, on which was kept the Shishir astra, on a silver tray. It was a crescent-shaped astra with a vertical hollow in the middle, where a person could slip his fingers in to hold it. It was off-white in colour and looked harmless and ancient, which it was, but only as far as its antiquity was concerned. It was primordial too and not of this world. It was given by Agni Dev to King Vishwarath, after he had performed one of the greatest Yagyas, which had continued for more than forty days.

Guruji gave Adheesh instructions and specific mantras to invoke Chandra Devata and the Shishir astra. Adheesh was used to all this, though he had not prayed to this specific astra, or even seen it till now. He was here for a week, constantly invoking the Shishir astra. Guruji would come from time to time and sit along with Adheesh and chant the same mantra, thus strengthening its power. On the seventh day, Adheesh saw the weapon acquire a bright silvery lustre, and he heard a sort of humming sound coming from it. At the same time, he felt a strong force envelop him. He knew that the powers of the Shishir astra had entered his body and that now the weapon was willing to execute his instructions.

He went to Guruji.

'I have checked up on the others. They have also practised hard and are now ready. I have told Jayant to bring the horses. Take water, the horses might need it,' Guruji said. Adheesh nodded and smiled. Guruji smiled back. It was because Guruji told him to take water for the horses but not for the people.

'With you around, I don't have to worry about your team, but you may be too preoccupied to pay much attention to the horses who are not used to so much heat.'

'Tomorrow is Purnima. Though they don't fear Purnima, the demons are just a bit uncomfortable during this period. On the other hand, all three of you will derive more strength from the full moon. You have the Moon's weapon too with you. You don't have to physically keep the astra with you. It will come to you automatically the moment you think about it. And Adheesh…'

'Yes, Guruji?'

'You don't have to worry about Aishani. She will be very well looked after.'

'I know, Guruji, I never had any doubts.' He touched Guruji's feet, and they both went out to meet the others.

Uday and Jayant were waiting for them along with the Farasi Bahari horses. They could have taken some other mode of transport, except that the Farasi Baharis were the fastest on land too.

'Once you release the prisoners, your job will be over. There will be another team to excavate the human beings and clean up the place.'

They knew this. During search-and-rescue operations, the Gurukul ran on smoothly oiled hinges. There were different teams designated for different work. Most of the time, these teams worked together without knowing each other.

They touched Guruji's feet. He blessed them and they left.

Adheesh had the coordinates with him that would take them to the opening inside the earth. They must have ridden for at least fifty miles without realising that they had almost reached their destination. The horses were so fast that they almost flew over the ground. They were gradually learning about the various attributes of the horses. The horses were interacting at a cerebral level with their riders. Even before they pulled them towards any direction, they would anticipate the intention of their riders and turn accordingly. In the beginning, the warriors were startled by such a prompt response and delighted that the horses understood them so perfectly. These horses were so superior that there was no surprise that they became extinct when Kaliyuga began. Perfection requires a perfect environment. The Farasi Baharis did not belong to Kaliyuga. The demons had almost taken over. The original goodness of mankind was covered with the shroud of negative traits, which would not go away till the end of the current era. The three warriors were from Satyug, the time of the Ramayan, which is why the Farasi Baharis responded to them.

They crossed jungles, rivers, and deserts. Once in a while they came across some people, but the horses were galloping at such breakneck speed that they became virtually invisible. Adheesh ordered the horses to stop only after they had reached the entrance of a cave. It was an inconspicuous cave in the middle of a jungle. They stopped because the horses had to be given their potion to ward off the heat and plenty of water.

Adheesh was on one horse: Uday and Jayant on the other. Adheesh looked at Jayant. Jayant nodded. His deep vision was going to begin from here on. Uday never needed any instructions. He was always ready and alert. They went inside the cave that was more like a tunnel. Initially, the Farasi Baharis walked gingerly, but slowly they regained confidence and their walk turned into a trot, and then they were galloping through the tunnel which had now become almost vertical. Jayant was keeping pace with the speed of the horses.

'Now, now, now, here!' Jayant whispered urgently. The tunnel's wall was made up of huge rocks. They stopped but did not see anything. They looked at Jayant. He was pointing towards some rocks on their right. Without hesitating, both Adheesh and Uday slashed through the rocks. Sure enough, four demons fell down dead. They continued their journey. The number of demons kept increasing as well as the heat but all three of them were unaware of it, so focused were they on their mission. These were simple guard demons. The real masterminds were deep inside the earth.

They carried on for a mile. Jayant spoke again, 'I can see them now, I can see the humans too. The demons are of all shapes and sizes. Some of them seem to be shapeshifters too. They are easily changing from one shape to another. Every demon is torturing humans in his own way. These humans are in a pathetic state. Most of them have given up. They are letting the demons do whatever they want to with their bodies. I guess they have lost their mental equilibrium also.'

Adheesh and Uday were ready. Apart from his sword, Adheesh had the Shishir astra, he just needed to invoke it.

Uday had his Pash in one hand and Einar's Gram in the other. He had practised using the Gram with his left hand.

'Okay, Jayant, tell us where the maximum congregation is. Keep an eye on the other groups of demons and inform us as soon as we destroy one group.'

Jayant nodded. He knew the drill. From the corner of his eye, he saw Adheesh close his eyes and silently chant some mantras. The air around them froze and suddenly with a whoosh, a weapon materialized in Adheesh's hand. Adheesh held the Shishir astra from its broader end. Showers of silvery energy were bursting out from the ends of the crescent, though flecks of white cold energy covered the entire weapon. For an instant, Adheesh looked at both of them and then fired the Shishir astra. There was a surprising roar that ended immediately. They could now see the demons on whom the astra was fired upon. They had been invisible earlier. Now they were covered with ice, transformed into ice sculptures. Uday was ready for this. With his massive strength, he began wrecking and shattering the ice sculptures. If Jayant had not been so preoccupied in his search for the other groups of invisible creatures; he would have stopped and marvelled at the carnage and mayhem that was taking place.

All three of them worked in perfect coordination, Jayant pointing to the camouflaged demons, Adheesh freezing them with the Shishir astra, and Uday smashing them to pieces. Some of the demons did catch on and tried to escape, but the astra spared none. Only a few sculptures were left for Uday to demolish when Adheesh went to the prison cells where the human beings were imprisoned. These cells were small caves.

Adheesh always carried a few explosives whenever he was on any mission. Now he blew open the entrance to the caves and waited for the captives to come out. A straggly lot did come out of the caves, but many were so broken, both physically and mentally, that they were unable to comprehend that they had been freed. The warriors helped the poor broken souls come out of the caves.

Adheesh blew up the roof of one part of the tunnel. After that, it was just a matter of time before the rescue teams from the Gurukul came and evacuated everybody to safety.

HOLIDAY WITH THE TWINS

'Guruji, we cannot go away just like that,' Aishani protested. 'There are so many things to be completed here in the Gurukul.'

'Like what, beta?' Guruji asked with a twinkle in his eyes.

Aishani thought, but she couldn't think of any pending work apart from demolishing demons. They had not heard of any demon incursions recently. That did not mean that the demon population had dwindled or that they were not plotting anything. Still ....

Guruji wanted them to take a vacation, far from the Gurukul but not too far. Guruji and Adheesh had even discussed the place where all four of them could go for a vacation. Aishani was not part of the planning because Adheesh knew that she would not readily agree to any plan.

She would have to be coerced to go on a holiday. Though both of them wanted their children to have as normal a childhood as possible, sometimes Aishani's desire to protect them was so strong that she would not agree to even the most mundane activities outside their home and the Gurukul. This was a chance for all four of them to bond as a family. Finally, she agreed to Guruji's advice and agreed to go on a vacation.

They were really fun times. Aishani and Adheesh were so engrossed in their primary job of destroying the demons that there was not much time to spend with their children. Though they did spend quality time together, there were few lazy afternoons or evenings, just being there together and doing their own thing. Both the parents were reassured that the twins were well looked after by the doting grandparents, a plethora of uncles and aunts, and above all Devnath. It was Adheesh's father Vidyadharji, who felt that Adheesh and Aishani were overworked, and that the twins needed them more. He also knew that his son and daughter-in-law would not agree if he asked them to take a break. So off to Guruji he went.

Aishani's logic was that since the Gurukul was the most beautiful place on earth, travelling to any other scenic place to spend their holiday seemed superfluous.

'Ash, both of us know that we have not been spending proper time either with each other or the kids. Now that there is a lull in our activities, we must use this opportunity to bond more with each other.'

Aishani was a warrior but also a mother. And like all mothers, she had feelings of guilt when she was away from her kids. She felt she was not giving enough time to the children.

So, she acquiesced. But they did not go to any seaside resort or the mountains. Instead, they checked into a posh hotel in Delhi, in the heart of the city. They had never before stayed in a big city. The twins took everything in their stride. There were cries of delight as the twins discovered the many amenities of the hotel. The novelty of everything delighted them. There was a huge playroom. There was never any want of toys at home, but they still squealed with happiness when they saw so many contraptions to play with as well as other children of their age. Both Aishani and Adheesh would accompany the twins to the playroom and the swimming pool. Aishani enjoyed just splashing around in the water.

This was the hotel. They were looking forward to discovering Delhi again along with the children. Aishani and Adheesh saw Delhi with new eyes. They had been here so many times but had never really paid attention to its heritage – the vast expanses, the beauty of the city. The malls and the markets were another matter altogether. Her busy life as a warrior didn't allow Aishani the time to discover this aspect of her personality; she had never done much shopping for herself. Before her marriage, her mother used to shop for her, later she shopped only for the most necessary things. She always considered shopping to be a frivolous activity.

She surprised herself this time. She had never indulged in this kind of freedom ever in her life nor had she desired to. But now, temporarily free from all her duties and being with the three people she loved most in the world, totally loose and unfettered, she was enjoying it. And a lot. She had been given a list of markets and malls by Ruby. Aishani had laughed, smug at the thought that she was not going to use the list. It all started when she went to the market to buy clothes for the twins. One thing led to another and before she knew it, she had become a shopaholic. She was running short of money. This had never happened before. She knew the value of money, but only as much as was needed to meet basic requirements. Hesitatingly, she talked to Adheesh about it. Adheesh laughed out loud. 'Who would have thought that you, of all people, would need money for clothes and things.' He stopped when Aishani gave him the look, but there was still merriment in his eyes. 'Not to worry, I'll just ask pitaji to transfer some money. God knows, he keeps on pestering me to spend more. He will be so happy and relieved that we are spending some money at last.' Aishani smiled.

The twins were thoroughly enjoying themselves shopping. They ran helter-skelter in the shops and were reluctant to change clothes for a fitting. Darsh would disappear and reappear suddenly. Both brother and sister would then giggle uncontrollably. If Adheesh was bored by all this, he hid it quite well. It was a typical happy middle-class family scenario.

Sightseeing was another joy they discovered with their children. Aishani was overwhelmed by the rich heritage, the temples and the parks of Delhi. Old Delhi was charming. Their Gurukul was very near to Delhi, and they had visited the city many times. But this was the first time that they were discovering Delhi, both as denizens and tourists. They took the twins to the Rail Museum and to the zoo. The twins were a bit young for the rail museum, but they thoroughly enjoyed the zoo. A visit to the Moghul gardens was a highlight of their visit.

'Adheesh, look at this flower! So different and so pretty,' Aishani said excitedly. Adheesh smiled indulgently. Even though there were no reports of any demons around them, he was fully alert. He had his precious family to look after. He was grateful that there were no signs of demons around them, but still, he could not shake off a feeling that something was wrong. He knew that he would have received a mental directive from Guruji if any such creature was nearby. Aishani was aware of Adheesh's discomfort, but she shrugged it away lest it spoilt their holiday. They went to the International Dolls Museum where again Darsh disappeared somewhere in the aisles, much to the delight of Divya. They giggled uncontrollably, when Darsh reappeared. Aishani was enjoying every moment of the excursions.

After a week of shopping and sightseeing, both Adheesh and Aishani wanted to take a break. They were a bit tired now. They were warriors, not used to a superfluous life. Also, looking after the twins was no small feat. At home they never had to worry about the children; they were looked after by family and friends.

'I'm sure everybody must be missing Darsh and Divya back home,' Aishani said with a laugh as they relaxed in their room.

'Thank God,' Adheesh answered fervently. 'We love our babies so much, but I don't think we are meant for this. Don't get me wrong, Ash. I love our babies, but I am exhausted.'

'I know what you are talking about. My mother left her vocation because of Jayant and me, and she had to look after the house. But I can't do it. Nor do I want to. Probably this is why God did not give us children in our previous births. He's given us only now. I think it's because there are so many people to look after them now. Let us be grateful for what we have and enjoy our lives with our babies as much as we can,' she whispered, overcome with emotion.

Adheesh nodded, relieved that Aishani had understood.

The twins were still sleeping though they were stirring, signs of waking up.

'Adhee, our children have already begun showing signs of their powers. We came to be aware of our powers at a much later stage, when we were mature enough to accept them and hide them from the normal population. Darsh and Divya are too young to recognize their powers as such, and won't be able to hide them. They will be starting school in a couple of months. There will be mayhem once the school authorities or the other children and their parents get to know about this.'

'Yes, Ash, I have been thinking about this too. We cannot send them to a normal school.'

'But Adhee, they have to be with other children of their age. They have to play and learn at the same time,' she said tearfully.

Adheesh hugged her. 'We'll sit with the elders of our families and discuss. Ultimately, we will follow God's directive. And Guruji's directive too.'

Aishani sniffed but felt comforted by Adheesh's words.

'What shall we do today, Adhee? I think the twins are also just a bit tired.'

'Why don't we stay here in the hotel? We can go swimming. In the afternoon, let us go to one of the beautiful parks in

South Delhi. Darsh and Divya will enjoy themselves as long as we are there with them.'

'Done,' Aishani said with a smile. 'We are blessed to have such children, Adhee. They are always happy. They even adjust and accept if they see any negativity around them.'

Adheesh hugged her and gave her a kiss. 'Yes, Ash, we are indeed very lucky to have such happy children.'

Divya got up, seemingly fresh and smiling. She poked Darsh in the ribs. He woke up and threw a cushion at Divya. They howled with laughter and Aishani rolled her eyes.

They had a light breakfast and went to the swimming pool. Both the children had taken to the water like fish. Around 3 o'clock, they went to a highly recommended park in South Delhi. They were impressed. Every part of the park was immaculate and in ship-shape condition. Its symmetrical landscape added to its bewitching beauty. There were small, jewelled ponds where the flowering lotus plants with large leaves almost looked like Monet's water lily paintings. There were a couple of bridges over the ponds too. The twins wandered around the topiary, where Darsh did the disappearing act again. Divya's delighted laughter wafted to Aishani and Adheesh. There were small hills covered with grass and shrubs. There was a cluster of bamboo trees and a children's playground with swings. There were benches scattered at regular intervals. Adheesh and Aishani sat on one of the benches facing the children, contentedly watched them playing There would be some minor tiffs, then loud giggling and squealing. Aishani closed her eyes and relaxed. Her head started to nod, and she fell into a light sleep, her head resting on Adheesh's shoulder. Adheesh put his arms around her and rested his head on hers but kept awake. There was an air of tranquillity around them, lulling them into a sense of security. The kids' sounds worked as a lullaby. Apart from that, there was no other sound. It was quiet and peaceful. Adheesh too closed his eyes for an instant.

His eyes opened suddenly. Where was he? He looked around. Aishani was still sleeping. It was too quiet. He could not hear Darsh and Divya. Immediately alert, he softly extricated himself from Aishani's hug, and made her comfortable on the bench. But Aishani woke up. She held his hand and said lazily, 'Adhee, come and sit beside me.'

'In a moment, love. You go back to sleep. I'll just go and see to the twins,' he said and hurried off. Aishani was fully awake now. The silence puzzled her too. Getting up, she quickly followed Adheesh. The twins were not where they had been playing earlier. Her heart in her mouth, Aishani followed Adheesh. He had his khukhri out. Aishani's weapons were always at her beck and call.

Suddenly they saw two huge figures facing each other. They recognized one gigantic figure as a demon. It was the other being they could not place. It was oddly familiar, but they could not place it. Mesmerized, they looked at the two characters, who were glaring at each other and gearing up to fight each other. The demon was clearly afraid. It had something in his hand, which the other person wanted. In spite of being afraid, the demon had a cunning smile on his face. He held the small thing in his hand and jeered at the other entity. The other person was becoming impatient now and did not seem to want to wait anymore. In a classic pose, it invoked a spear and with full force, pushed it into the demon's heart. The demon howled in pain and tried to retaliate but was no match. The demon fell down dead. His fist opened and out fell a small creature, who got up, brushed himself and ran towards the other being. The other being was still in the classic pose of plunging the spear into the demon's heart. It was still panting and heaving from the force of its own attack.

Adheesh and Aishani were hypnotized by the scene. For a minute, they forgot why they were there. Now the huge creature looked at the small one that had come up to it. It smiled and everything became clear to Aishani and Adheesh. The small creature grew in size. It was Darsh and the huge creature, scaled down in size, was Divya! In front of their horrified eyes, the twins embraced each other amid peals of laughter. The body of the demon had vanished. Darsh and Divya embraced each other once again and giggled some more. They turned and saw their stunned parents. They ran towards them and hugged them. Adheesh and Aishani lifted their children in their arms and hugged them. They were still bemused. They knew that their babies would inherit some of their powers, but they had never imagined that they would begin showing their powers so soon. It seemed that Darsh had been changing his size for a long time now and Divya was not going to put up with any nonsense.

Divya hugged her mother and said in a small voice. 'Mummy, I want to sleep.'

Aishani stroked her head and kissed her. 'Yes darling, but what happened? Did that person frighten you?' Divya perked up a bit. 'Mummy, Darsh and I were playing pakdam pakdai. Darsh would become very small and I would search for him. Suddenly that dirty uncle came and caught Darsh in his fist and pressed him. He was hurting Darsh, Mummy. I called out to both of you, but you didn't come. So, I took out my spear and beat it. It became scared and left Darsh,' Divya then fell asleep.

'Aishani caressed her daughter's head. Adheesh and she knew that it was not a normal sleep. It was a rejuvenating sleep. Divya had grown up to the demon's height and killed it with her toy sword and she had become her real size again. This had taken a toll on her body and nerves. They knew that she would sleep for a long time now. She was too young for all this. She needed training and meditation for such endeavours. On one hand, Aishani was very proud, and on the other hand, she was very worried. Her children had not even begun their lives and they had already carried out this feat. She looked at Adheesh. He too looked extremely worried. Darsh was slightly more alert. They now understood that, when Divya and Darsh were playing in the malls and the hotel, Darsh would reduce himself to a small size and Divya would go and search for him. That meant that they had been playing this game for some time now.

'You want to sleep too, Darsh?' Adheesh asked his son.

'No, I'm not tired papa, I want to play pakdam pakdai with Divya,' he said.

'Divya is sleeping, beta. We'll put her to bed, then we will play together or go to the swimming pool.' Darsh perked up at this. They went back to the hotel and put Divya on her bed.

Adheesh took Darsh to the swimming pool, while Aishani stayed with Divya. Adheesh and Aishani looked at each other. They wanted to discuss all this, but it would have to be later. Darsh was getting restive. Aishani sat on Divya's bed. She was sleeping soundly, as if she had just got come through an ordeal, which indeed she had. A plethora of questions was in Aishani's head, and she wanted answers.

Adheesh and Darsh returned finally. By now, Darsh was also sleepy. Adheesh said, 'No need to feed him, I took him to the pool cafeteria. Let me put him to bed, then we'll talk.' Aishani nodded. Both of them were burning with questions. Finally, they were alone, seated on the sofa in the other room.

'Oh Adhee, I just cannot fathom today's incidents,' she said, not able to control her tears.

'Why are you crying, baby? It's our honour to have these babies. The great Hanumanji could turn as small as a fly and then large enough to swallow the Sun, and even burn demon king Ravan's Lanka. Our children have these powers from God. It is inside them; they don't have to invoke these powers like we do. We have to pray and meditate for days to acquire these powers. We are one lucky set of parents,' he said with a smile, but she could make out that he too was worried.

'Yes Adhee, just like our parents felt that they were blessed to have us as their progeny, we are blessed to have Darsh and Divya. But they are so young, they are not even aware of their powers. Or that they are different from other children. How will they hold their powers? We were not even aware of our powers till we joined the Gurukul. After that, we could successfully conceal and withhold our powers.'

'Yes, Ash, at the moment the only solution I can think of is that the twins cannot be sent to a regular school.' He stopped when he saw the horrified look on her face, 'Now wait, I didn't say that they would not be educated in the traditional disciplines, just that they would not be sent to traditional schools. I think the elders would also arrive at the same conclusion, that in the beginning the twins should be taught at home, till they become mature enough to understand things. Bear with me, baby. We have to deal with the situations as they come.'

Aishani sniffed again, but she was mature enough to realize that there was no other solution. 'I know, Adhee, it's just that the revelation is so sudden that I'm finding it difficult to grasp it all. We will have to go about it in a very different way. Some more of our people have to be taken into confidence. Guruji is always there to guide us out of this dilemma.'

'Doll don't worry so much. Whatever happens, happens for the best.' Adheesh said, pressing her shoulders. We will have to be very careful, Adhee. What if the babies have more than one power? What about Darsh being attracted to blood?'

'Ash, I am also flummoxed by these happenings. We should go home and call an emergency meeting with our inner circle.'

'Yes, let's do that,' Aishani concurred. They left the next day after making sure that Divya was fully rejuvenated.

The meeting was held in the room beside Guruji's cottage. It was a small room but large enough to accommodate approximately more than 20 people. Guruji was sitting at the head of the table. The inner core team of Aishani, Adheesh, Uday, Ruby, Jayant and Tejas were there, along with the peripheral team of Aishani's mother Madhu, and Adheesh's father Vidyadhar. Devnath was very much part of the inner team, but he took his position as a servant and guard duties, seriously and thus stood behind everybody, mainly guarding Adheesh, and following his orders.

There was a long silence after Guruji's revelation that the children had magical powers. It was not a shock, as each of them already suspected something like this. They had their own experiences too, with the twins. Both Aishani and Adheesh would be away for long periods of time, and they would all pitch in to care for the babies. This was where some of them had noticed a few things different about the twins. There was a time when Darsh had disappeared inside the wall and Divya had smashed the wall and found Darsh. All these things were laughingly done. In the case of the wall, it was laughingly put back together by the children. This happened when Madhuji was looking after the children in her house. At that time Madhuji had thought, that somehow, the house had a hand in it. But she was not so sure now. All said and done they were all very proud of the children and their powers. They were Aishani and Adheesh's children. They had to have their powers. Generally, it was decided that the twins would be home-schooled by the members of the household itself. Then each member would try to train the twins to use their powers in the right direction. They discussed many other points as well.

'Guruji,' Vidyadharji addressed Guruji, 'At the moment the most pressing requirement is the twins' safety and security. I will get the best watch persons for my grandchildren. I know where to get them from.'

'I know Vidyadharji, I know that you will leave no stone unturned to keep the children safe, but the lesser number of people know about it, the better it is. In any case, the number of people in the know, will increase slightly as your wife and your brothers have to be told, so that everyone is alert around the children.'

Vidyadhar nodded. Guruji was right. The fewer people knew about it the better it was. There were many points to be discussed after the revelation.

'Now that the truth had been uncovered, there were many important points to be discussed. We cannot discuss all of them now. We will tackle them as and when we come across them. The core team will have to go out on their assignments. We will try to make sure that at least two members of the core team are always around the children. One or two places, where I would think that more security will be required, will be Madhuji's and at Uday's home.'

They all nodded in agreement.

Guruji looked at all of them. They were still in a daze, very proud, but anxious too.

'Together we can overcome this predicament easily. It's just a matter of time before the twins understand their powers and their position in our circle,' Guruji stated and looked at Aishani, who winced at this sentence but kept her head down.

ADHEESH WHO?

They were sitting in the writing room of the library. A couple of other instructors and gurus were also there. Approximately ten per cent of the inhabitants of the Gurukul were allowed in the senior library, out of which only the 11 most capable warriors were allowed in the writing room. This was where they wrote down their experiences, and their encounters with the demons. This would be later edited by experts and turned into books for keen and inquiring minds. True, there were other warriors who also went on missions to destroy demons. However, these warriors were in the minor league and were sent on less hazardous missions, to demolish minor demons. These warriors gave their reports to the librarian in the general library, who after perusal, sent them to the concerned departments.

'Adhee, we have to wind up early today,' Aishani said. Adheesh gave her a preoccupied stare. He was giving the final touches to their last report. He wanted to wind it up so that they could move on to fresh issues. Like any soldier on active duty, writing reports was a boring chore for both of them.

'Ruby will be staying at our place with Darsh and Divya for the next month or so. We are going to the south as Guruji has directed us. She will be coming this evening along with her son. We have to make her comfortable before we leave.'

'Hmm, just a few minutes more, then I'll be totally free. Otherwise, I'll have to complete the report after coming back. You know how these people are, they want even the minutest detail, which I might forget after a month.'

Aishani nodded in understanding. 'Okay, I'll wait.'

Adheesh completed his report and submitted it. 'Let us take the shortcut home. We have to spend some time with her and her son, and Darsh and Divya too.'

They walked through the deserted pathway in the jungle. The jungle around the Gurukul stretched to the outskirts of the town. They generally avoided this route because it was dirty. Dirt meant demons. They knew it was not so, but the thought was never far from their minds. They held hands and walked fast. Another five minutes and they would have cleared the fringes of the jungle. Dusk had started to fall, and mosquitoes began their ferocious attack. Adheesh and Aishani kept slapping their hands and necks to get rid of the mosquitoes.

Suddenly Aishani stumbled. Adheesh tried to steady her, but he couldn't, and she fell down. Adheesh was alarmed.

He knew that Aishani was as surefooted as a mountain goat. She had not stumbled. He pulled her to a standing position, but she fell down again. Thoroughly alarmed now, Adheesh picked her up in his arms. Aishani had fainted.

'Ash!' he tried to bring her to consciousness, but she had gone limp and would have fallen again had he not held her. He checked the nerve on her neck. It was pulsating. It was then that he noticed something alarming. An exceedingly small dart was embedded in her neck. He pulled it out, picked up Aishani and walked back to the Gurukul. He took her straight to the Vaidyashala. The Vaidyashala was manned by three doctors 24/7. One was an allopathic doctor, the others were well-versed in Ayurveda and homeopathy. And then there was another doctor, designated by Guruji personally. This doctor dealt with all kinds of supernatural sicknesses and afflictions. Initially, the warriors of the Gurukul needed this doctor more than the others. After this healer diagnosed and alleviated the warriors of paranormal afflictions, the other doctors stepped in.

The doctors and the attendants quickly herded Aishani into a fully equipped room in the Gurukul's hospital. They were familiar with these two exalted warriors. They came here at regular intervals for their treatments and rejuvenation. The doctor who attended to Aishani, immediately found the reason for her unconsciousness.

'She has been shot in the neck with the Anamnesis serum. This will make her forget the person who was with her at the time of the attack, and the person she loves most in the world. She will recover from her unconsciousness but would have lost most of her memory.'

Adheesh was thunderstruck. But he was too experienced to take the doctor's word for it. He was not going to give up on any person based on an initial diagnosis. The only thing was that this attack had come at an inopportune time. They were supposed to leave the next day to deal with some demons who were attacking the people in sparsely populated places. Now he would have to go alone or with somebody else. First, he made sure that Aishani was comfortable, or at least as comfortable as possible, under the circumstances. Then he rang up Ruby.

'Adheesh, is everything alright? I was expecting both of you much earlier.'

'Things are not too good at the moment, Ruby. We will not be able to come now. I will explain everything when I meet all of you. Aishani has made arrangements for your stay, but she wanted to make you more comfortable. I may be leaving tomorrow alone or with Jayant. The twins will be absolutely comfortable with you and your son.'

'Of course, Adheesh, that goes without saying. But where is Aishani? Why will she not go with you? Is she in the Vaidyashala?' Ruby asked intuitively.

'Yes,' he said shortly. 'Ruby, I'll talk to you later, Guruji has arrived.'

'Okay, Adheesh. I'll wait for your call.'

Adheesh touched Guruji's feet. Guruji blessed him and then went straight to where Aishani was lying so still. Guruji looked at her for some time and then turned to Adheesh. 'She will regain consciousness in a couple of hours, but she will not be in any condition to accompany you on this mission. You will have to go with Jayant.'

'Yes, Guruji, I understand. Vaidyaji was telling me that she may have lost her memory.'

'We'll have to wait and watch, Adheesh. We'll know soon enough, after she regains consciousness.'

Guruji chanted some mantras and softly blew on Aishani's head and left. Adheesh sat down on the veranda outside. There were too many questions in his mind. Would she really lose her memory completely or just partially? Only time would tell.

He spent the next 15 minutes informing his father and Jayant about Aishani, and the change in his schedule. He knew Vidyadharji would inform the concerned people and take charge of everything. There was nothing to do but wait. It had started to drizzle. There was a soft breeze blowing, which cooled his body and eased his tension. He looked at the verdant stretch of herbs, shrubs and flowers, which looked beautiful but grimy because of the fine misty rain. He sat down in a corner of the veranda, closed his eyes, and started to meditate. He meditated for one hour, then got up and went to the room where Aishani was. Two doctors were there, and one of them gestured to him to come inside. Aishani had opened her eyes. He went to her. She tried to get up.

'No, Ash, don't try to get up,' Adheesh put his arms around her. She shrugged him away and lay down again. She looked tired. She looked at him uncomprehendingly. Adheesh was expecting this. But he still didn't know whether she had recognized him or not. There was some movement outside. Guruji had returned. Aishani saw Guruji and made the gesture of touching his feet. Guruji blessed her.

'Guruji, why am I here? Did I have an accident? Why are the doctors here?' she completely ignored Adheesh.

'Relax, beta, nothing much has happened. You had a minor accident. You will be fit in a few days. How do you feel now?'

'I am all right, Guruji. I have this heaviness in my head and my neck is hurting. I'll be alright after I take an aspirin.'

'No, beta, we'll be giving you some other medicines. I'll send the medicines to you very soon. In the meantime, Adheesh and the others are here in case you have any problems.'

Aishani looked at Adheesh. 'Are you a doctor here?'

Adheesh glanced at Guruji, who gestured to him to be quiet.

'No, beta, he is a warrior here. Sometimes he helps in this hospital.'

Aishani gave him a formal smile. Adheesh smiled back and then followed Guruji out of the room. When they were out of earshot, Guruji said, 'She does not remember you. We have to find out what she remembers and whom she remembers. We cannot put any pressure on her mind. This will be a gradual process, helped along with medicines and herbs and specific tantric rituals.

'Things are not so serious that you have to delay your mission. I will continue with her medication, and I will regularly give you updates on her recovery.'

'Yes, Guruji, I hope she remembers the twins. I understand, but they will be heartbroken,' he added worriedly. 'I have to go on the mission, but I would rather have be here with them at this time.'

'Darsh and Divya will be very well looked after. You could have brought them here today itself, but Aishani is not in a fit condition to meet anyone, at least for a few days. Besides, we have not been able to assess their full powers as yet. If Aishani does not recognize them, they might use their powers unconsciously. And we don't know what the results will be.'

Adheesh nodded. 'Yes, Guruji, I'll go and complete our mission, and immediately on my return I am going to hunt for the demons in the jungle beside the Gurukul. There must be more than one of them, or they might be from the town itself, camouflaged as humans.'

Guruji concurred. 'That is a possibility. In your absence, I'll designate a few warriors for this job. And Adheesh, before leaving, I would like you to come here and give Aishani a concoction to drink. This will be the beginning of her treatment for memory loss. It can be given only by you because at the moment you are the first person that she does not remember, and you were with her at the time of the mishap. Another precondition for this drink is that it can be administered only by the person who loves the victim unconditionally. This potion will last for a couple of days, by which time you will be back, and then we will give her the next dose.'

Adheesh agreed, touched Guruji's feet and left saying, 'I will be back in the morning.'

Guruji was already there when he reached the Vaidyashala early the next morning. Together they went into Aishani's room. She was awake. She folded her hands in Namaste to Guruji and again ignored Adheesh. She probably took him to be one of Guruji's assistants. Adheesh's heart sank when she didn't even look at him.

'Aishani beta, I am going to chant some mantras. You have to drink this potion during the chanting. Here, Adheesh take this glass and help Aishani drink it.' Guruji handed the glass to Adheesh. Then he put his hands on Aishani's head and began chanting. Even though she didn't want it, she allowed Adheesh to help her drink the medicine. She was surprised when her body almost swayed towards this man, this stranger, and she didn't feel uncomfortable. She brushed away the thought. No more. Next time she was going to take the medicine herself.

Guruji chanted for some more time, then blew on her head. Then he left with Adheesh. They went to the outer periphery of the veranda, out of Aishani's earshot.

'Guruji, I am leaving with Jayant now.' There was nothing more to say. He just wanted to conclude his business in the south and rush back to Aishani. He knew that she would be well looked after but he wanted to be there to witness every small recovery of hers.

Six days went by. In the deep jungles of the South, Adheesh and Jayant were systematically destroying the demons who had infested the jungles and if not deterred, could come to the villages and towns too. But it was a bit different. These were not the intelligent demons of yesteryears. These were demons in the true sense of the word. They were huge hairy creatures; with sharp, pointed teeth; many of them too large for their mouths. The teeth were like an entity in themselves. Even before the demon had spotted an enemy, the entire jaw along with the sharp teeth, would jut out of the mouth and latch on to the enemy or food. Its owner would then follow slowly moments later. After which they would demolish the enemy, in whichever way they could. Some of them had sharp horns. Some had two and some had a single horn in the middle of their head. They had sharp, pointed ears, but others had very small ears. The worst thing was that they reproduced very quickly. There were hundreds of them in the dense jungle, too many to count. The good thing was that Adheesh and Jayant outmatched them on every level. The demons were ferocious, but they were like large, wild beasts without brains. Their brains were conditioned only to kill, maul and eat. Adheesh and Jayant were master warriors and they killed mercilessly. The greatest problem they faced was the speed at which the demons reproduced. No sooner had they demolished ten of these creatures, than another ten would spring to life. After three days, they were at their wits' end. No way would they be able to destroy these demons in the next week.

On the fifth day, Adheesh made a safe place for himself under a tree and meditated. Guruji immediately came into his thoughts.

'Guruji, this is very frustrating. The more we kill, the more they reproduce. Annihilating them is not difficult; the problem is their pace of reproduction.'

'Hmm... I think some divine intervention is required. You need a divine weapon like the Pishach Astra. These demons are more like ghouls or Pishach. This jungle is famous for breeding them. They had infested these jungles in ancient times too. Then they disappeared. They have resurfaced now. They had probably been eradicated by the devatas with the help of this weapon. I will invoke this astra and give you the mantras to conjure it there.'

'Guruji, how long will it take to come to me and how long will it take to demolish the demons?'

'When you release the Pishach Astra on any demon, it hurtles towards them, splits into many small sacs with needle like spikes which suck up their blood, effectively killing them. Since you are not here, it will take slightly more time for our thoughts, mantras and meditation to align with each other. It should take anything between four and five days for the mantra to come in your physical possession and another five-six days to rid the jungle of all the demons.'

'Guruji, that means another three weeks. I can stay here for any number of days, but you had told me that Aishani can drink the memory potion only from a person who is totally dedicated to her.'

'Yes, so it is, but recalling you will wipe out all that you have done there. Aishani is the most valuable asset of our Gurukul. She is our leader. No harm can come to her. You finish your work there, Adheesh, and I will ensure that Aishani's recovery is smooth and fast,' Guruji reassured him.

Adheesh came out of his meditation. He was not worried that Ash would forget him. That could never happen. They had lost and found each other through the ages. If not immediately, then a little later, they would be back together. But she was attached to so many threads and lives and so much depended on her. He had full faith in Guruji, however. He would find an alternative to the memory potion. He began preparing himself for the mantra of the Pishach Astra.

Back in the Gurukul, Guruji knew exactly who was

totally dedicated and devoted to Aishani, who could give her the magic potion in lieu of Adheesh. This was Uday who had fallen in love with Aishani even before she had met Adheesh. His love was nipped in the bud by Guruji who had stated that Aishani and Adheesh were soul mates. Uday had kept his love for Aishani under wraps, but Guruji knew that he would always love her. But the risk was that Uday's heart would be broken again and Guruji didn't want one of his best warriors to be emotionally hurt. But tough times call for tough measures. Guruji sighed and sent for Uday.

Uday entered Guruji's cottage and touched his feet. Guruji apprised him of all that had happened in the last few days. Uday listened intently. He now understood why he had not been sent with Adheesh. It had puzzled him but now it was clear. Guruji wanted him to hunt for the demons who had attacked Aishani. But it was surprising that Guruji would keep him here only for this reason. He waited for Guruji to tell him more.

'Uday,' Guruji paused for a moment. 'Adheesh was supposed to return in a week's time. Unfortunately, his stay had to be extended. I am giving Aishani a memory potion, which has to be administered once a week.'

Uday waited for more. The Gurukul's strict policy of not letting even the left hand know what the right hand was doing, meant that he did not know about the severity of Aishani's accident. He knew that she was sick, but not that she had lost her memory. He was shocked but kept quiet.

'Now this magic potion can be given to Aishani only by a person who loves her unconditionally and is truly devoted to her.'

Uday stiffened. Maybe Guruji would now send him to the south and recall Adheesh. He saw that Guruji was looking at him without saying anything. After a couple of minutes, he became uncomfortable.

'For the medicine to be effective, you will have to give it to her. Apart from Adheesh, there is nobody more devoted to Aishani than you. If you give her the potion at regular intervals, her recovery will be gradual but steady. If not, we will have to wait for Adheesh, by which time it might be too late and more rare herbs will be required.'

Uday was thunderstruck. He would do anything for Aishani, that was true, but how did Guruji know that? Did others also know? It was something that he had never acknowledged or confessed even to himself. So many questions raced through his mind. He looked at Guruji numbly.

'Don't worry,' Guruji said. 'Nobody knows.'

'Let us go to the Vaidyashala. You can give the potion to Aishani, while I chant the mantras.'

Uday followed Guruji to Aishani's room. Now that he knew the task that was given to him, he was nervous. What would Aishani think? Did Aishani even know? Would she even recognize him after the attack on her? These thoughts ran through his mind even as they entered her room. She was awake and sitting up on the bed. She folded her hands in namaste to Guruji and then turned to Uday and smiled at him. Uday heaved a sigh of relief and so did Guruji.

'Guruji, can Amma and Ruby visit me? I think I am recovering rather well.'

She had asked for her mother and her friend Ruby, but

she did not ask about her children or Adheesh, Uday noticed. She would have to remember very soon, as the twins would begin asking for her, Uday knew. His heart ached. He knew she could never be his, but that didn't stop him from loving her. Adheesh was a dear friend and both of them were his leaders. He would go to any length to help them.

'They will definitely come to visit you, beta, but after a few days. You need to recover fully before I can allow anybody to come near you.'

Aishani looked confused. She looked towards Uday. Guruji understood.

'Uday is here to help me administer the potion while I chant specific mantras,' Guruji said. Aishani accepted Guruji's explanation.

Guruji asked Aishani to sit cross-legged on the bed and he lit some specific dhoops and diyas, sprinkled holy water on her, and began to chant. Uday took the glass of potion from the table and gave it to Aishani. As soon as one stanza of the mantras was over Guruji gave the signal. Aishani sipped the potion obediently. The whole process took approximately one hour. By this time Aishani was very sleepy. Guruji blessed her and he and Uday left the room.

Uday's heart ached to see Aishani like this. It was as if a large chunk of her life had been deleted and she was not even aware of it. She did not remember that she had two beautiful children and a loving and devoted husband and partner. She lived an extraordinary and enchanted life. Fate had dealt a cruel blow and she was not even aware of it. The lives of three more people were affected by this – that of Darsh, Divya and Adheesh. Uday took a deep breath. He vowed to himself that he would do everything in his power to restore Aishani's memory and also punish the demons who had done this to her.

Uday would give Aishani the memory potion while Guruji chanted the mantras. It was quite a simple procedure, just giving her the greenish concoction to drink. Or so it seemed to Uday. The fact was that had it been given by any other person, apart from Adheesh or him, the potion would have become ineffective. Even a minute difference in a person's love and dedication would affect the efficacy of the potion. Guruji knew this, even if Uday didn't.

After a few days both Guruji and Uday began noticing subtle changes in Aishani's behaviour. She began showing signs of restlessness, as if she was missing something. One day, after Guruji had completed his chanting and she had taken the potion from Uday's hands, Aishani blurted out, 'Guruji, everybody I am related to has come to visit me. Then why do I keep on waiting for more people? Do more people know me, and do I know more people? Who are these people that I am missing, Guruji?'

'Do you have visions too, Aishani? Or dreams?'

'Not really, Guruji, but sometimes I see myself playing in a garden and feeling extremely happy. I don't see the people I am playing with.'

'That's good progress, beta. We will go now, and you relax. Don't put too much stress on your brain.'

Aishani agreed and lay down again.

Meanwhile, Uday had gone to the forest where Aishani was attacked. Tejas was with him. He flew up to the treetops while Uday walked along below, carrying his weapons, the Pash and the Gram. After two days of reconnaissance, they came across two demons. Tejas signalled to him and Uday caught them one by one. They began blabbering and crying hysterically before Uday could land the first blow. He paused for a moment. There was something about their entreaties that caught his attention. Both Tejas and Uday waited for their explanation. It turned out that these demons were petty thieves. Their ancestors had mingled so much with humans that by this generation, they were more human than demon. But some demon attributes remained, such as stealing memory from others. This was the reason for Aishani's memory loss.

'Bhaiya,' Tejas whispered to Uday, 'Guruji keeps the truly repentant demons in an enclosure in a secluded part of the Gurukul. Do you think we should take these demons to Guruji to decide their fate? You know Guruji sometimes uses their powers to destroy more demons.'

Uday appreciated Tejas' astute reading of the situation. What his playful, younger brother said made a lot of sense. He nodded. Uday and Tejas tied up the demons with ropes interspersed with iron knots. They then took them to Guruji who handed them to the Gurukul's security guards and one of the teachers.

Uday continued to help Guruji administer the memory potion to Aishani. It was three weeks now and she was much better. She had become more and more restless, a positive sign of her recovery. On the first day of the fourth week, Adheesh returned with Jayant. He went straight to Guruji, gave him a brief report, and then went to Aishani, with Guruji and Uday.

Aishani wished Guruji, smiled at Uday, but did not recognise Adheesh. Disappointed, Adheesh looked at Guruji but did not say anything.

'Aishani is much better now. In fact, except for one or two aspects, she has recovered fully,' Guruji informed Adheesh. Aishani was slightly puzzled as to why Guruji was explaining things to this man she did not recognise.

Guruji saw her look and said, 'Adheesh is a very senior warrior of our Gurukul. Now that you are much better, Adheesh will take you around to various parts of the Gurukul so that you feel more at home here. This will help you settle your restlessness too.'

Aishani was puzzled but she did not question Guruji. They went out of the Vaidyashala. Guruji walked with them for some time. Leaving the Vaidyashala, Adheesh saw Uday standing on the veranda. He was a bit surprised to see him there but did not think about it too much. His priority was to help Aishani regain her memory. Guruji escorted them to a secret part of the Gurukul where both of them had found themselves. Guruji nodded to Adheesh, who then crossed with Aishani into their personal paradise.

Aishani and Adheesh were walking beside a stream, the same stream which used to talk to them and had reminded them of their past births.

'I think I've been here before,' Aishani said. Adheesh kept quiet. He did not want to rush her. He knew that regaining memory was a complicated matter.

They kept on walking. It all seemed so natural, walking here with Adheesh, Aishani felt. They came to the tree where they had received their emancipation.

Aishani suddenly blurted out, 'Look Adheesh, our tree, those are the branches where we used to sit on.'

Adheesh looked at her in shock and surprise but did not say anything.

'Adheesh, why are you looking at me like this? Weren't we supposed to go to the south to annihilate the demons there? Why are we here?' Then she sat down, dazed by her own words.

'Who are you?' she whispered, still in a daze. Sitting down on the stump of a tree, she gingerly stretched her hand towards him. Adheesh took her hands in his and came closer.

'I am your Adheesh, sweetheart. You had an accident, and you forgot many things and many people including me,' he said with a tremulous and tender smile.

'What are you talking about, Adhee? How can I forget you? I remember everything.'

He sat down beside her. Thank God, she remembered him now, but she still did not recall the most important aspect of her life, her kids. He would just have to wait.

She took his hand in hers. 'Let me tell you what I remember, Adhee, and you can fill in the details when I forget something.'

He nodded.

Aishani began from the time they had met in her father's library, how they fell in love with each other; their going to the past and reuniting with her father; getting married in previous births, then getting married again; going to Mount Kailash; coming back and rebuilding the Gurukul; getting pregnant and giving birth to her twins. Aishani stopped, stunned by her own statement. Memories flooded her like an avalanche. She had children, her beautiful Darsh and Divya!

'Adhee,' she said brokenly, 'Where are my babies? I forgot them. Take me to them now!'

Adheesh heaved a sigh of relief.

'Yes, doll, let us go to them immediately. I haven't seen them for a long time too.'

ASURI

'Guruji, people are falling sick left, right and centre. And dying too. Ten of our warriors are sick, extremely sick. Two of our warriors have died. Towns and cities are becoming graveyards and crematoriums.'

'Yes, Adheesh, we have no time. We have to work backwards to salvage the situation,' Guruji sounded worried. 'While we cannot do anything about the souls who have left us, we have to do everything in our power to halt this endemic and put an end to the rising death rates.'

All of them were in Guruji's cottage. Along with the core team, there were three more warriors. The three had time and again proved their valour and ingenuity in tackling various issues. Two of the warriors had been with them in the Northeast, when they had gone there to annihilate the demon,

Mantis. They were Ashutosh and Divyansh. The third warrior had recently joined them. He was Pascal. They had worked with him in the Chhota Nagpur forests.

Doctors and scientists were working overtime to defeat this menace, but things were moving extremely slowly. The disease was spreading fast and there was no real cure in sight.

'As the saying goes, 'When the going gets tough, the tough get going.' We have to find the cure by ourselves, our way,' Guruji said.

Everyone paid attention to what Guruji was saying. They knew that the doctors and Vaidyas were extremely efficient. They were remarkably good in esoteric medicine too. But nothing was working against this contagion.

'We know about the Asuras,' Guruji said, looking around at the warriors gathered there. 'They are male rakshasas or demons. The female Asur is called Asuri. Initially, the Asuras and the Asuris were very benevolent, honest, and true beings. There was no difference between them and the devatas. But later the Asurs changed, and their negative traits came to the fore. They became rakshasas. But they still retained their intellectual and esoteric powers. While almost all the Asuras came to be called rakshasas, because of their negative traits, some of them, especially the female Asuris, remained true to themselves and humanity too. They learnt a lot from the Rig Veda and later the Atharva Veda. The Vedas teach how to live, how to deal with everyday life, and the Asuris learnt and are taught as well. They cured diseases too. They had vast knowledge of herbs and medical remedies, mystic cures, and charms. But gradually these Asuris faded into oblivion as all the Asuras turned into demons. But the Asuris survived through the ages and some of them are still here on the earth.'

Uday asked, 'Guruji, are you implying that these Asuris may have the cure for the endemic which has affected all of us?'

'Good inference, Uday. These Asuris have survived in this country for ages. Nobody believes in them anymore, but they know more about sickness and disease than many doctors. They know this country like the back of their hands, they know exactly what we are immune to as well.'

'The medical fraternity is desperately searching for a cure, but it has all been in vain so far,' Adheesh said. 'Our workers are already helping those hit by the disease. As you say, we must not leave any stone unturned. We have to go to these Asuris for the antidote.'

'Easier said than done, Adheesh,' Guruji answered, 'Even I do not know where they can be found in the 21st century. Needless to say, they will not be found in densely populated areas. They will be found in towns or villages, bordering jungles.'

'Even if we reach them, Guruji, how will we recognize them?' Ashutosh asked.

'That is the major problem, Ashutosh. We have no means of recognising them. There are too many alternative medical doctors, and some of them are good too, making it impossible for us to identify the Asuris. We can go in all the directions and try to find them. We can deduce that being female Asuras, they must be tall and strongly built. There won't be too many tall and sturdy female medical practitioners in the country. Of course, we are clutching at straws, and everything is speculation.'

Pascal asked, 'Guruji, in the place where I come from, there is a language known as Asuri. There could be some connection between the Asuri people and the Asuri language. Maybe the Asuris settled there, and their language came to be known as Asuri too.'

'Excellent deduction, Pascal,' Guruji praised him. Pascal flushed with pleasure. To begin with, he was in such hallowed company, and then to be praised from the highest in the Gurukul!

'Tell us what else you know about this language, Pascal?' Guruji said.

''This language is spoken in Jharkhand and in the Chhota Nagpur areas in Gumla and Lohardagga districts. There are smaller groups speaking this language in the nearby states of Chhattisgarh, West Bengal and Odisha, and some parts of Maharashtra too. The tribes that speak the Asuri language are the Munda and the Oraon.'

Turning to others, Guruji said, 'All of you have tonight to do as much research as you can. I know it is short notice, but people are dying everywhere in the country. We don't have much time. Go to the library and find out as much as you can. Ruby and Aishani, you will not be required in these places, as this is only a search operation. Take time to recoup from your last operation. Just help your colleagues in the research.'

Agreeing, they all got up, touched Guruji's feet, and left. Only Aishani, Adheesh and Uday had access to the senior library. The rest went to the main library.

'We will meet tomorrow morning in Guruji's cottage,' Adheesh said as they went their separate ways.

The next day they decided that they would first go to Jharkhand in pursuit of the Asuris. If their mission failed here, then they would divide themselves into four teams and go in all four directions. Adheesh decided to take Devnath with them as he had some knowledge of the areas. Also, Devnath never complained. Though he took special pride and pleasure in looking after the twins, he was brought here as Adheesh's bodyguard, and he considered Adheesh his responsibility. Adheesh understood this, but he could trust no one else with the twins. With Aishani and Ruby at home, however, he felt the twins were safe and so he could take Devnath along. Devnath did not say anything, but Adheesh knew that he was excited.

They reached the Muri railway station and from there, took another train to Ranchi. The second leg of the journey was short, just an hour. After that they divided into two groups with Adheesh and Uday leading one each. Adheesh had Devnath, Jayant and Ashutosh in his group, while Uday had Tejas, Divyansh and Pascal. Adheesh and his team were to go to Khunti and Uday and his team to Tamar.

Though Uday was the leader, for all strategic decisions, he looked to Pascal to lead because he was familiar with the geographical area. Also, he was highly intelligent and Uday trusted him as he knew he was committed to the cause of the Gurukul. They had to go to a place called Bishunpur. The name of the village must have been Vishnupur. Through time, it came to be known as Bishunpur in Gumla. They had to cross smaller tribal villages to reach this place.

'The main tribes around here are the Asur, Brijiya, Korwa and Birhor,' Pascal told Uday. 'We will have to search for a woman healer. Such healers are not uncommon here. In fact, many people prefer going to these natural healers. I will try to find out as much as possible. The famous residential school Neterhat is just about twenty kilometres from here.'

Divyansh added, 'Guruji told us that Asuris are likely to be tall and strongly built. It should not be too difficult to find such a healer here.'

They were pleasantly surprised to see that the district Gumla was more developed than they had expected. They checked into a hotel, freshened up and then went to the restaurant to eat something. There were a few people in the restaurant. It seemed to be a friendly place with a couple of talkative waiters. The menu did not have too many items. In any case, at this time, they were serving only samosas, kachoris and, a local dish called Dhuska. It was a fried cake made up of rice and lentils and served with potato curry. They ordered it on Pascal's insistence. It was so good that they ordered another round.

Pascal turned to one of the waiters, 'One of our friends is extremely sick. He has a rare skin disease. We have taken him to many doctors and many experts, but nothing has helped. In fact, the disease has worsened so much that he is unable to leave his house. He is suffering because of the pain of the pustules on his body and the disfigurement as a result. He is in despair. He now knows that there is no cure for his disease. He just wants to die. We desperately want to help him. He has a wife and children.'

The waiter, whose name was Buddhwa because he was born on a Wednesday, as he told them, made a few sympathetic noises, but offered nothing more.

Pascal talked in the same local language. The others could only guess what he was saying, 'We have heard that there is a female healer here who treats people. We have also heard that people have great faith in her.'

Buddhwa shook his head and said, 'Maybe, but I have not heard of her.' Later as an afterthought, he said, 'You can ask the owner, Ramdev Chacha, who has been here from time immemorial.' They laughed loudly at his attempt at humour. He led them to the owner, who was sitting at the cash register. Ramdev Chacha was very old and hard of hearing too. Pascal was planning to speak softly as when you try to take a person into confidence for a favour, it is good to speak in a low tone. But the whole effect was spoilt when Pascal had to shout to get his sob story across to a man who wasn't even interested. It would have been funny, had it not been so frustrating. Disappointed, they paid their bill and were about to walk away when Ramdev Chacha spoke.

'I see that you are talking about Gundurasuri, the one who cures leprosy and skin diseases. She is old now and lives deep in the jungle. She is not too interested in curing people now. She takes up only those cases that she finds interesting. Otherwise, she just roams about in the jungle, looking for tree bark and digging up roots. She smells of the jungle and the Asuri.'

They stopped short. The man had spoken very clearly. They turned towards the old man. Pascal's translation was like a running commentary. Uday heaved a sigh of relief. Maybe the old man would take them to this female healer.

Pascal said, 'Chacha, please tell us where she is. You will be saving so many lives.' He folded his hands in supplication.

But the old man was lost in his own world again. He looked at them uncomprehendingly, merely giving them a beatific smile. They looked at each other frustrated. They were warriors, not nursemaids to coax geriatric men to talk about their lives and acquaintances. They sat down at one of the tables again, waiting for the old man's focus to return to them.

Buddhwa came to them and said, 'No use waiting here. He may or may not talk again today or even tomorrow. Definitely not today. You can come tomorrow and hope that he remembers.'

They left reluctantly. Throughout this time, Tejas had been noticeably quiet. Now he whizzed past them and was up on the treetops in a matter of minutes.

'Ooh! I can see the whole place from here, even the outskirts of the town where the forest begins. I wish you could come up here and see the quaint thatched mud huts in the jungle.'

They smiled good-naturedly at his antics. Even Divyansh, who was comparatively new to the group, grinned. He was just getting to know the people he was being associated with, and every day he came across a new facet of their personality. But what was most striking was their total commitment to their cause and the cause of the Gurukul, which was to annihilate all the demons on earth and spread peace.

The next day, Adheesh and his team joined them in Gumla. They too had not had any luck in finding the Asuris. But during their conversations with the locals, they too had heard about a female healer who had now given up as she had become very old.

'If she is the same person, then she has to be the descendent of the Asuris. In the Atharva Veda, all kinds of medical remedies and charms are projected as Asuri which is manifested in plants and animals. Asuri Kalpa is an expertise, comprising special knowledge of healing rites and magic,' Adheesh said.

'The villagers gave us her name, quite a quaint name, Gandur. They gave us one more name Birsi. Do you think there is more than one healer?' No one answered though they were all thinking hard.

'We will have to keep on searching and fast. Once she understands what is required, she will have to search for the plants and roots and make the medicine. That will take some time. After that, we will hand over the formula to the concerned authorities, who will have to make it in bulk. I can vouch for us, but what about the rest of the people?' Uday said. 'What do you say, Devnath?'

Devnath had been unusually quiet the whole morning, but when they turned to speak to him, he was not there. Surprised, Adheesh looked around for him. He realised that Tejas was not there either, but that was not surprising. They all knew that Tejas could not stay still in one place, he had to move around. Suddenly he heard a cooing sound. It sounded like a bird, but Adheesh knew that it was Devnath. But where was he? Adheesh cooed back. It was their secret language. The sound was coming from somewhere up above. Surprised, Adheesh looked up. After a bit of searching, he saw Devnath hanging from the top of a tree, along with Tejas, who was grinning from ear to ear. Devnath too was smiling. Adheesh knew that they must have seen or felt something. Devnath's intuition was always strong. They all gathered at one of the corner tables at the dhaba nearby.

'What did you see, Devnath? Or did Tejas coerce you to join him on the treetop?' Adheesh asked with a smile.

'Bhaiya, Tejas asked me to come up to the top of the tree. He wanted to show me something.'

They all waited. They knew Devnath must have unearthed an important clue.

'Tejas called me because he knew that I would be able to swing from the branches. Not as much as him, but I managed. Now what I saw and felt could be good news for all of us. We could see the jungle all around. In between the trees, we saw small mud huts with thatched roofs. Then I got a whiff of uncommon kinds of vegetation. This was not the fresh smell of the jungle nor was it of rotting vegetation, rather it was the smell of barks and roots drying in the sun. Almost like the Ayurvedic medicines which Aishani bhabhi uses.'

'Could you see anyone, Devnath?' Uday asked.

'Yes, but I could not really make out. They were too far away. There were just three or four people moving about. One of them seemed like an old lady, bent at the waist. If she could stand straight, then she would have been a very tall person.'

Their eyes widened. They jumped up from their chairs.

'Take us to that lady,' Adheesh ordered Devnath. He was more than willing.

Suddenly they saw Buddhwa, the waiter who had served him at the hotel, hovering around, 'He had heard their conversation. He said, 'Bhaiya, I know whom you are talking about, but she is terribly old, almost as old as Ramdev Chacha. She talks to herself, rather she keeps on muttering to herself. She doesn't remember anything. I have been seeing her for the last twenty years.' He added with a laugh, 'That is my age.'

'We'll take our chances, Buddhwa, we don't have any choice,' Adheesh said, and they left for the forest. It took them about forty-five minutes to reach the old woman's hut. There was another woman with her, younger, probably her daughter or daughter-in-law. She looked at them curiously.

Adheesh folded his hands in greeting and said, 'We have come from the neighbouring state. Some of our people are extremely sick from the endemic. We have taken them to many doctors, but to date, we have found no cure. We are desperately looking for a cure. This endemic is spreading to all parts of the country. We have heard that your mother heals people through natural remedies.'

'My name is Birsi, and she is my mother-in-law. She is very old as you can see. She cannot remember anything. In her lucid moments, she has told me that she doesn't want to live anymore but is waiting for someone or something before she finally departs from this world. I don't know how she can help you.'

Pascal was watching her closely. So was Devnath. His intuition was telling him that she was hiding something. Pascal spoke in the local language, 'Birsi, you and your mother-in-law are famous throughout this land. With your help, Gundurasuri has cured so many people. Now there is a chance again to help and cure many more people. I implore you, please help us.' He folded his hands in supplication.

The others did not understand what he was saying, but they understood the gist of it. Birsi stood there without saying anything. She appeared undecided about something. She looked at them. She realized that they wanted her help. Tears came to her eyes, and she started to cry. They were surprised and looked at her helplessly. Slowly she spoke through her sobs, 'They killed my husband Sanischara. One day my mother-in-law sent my husband to get some roots for a patient. By the time he got them, it was too late for my mother-in-law to infuse her magic in the concoction. The patient died. The furious relatives held my husband responsible and killed him. My mother-in-law has never forgiven herself. Both of us were heartbroken. We left the town and started living here in the jungle. Since then, my mother-in-law has not healed anybody. What was the use when she could not save her own son? But sometimes she mutters about saving humanity. She spoke all this in Hindi.

Jayant was looking around. Through his special vision, he was almost sure that they had come to the right place.

'Maybe she was waiting for us and this endemic You have enormous amounts of herbs, just waiting to be converted into medicines,' he blurted out, then stopped short. It was not his place to interject when seniors like Adheesh and Uday were there.

Birsi was shocked, 'How do you know that my mother-in-law had hidden everything with her magic.'

Adheesh smiled. 'We too have a bit of magic, Birsi. That is why we think that Gundurasuri's magic might help the people of this country. Please, let us meet her once so that we can validate that she is the healer that we are looking for.'

Birsi was still undecided. She looked at their serious faces. Finally, she made her decision. 'Ok, follow me, but don't ask too many questions,' she warned them.

They all breathed in relief and followed her to the back of the hut. It was a sparse place with just a string cot on which the old woman was sitting, mumbling to herself. She was bent double, so they could not make out how tall she was. She was not looking at them. It seemed as if she wasn't aware of their presence. But Devnath knew that she was aware that they were here.

She got up from the cot to reach for something on the shelf. She was taller and heftier than many young women of her tribe. Her fingers were gnarled and knotted; her loose and saggy skin was somehow holding her bones together, but they saw only her eyes. They were sharp, intelligent, and alert, but they were full of deep despair. She had a crop of pure white hair.

Though the rest of them could see only a sparse and a scanty place, Jayant could see mountains of herbs and roots, some dried, some drying, and some even soaking in the nearby pond.

Adheesh and Devnath went with her while the others stayed behind. Birsi warned them not to excite the old woman. Adheesh and Devnath touched her feet. There was no response.

'Maiya,' Adheesh began, 'We have come here as your children. You have many more children who are extremely sick. They need your help. You have to provide them succour, mother. Please cure them and give them a new life.'

No response.

'Maiya, remember how Sanischara would dance and sing the Dumkach with all his friends. You would sing along with them. Birsi too would dance along with him. All of you used to be so happy. You used to make mounds of Dhuska, along with your world-famous potato and chickpea curry.'

Gundurasuri's hands began to shake. She again began to mumble. A tear dropped from her right eye. Doggedly Adheesh continued, 'Maiya, all of Sanischara's friends are your children. They are all in danger now and only you can save them.'

There was no change in her demeanour, but he knew that he had her attention. 'You have collected an extraordinary amount of medicine, more than enough to cure our whole country. You or your ancestors must have known that your magical medicine will be required at this time in the Kaliyuga. This is the moment you have been waiting for, Maiya. Come out of your fog of despair and resentment and help the rest of the world.'

Gundurasuri stopped in her tracks. Yes, this was the moment she and her ancestors had been waiting for, for eons. She was human now; her heart was heavy. Her only child, her baby was gone, and she was being asked to cure other children. She looked at the men in front of her. She knew that they were no ordinary men. They had been sent to her by the highest authority. She held out her hands to them. They came to her, but she shrugged them off and beckoned Birsi. Both of them held each other and cried as if there was no tomorrow. They cried for the son, the husband; they cried for the happy life they could have had. They cried for almost an hour.

Then Gundurasuri got up, wiped her tears with a rag, and looked very business-like. She had purged her grief. Once she began, they were taken aback by her decisiveness and speed, and authority. There was no dilly-dallying with her. She directed each one of them to do a job. On their part, they were more than willing to do her bidding. Gone was her apathy, indifference, and despair. They guessed that she was behaving like the Asuri of the Atharva Veda, who knew exactly what was needed to make the medicine to cure the deadly disease that had encompassed the country. Her behaviour was an amalgamation of the present Adivasi woman and the Asuris whose treatments were written in the Vedas. There was a purpose in her stride now. She continued to mutter to herself, however.

Firstly, she made visible all the piles of herbs, roots, and bones she had collected. Then she designated to each of them a specific chore. Not even a moment's slacking was allowed. And they were definitely not slackers. The work was different from their usual work, but they were learning fast. Despite her appearance and sorrowful expression, they knew that behind the wrinkles was a strong and sharp mind.

Once Devnath was near Adheesh who was segregating the herbs, 'Reminds you of Kailash, doesn't it, bhaiya? But Aishani bhabhi was so much softer to deal with, not like this sergeant major.'

Adheesh grinned at the comparison. He looked around at the others, who were also reeling under the impact of Gundurasuri's tongue. She was like a woman on fire. He turned to Uday, 'Hold the fort, Uday, I'll go and update Guruji on the happenings.'

Uday nodded. Only Adheesh, Aishani, and maybe Ruby had the power to communicate mentally with Guruji.

Adheesh went into the forest and sat down under a Sakhua tree. It was a huge tree with large leaves. It was a peaceful and quiet place. He sat and meditated. After ten minutes or so, he heard Guruji's voice.

He mentally wished Guruji, who blessed him.

'Yes, Adheesh?'

'I think we have found the descendent of the Asuri, who knew the cure for so many diseases, including leprosy. She has a history as a human being, but she has now agreed to make the medicine and infuse it with her magic. We are all assisting her in putting the contents of the medicine together. I guess she will weave her magic into it once the medicine has been made.'

'Observe everything closely and inform me.'

'Yes, Guruji, there will be tons of the antidote. How will it reach the government? How do we know that this will the right medication?'

'Pertinent questions. I can understand your apprehension. There are other people for these jobs, as you know. Your job is to make sure that the medicine has been developed along with her special powers. You will bring a bag of it so that the scientists can confirm its efficacy. Once that is confirmed, getting the medicine to the government will not be a problem. No one will get to know about it till the medicine is packed and ready to be sent to the hospitals, pharmacies, and the market.'

'Okay, Guruji.' Adheesh wished Guruji again and went back to the others.

It took them two days to assemble everything. It was only because they were diligent workers that the work was completed in two and a half days. Normal human beings would have taken more than a month to perform the same task. That is, if they survived the strong poisonous fumes and heat, and the stinging of the herbs and roots. To their surprise, Gundurasuri ordered them to go back into the village and come back after one day.

On the way back, Devnath said, 'She will now begin her incantations and rituals and put her magical powers in the medicines. This has to be done in absolute secrecy. Otherwise, the antidote will not be potent.'

Adheesh nodded as they walked amongst the Sakhua and Karanj trees. He was aware of this. Another day to go and they would have the medicine in their hands. When they returned to the jungle the next day, Gundurasuri and Birsi were waiting for them with the medicine in a bag. Adheesh had told them that he would come with the others to collect the rest of the medicine after a few days. They bid farewell to Gundurasuri and Birsi, promising that they would visit them whenever they came to this part of the country.

Gundurasuri blessed them. They knew that they would not meet her again. Now she could die content with the thought that she had saved the world.

In a matter of two weeks, the government announced that the cure for the deadly disease had been found and was available at cheap rates throughout the country.

BHAUMASTRA

'I had a meeting with the Prime Minister,' Guruji informed the warriors gathered before him. They were a bit surprised, but not overly so. The Gurukul and its inhabitants were the mysterious and unrevealed face of defence in the country. Nevertheless, some straight-thinking and good people of the country did know about them. Maybe all of them did not have a full grasp of the might of the Gurukul, its head and its warriors. A few of them did, however, know about it. The Prime Minister was one of them. The number of people whom Guruji trusted, apart from his warriors, could be counted on the fingertips.

They were sitting in the annexure of the senior library. Vashishtji, the librarian, was aware of the importance of the meeting as it was being held in the annexure. He put a spell on the entrance of the annexure, making it invisible. There were only three warriors with Guruji – Aishani, Adheesh and Uday, the most senior warriors at the Gurukul.

There had been a number of major robberies through the years. Robberies and stealing are the two most common aspects of Kaliyuga. But what was jarring was that such subtle and smart methods had been used during the heists that the government was almost on the verge of economic collapse.

'For the first time in many years our economy is showing signs of growth and stability,' Uday said. 'And now this. We have a good Prime Minister, and his core team is also good. We have to do everything in our power to help him and our country.'

'Yes, Uday, this news cannot be allowed to leak out. There will be panic. People will begin hoarding, except that there will be nothing left to hoard. There will be anarchy all around,' Guruji said.

'What about the police or the secret service? Surely, they are very efficient?' Adheesh asked.

'Yes, they are. They would have caught the criminals, had they been humans,' Guruji said, pausing in his speech.

Aishani smiled to herself. There was such a child-like sweetness in Guruji. He was the greatest person she had ever met. And here he was innocently pausing for effect. The others did not notice it, though.

'So, this is where we come in,' Adheesh stated. All three nodded in unison.

'What do our intelligence agencies say, Guruji?' Aishani asked.

'This is definitely the work of demons, albeit a different kind of demons. They are the ancient species of demons who had hidden inside the earth for survival. They stay deep within the bowels of the earth. They rarely come up, and then only to kill for their survival. They carry their victims with them and don't surface again till they need to for their food.'

'So where does the money come into this?' asked Aishani.

'This must have happened in the last few decades. They have been attracted to shiny bright jewels which were plenty on the surface. They began to kidnap and kill women who wore bright jewellery. These women must have offered them money and in their perverted thinking, they must have thought that money was more important than jewels. Anything to bestow pain on the humans, now that the devatas and gods have left the earth,' Guruji replied.

'How do we tackle this, Guruji?' Adheesh queried. They all knew that Guruji would have a solution to the problem. He knew every demon and their shenanigans. Sometimes the warriors would discuss this in a light-hearted manner. It was as if there was a motherboard in Guruji's brain with bulbs of different colours, red, green and orange, for example. Green stood for the demons who were still sleeping or were in hibernation. Orange indicated demons in the process of waking up, while red marked those who had come out of hibernation and were now raring to go. Smiling to themselves, they waited for Guruji to give them instructions.

'To begin with, I have yet to get news on the exact location of the massive trove of money and jewellery. This stash is in such a desolate place and so deep inside the earth that it cannot be reached using technology that is available to humans. Supernatural forces have to be used and this is where we come in.'

'Guruji, if they hoard their stash so deep inside the earth, then how do they live there? And how do they use all their stolen items?' Aishani asked.

'The demons don't live near their cache, nor do they use it. They just hoard it. They're thieves and robbers. They are not superlatively strong either. They're just peculiar. Nobody can reach their hideout and so it's got to be us.'

All three of them nodded in unison. Guruji turned to Adheesh. 'I want your team to visit and find out as much as you can about this money, gold and jewels, being hoarded by the demons. Report to me tomorrow, at the same time.'

They nodded, touched Guruji's feet and left. Ruby, Jayant and Tejas also joined them. Adheesh briefed them other about the issue. They heard him out, then went to work immediately. After some time Uday left for the seniors' library, just in case.

The next day they reported to Guruji, who waited to hear their plan.

Uday began, 'Guruji, there is a small mention of the hoarding demons in the archives but not much importance is given. There is very less material about the method of getting back the cache of riches from these demons. Apparently, they are not considered real demons by the demonic clan as they are soft and too effeminate. They are, however, too fierce by human standards. What we could decipher from the archives is that their only vice is stealing money and gold and hoarding it. But though they are unearthly and demonic hoarders and nearly harmless, they have stolen almost all the government's money,' he said wryly.

Guruji looked at Uday. 'Tackling the demons will not be a big problem for us.' he said, without arrogance. He was just stating a fact, 'What will be difficult, however, is how to go deep down to the centre of the earth and retrieve the money.'

Everyone was listening to Uday. He resumed, 'We can reach these depths only with the help of a super-powered weapon. In the archives of the senior library, I came across one such weapon known as the Bhaumastra, or the weapon of Mother Earth. This was created by Bhumi Devi or Earth itself. It can create tunnels deep inside the earth and we can then retrieve the cache of jewels, money and gold. The main feature of this Astra is that it drills into rocks and soil without leaving debris.'

Adheesh added, 'The debris of the rocks and soil has to be in metric tons. It seems impossible that no debris is left.'

'Yes, Adheesh, it seems impossible for humans and their drilling contraptions. The Bhaumastra was used extensively in the construction of temples in ancient times. The debris which would naturally be in tons, would be piled up nearby in the air to be disposed of later, and in some cases, the temples were made with the detritus of rocks and soil. It is said that the Ellora caves have been made with the help of the Bhaumastra.'

Guruji looked at them appreciatively. Whether it was fighting the demons or researching on their antecedents, his warriors were meticulous. He was very proud of them. It was not in his personality to praise frequently. A nod here, a smile there, was enough to boost his warriors' spirits.

'Reports have arrived just now. The demon hoarders have kept most of their stash in parts of the Deccan plateau, the largest of which is near Hyderabad. You will go there, protect Aishani from all sides and the demons too, while she is using the Bhaumastra.'

'What will happen to the treasure, Guruji?' Ruby asked, curiously.

'It will be taken to a safe place and then eventually handed over to the government to be used for the development of the country. We have to sift out honest and committed people in the government, who will actually use the treasure for the good of the people. Human beings are no less wicked than demons when it comes to hoarding money and gold,' Guruji commented, wryly.

'You will go to Hyderabad, where a local guide will take you to the exact location. Most of the stolen gold, silver, jewellery, and money is stashed miles underground. It is humanly impossible to reach there. There are other places also where they have hoarded the money, but this is the largest cache. This is where all of you come in the picture. The guide, who I have designated for you, knows all of you very well, though you may not know him. He is also a junior in our ashram. His name is Bhuvan. He is from Hyderabad, and he speaks Telegu, Hindi and English, and of course the mandatory Sanskrit. Begin your work at night and try to finish it before dawn.'

'Who do we hand the treasure to, Guruji?' Adheesh asked.

'The Maruts will be there to take care of the treasure, Adheesh. They will be there with all of you, but they will make themselves visible only when you conclude your work.'

'Guruji, what I know about the Maruts is that they are storm deities and are provoked to anger very easily.'

'Yes, Adheesh, that they are, but they are also many in number, forty-nine to be exact. They are sons of the Rudra Devata. They are the sons of Devi Diti. Diti means the earth. If their mother is uncomfortable, they will naturally rush to help her. In this case, Mother Earth is being burdened with stolen goods. The Maruts will help anyone to get rid of the unwanted cache of money and gold. They are also helpers of the Indra Devata, the king of the heavens. The Maruts have golden chariots, which are drawn by huge horses. Such is the anger and force of the Maruts that the whole world trembles in their presence. But they have a sense of compassion and fair play too, which they have inherited from their mother Diti. In our case, nobody will dare steal the gold from the Maruts. It will be in their safekeeping to be given back to the concerned government departments, as and when required.'

'Wouldn't they want to keep it for themselves?'

Guruji answered, 'While it is true that Swarga is made up of all kinds of riches, but they are not ill-gotten. If that was the case, then it wouldn't be heaven at all, it will be Pataal or Hell.'

They nodded in unison.

The next day they left for Hyderabad. Bhuvan was with them as a guard. Since he was a junior warrior, he was instructed by Tejas to go along. They had deliberately sent Tejas to Bhuvan, so that he could be relaxed in their presence. Adheesh, Aishani, Uday and their party had become a cult among the Gurukuls of the world. People who knew about them looked at them with awe and veneration. The juniors were dumbstruck around them. In their own way, they tried to make him comfortable. Bhuvan did let go of his reservations about them after some time. He realised that they were normal people just like him. He couldn't, even in his wildest imagination, have dreamt that they were such a strong storehouse of superpowers. They, in turn, were surprised by Bhuvan's intellect and knowledge. He was not as young as one would have expected a junior student to be. Maybe he was one or two years older than even Adheesh. He was a mining engineer, and he had a good job in Hyderabad. One day, a past memory rose when he was sleeping. In his dreams he had a vague glimpse of a couple of his past births, in which he was a warrior and fighting beside other warriors. The dreams kept repeating and every time a new dimension was added to them. Bhuvan was not the same man anymore. He had a strong urge to rid the world of all demons. Believing in his dream, he embarked on a journey to take on the world alone as a warrior from ancient times. He wouldn't have lasted more than a week. This was the time that he met Guruji. It is said that the Guru comes when the student is ready, which was precisely what happened and here he was with such elite warriors.

They alighted at the Hyderabad railway station. From there Bhuvan took them to the bus stand. He bought tickets to a place called Patencheru. Adheesh had given Bhuvan the coordinates while at the Gurukul. They could have come to this place by themselves, but it always helped to have a local with them. It gave them time to meditate and mentally prepare themselves for the tough tasks ahead. It also gave them time to familiarise themselves with the topography and the people.

They reached Patencheru in about an hour. They looked around. While they were on the outskirts of the city, they could see huge rocks and boulders everywhere for miles around. Just the right place to store stolen goods, Aishani thought to herself. She looked at Adheesh, who nodded and reinforced her thoughts. She glowed. There were so many moments like this when they instinctively thought of the same things.

Bhuvan had been here earlier. The warriors checked into a lodge and retired to their rooms to freshen up. In the evening, they went out with Bhuvan. Travelling by autos, Bhuvan directed the driver to a place outside the city limits. They began walking towards a hillock of rocks and took lots of pictures. There was nobody there. They acted like tourists, marvelling at the formation of innumerable rocks and boulders.

Soon it was night and time for them to begin their work. They saw a few shadowy figures moving among the boulders.

'Shh!' This was Ruby. 'These must be the demons guarding the treasures. Don't bother, I will look after them,' so saying, she walked towards the shadowy figures. They stiffened when they saw her going towards the largest boulder. The guards had a very boring job. On top of that, they did not know what they were guarding. It was a cakewalk for Ruby. The guards had never seen such a beautiful woman before. 'She is an apsara,' one of them whispered to the other, not realising that what he said was the absolute truth. Ruby beckoned them to come behind one of the rocks. They followed her. Tejas was waiting for them. He struck them twice and they fell. That was that.

'Didi, should I bind them up?'

'No, idiot! You will not do anything of the sort! We will wait here till the others complete their work. Then Adheesh or Uday will decide what to do with them.'

'Okay, but can I go to the other side of the rock and see what they are doing?'

Ruby nodded reluctantly. She too wanted to witness the action, but somebody had to sit with these demons. After some time, Jayant joined her. They passed the whole night keeping an eye on the demons. The moment the demons regained consciousness or made the slightest move, Ruby would beguile them with her eyes and Jayant and Tejas would whack them back to sleep. Their instructions were not to kill the demons. They were not killer demons. They were not so harmful that they had to be slain.

It was dark. Adheesh and Uday were alert to any danger. Their weapons were out, ready whenever needed. They pointed to the area Aishani had identified as wonderful.

Bhuvan's heart was beating faster. He was going to witness one of the greatest feats of his life, by the greatest people in the world. He knew that he might not get a chance like this again.

At the precise time given by Guruji, Aishani summoned the Bhaumastra. It was there with her all the time, only now it was visible to the others too. Aishani closed her eyes, chanted the mantra, and shot two arrows into the night sky. These arrows were shot from the same bow at the same time. In appearance, they just looked like antiquated iron arrows, slightly thicker and longer. They did not look very powerful. The arrows went up in the air for approximately 500 feet, then turned and began their descent down towards the earth. Their shape began to change, and a hum could be heard. When the arrows came nearer to them, the humming grew louder. They realised that the sound was like a piece of heavy machinery, moving on its own axis. The arrows were not arrows now, rather they were like gargantuan drilling machines. They fell exactly where Aishani had calculated them to fall. The Astra was conditioned to fall and drill tunnels where the maximum amount of treasure was stashed. Bhuvan stood in awe at such an astonishing scene. Not only Bhuvan, but the others were also filled with amazement. Every time such an extraordinary thing happened; they were thrilled.

A hundred earthly drills would not have been able to drill a hole in these ancient rocks and boulders, but the Bhaumastra not only penetrated the huge boulders as if they were made of paper, but it also made tunnels in them that went deep into the earth, pinpointing exactly where the treasures were hidden. It was an awesome sight. The debris was massive, but it hung and floated in the air. The warriors didn't know where to look, at the hills of debris or the deep tunnels which were being drilled by the Bhaumastra. They had to go into the tunnels to retrieve the gold and other valuable items. But Adheesh knew that it would be a gargantuan task. The loading itself would take more than a week. Besides, they were not equipped for it. They were human warriors, not carriers. This was why Guruji was taking the help of the Maruts.

For the better part of the night, the Bhaumastra kept making tunnel after tunnel. In some places, they could catch a glimpse of the gold too. They had to wait. They could not go in while the Bhaumastra was drilling the tunnels.

'This must be some cache,' Aishani whispered to nobody in general, but both Uday and Adheesh heard her.

'That is why Guruji wanted us to come here. These hoarders have not only looted our country, but I'm also sure there are treasures belonging to other countries too.'

It was almost dawn now. The Bhaumastra had stopped digging in two or three places, which meant that the treasures had been found. It was still working in other tunnels. Aishani was beginning to worry now. Though it was a lonely place, there was no guarantee that people would not come here now that it was daybreak. And they still had to gather all the treasures. It was time to hail the Maruts.

Suddenly there were loud booms heard across the sky. It seemed as if the sky would fall apart. Thunder rolled in like the fury of the gods, which indeed it was. They knew that the thunder gods or Maruts were coming. Lightning flashed, lighting up the rocks and boulders with thousands of zigzagging bolts. This was the raw power of the Maruts warning anybody and everybody who came in their path of their anger and power and its repercussions. They threw jagged lightning bolts everywhere, even into the smallest of crevices. The inky sky was filled with flashes of brilliance and radiance. The blinding incandescence and the loud boom of the thunder heralded a tempest.

They looked up. In patches, the sky was dark and ominous. Then it would become blazing white for a few moments, lighting up the whole area. In these few moments, they had a vision of large giants riding on huge golden chariots, driven by enormous horses.

'Maruts!' Uday exclaimed.

'Yes,' Adheesh confirmed. Aishani was quiet. She was still busy with the Bhaumastra. Till the mission was over, she would be totally focused on it. The others were watching the whole scene with their mouths open in surprise. The golden chariots began to descend. They could now see the Maruts at close quarters. They were tall, imposing figures. They looked like devatas, but they looked like rakshasas too. The warriors folded their hands in supplication. The Maruts acknowledged them with an arrogant nod of their heads. The work of the Bhaumastra had concluded and Aishani was putting the arrows back into their quiver.

The Maruts turned to Aishani and froze. All the rage and bluster vanished from their demeanour. They recognised her. She was Maa Durga, albeit in human form. They saluted her. All forty-nine of them folded their hands and bowed to her in respect. Everybody was astounded. They, of course knew through hearsay who she was, but to have a heavenly being recognise and bow to her was too much even for them. It was a shock for Aishani too. She had never considered herself other than a human. This was one of her qualities that Adheesh found so endearing.

After taking her permission, in one grand motion, the Maruts sucked every bit of the treasures onto their golden chariots, and then took off as noisily and as they had come, full of thunder and lightning.

The others heaved a sigh of relief, but Aishani had a bit of work left still. Adheesh, Jayant and Uday were at her side, guarding her. She took out her bow and arrow, touched it to her head, and chanted a mantra. Once more she shot the arrows into the sky. This time when the arrows came down, there was no drilling. All the debris from the drilling was pushed back into the tunnels. Soon, the tunnels were closed, and the rocks and boulders were as they had been before.

They looked around. There was an eerie silence. Bhuvan was in a trance. His power of reasoning had deserted him for the time being. Ruby, Jayant and Tejas came out from behind the boulders where they were guarding the demons. The demons were still unconscious. They picked up their weapons and began walking towards the main road. Dawn was giving way to early daylight. Very soon they would find a means of transport to take them back to the main city.

SO MANY CHILDREN

Adheesh and his uncles, Kedar and Kalpesh, were sitting in the living room, enjoying their beers. Rather Adheesh and Kedar were having a beer. Kalpesh never consumed liquor as he just didn't like it. Among the three of them, he was the sober kind, sober and happy. The other two were a bit boisterous. Adheesh's uncles were nearer to him in age than their elder brother, Vidyadhar, Adheesh's father. All three of them were chums, though none of them had much time to spare as they were all so busy most of the time.

Much water had flown under the bridge since the time when they used to go hiking as youngsters. They had not gone out together for many years now. Adheesh reminisced about the time when they had gone hiking and a big bear had torn open Kedar's stomach with a swipe of its giant paw. They had only a basic first aid kit with them, which wasn't of any help. It was Kalpesh, an Ayurvedic doctor, who had sewn up his brother's stomach with the pincers of giant ants.

All of them were now older and married. Adheesh was the first one to have children. Not to be left behind, Kedar too had twin boys. Kalpesh and Padmaja had a baby girl. These days there was a constant smile on the faces of Vidyadharji and his wife Anuja. They couldn't thank God enough. From a house that was mainly silent because the grownups were too engrossed in their respective professions to a house that was never silent even for a moment.

'Runs in the family,' Adheesh informed Kedar, referring to his twin boys. Kedar guffawed. Kalpesh's daughter, from the time she was born, was as quiet as her parents. There were now six children in that generation – the five children in this family and Ruby's boy, who was in many ways a part of this family. The lovely baby smell, the milk, the formulas, and the cooing of babies were to be heard all around them. Anujaji was the busiest as the children's parents were all working professionals. They did love and care for their children, but Anujaji had taken it upon herself to look after the children. She loved every minute of it, even if she was harried all the time. She did have a couple of maids to help her, but she liked to do most of the things herself.

Though extremely happy, Vidyadharji was worried too. He knew that his family needed extra security. Adheesh and Aishani were in a different class altogether. Nobody had a more dangerous and risky vocation and calling than theirs. Now Darsh and Divya had inherited their parents' supernatural traits, and more.

Vidyadharji had brought Devnath to guard Adheesh. But now Devnath was being overstretched. He had volunteered to look after Aishani and later her children. Now there were four more children. Only God knew whether these children too had any special powers. They did have his blood. His brothers too shared his bloodline. Any child could be bestowed with some of Adheesh's powers. Vidyadharji had full faith in his servants' loyalty but now he needed more committed guards and helpers. He knew where he had to go. He decided to go to Aghori Baba in Varanasi. He knew that only Aghori Baba could provide him with the most dedicated helpers, on par with Devnath.

Aghori Baba was waiting for him at his ashram in Varanasi.

'Come, Vidya,' Baba was genuinely happy to see Vidyadharji. Their friendship went back decades, probably even to their past births.

'Sit down, Vidya,' Aghori Baba pointed to a mat in front of him. Vidyadharji sat down. There were a few bones, a skull and some ash kept in a small mound. Vidyadharji knew that they were from the crematorium.

'Tell me everything, Vidya. Fill in the details since the last time we met and tell me the purpose of your visit.'

Vidyadharji folded his hands in supplication, 'You know everything Baba. Nothing is hidden from you. You know the purpose of my visit too.'

Aghori Baba gave a hearty laugh. 'So, it seems Vidya, so it seems. I am not God. There are so many things that I don't know.'

Quickly Vidyadharji gave him a short summary of his

family and their feats. He also told them about the children.

Baba narrowed his eyes, 'Vidya you are worried about the children and their safety.' Vidyadharji nodded his head in agreement.

'Yes, Baba, you know my family is not a normal one. Anuja and I are blessed to have so many talented children. The children too have powers, even Ruby's son seems to have some special qualities. I haven't been able to ascertain each child's power or strength. The children are too young to understand that they have special powers. They don't have the maturity to control their powers. They don't know that they are different. That is why they are being home-schooled, though for how long we don't know. A plethora of demons is always on the lookout for such powerful youngsters. They may get kidnapped anytime. We can't be too careful.'

'What do you know about their powers? What kind of powers do they have?'

'Well, Baba, they are still too young to fully comprehend the kind of powers they have. I think the children do not know about their powers either. They just play and improvise on their powers. If something happens or not, either way, it's fine with them. Three of them are my nephews and niece, but they are more like my grandchildren. Then there is Ruby's nephew or so she says. I have a feeling that he is her son. Ruby's son is of a serious bent of mind. He has read almost all the great Indian epics. He can recite mantras which I haven't even heard of. Both mother and son have become part of our family. Baba, sometimes I get very scared. All of them are mine. How am I going to protect them?'

'I understand your feelings, Vidya, though I may not approve of them. Everybody comes into this world with his or her preordained destiny. We cannot escape our destiny. You are scared, Vidya. But you are probably one of the most blessed men on this earth. Human beings do not have any single special power, and here you are with special children present around you. You must have done some wonderful things in your past births to be so blessed in this life.'

Vidyadharji nodded. He was aware of his good fortune. He prayed and thanked God for it every minute of the day.

'Yes, Baba, but I am a human being with all the strengths and weaknesses of a human. That means that while I am grateful for my blessings, I have also the human frailty of being attached to my loved ones and being concerned about their safety.'

'I have selected a bodyguard for your grandchildren. There is no match for Devnath's strength, loyalty, and commitment. This boy is of the same calibre as Devnath. He will guard your children against human as well as supernatural evils.'

Vidyadhar folded his hands in gratitude. If anybody could assess his need, it was Aghori Baba. Baba looked at somebody standing near the entrance. He came inside. He was a slim, young man, as old as Devnath had been when he had joined Vidyadharji's household.

'This is Nirved. Don't go by his youth and innocence. He is much more mature and sharper than any human. He knows quite a lot about each of you.'

Vidyadharji looked at Baba inquiringly. Baba nodded. Vidyadharji nodded to Nirved and gestured to him to wait outside. Nirved folded his hands respectfully and went outside. Vidyadharji turned to Baba and asked, 'He knows about us?'

'Yes, Vidya, utmost loyalty has to be given to a person you know. In the absence of that, such people are made familiar with the persons they have to guard and be loyal to.'

'Does that mean that I will be coming to you for more of these protectors? Are you grooming some more boys or girls, Baba?' Vidyadharji was very curious.

'All is in the hands of Shiva. If Shiva wishes that I train more protectors, then so be it.'

Vidyadharji waited for some more clarification, but none came. He had to be satisfied with this answer. He thanked Baba for Nirved, folded his hands, and left.

On reaching home he introduced Nirved to Anuja. Lately, she had been worried about the children too. 'I think I will involve Aishani in this. She has also been worried about their children's training, and their future. But dear, even with these two, Devnath and now Nirved, the children will still have to interact with the outer world. Home schooling may not be such a good idea after all.'

'Yes, I know, Anuja. Plus, whatever powers they have must be given direction and honed. I'm afraid, we have to consult Guruji on this.'

Anuja nodded, not entirely happy with the way the conversation was going. She knew that Guruji would suggest sending the children to different Gurukuls, so that their powers get honed, and they become independent. Here the children made a closed group, into which no adult was allowed. But would the parents agree?

'Anuja, we do not have any choice, nor do the children. Adheesh, Aishani, and Ruby are always out with the others. You know that their commitments are such that they cannot stay at home, even if they want to. We won't be able to control the children and their powers. Devnath and now Nirved will be able to provide security. Our children need much more than that however.'

There were tears in Anuja's eyes. 'God has given us much more than we desired. Have we inadvertently committed any mistakes? Is God taking our happiness back?'

'Don't go in that direction, Anuja,' Vidyadharji reprimanded her softly, 'These are our children, our flesh and blood. We have to ensure that we give them the best in life. That means proper education and guidance.'

Anuja nodded. Suddenly she perked up. 'As of now, we have only witnessed Darsh and Divya showing some supernatural powers. They have to be given special education. What about the other children, that is Kedar's and Kalpesh's children or even Ruby's son? Their parents do not have any superpowers, or do they?'

'We don't know, Anuja. As far as Kalpit is concerned, if he is indeed Ruby's son, why has it been kept a secret? Did Kalpit's father have any superpowers? Was he a warrior or some distinguished guru? Is he a child prodigy or does he really have superpowers? Ruby is Aishani's best friend apart from being a female warrior. If Aishani finds Ruby blameless, then it must be so.'

Vidyadharji had inadvertently landed near the truth without knowing it.

'What about Kedar's twins Ridhan and Nehal, and Kalpesh's daughter Avni?' Anuja was not giving up hope so soon.

'They all have the same blood as Adheesh. Though Ridhan and Nehal have not shown any signs of superpowers yet, have you noticed Avni? She seems to see the future. She informs us about incidents that are yet to take place. She cannot even speak properly, but she can see the future.'

Anuja nodded. She didn't know whether should be proud or anxious.

'We will talk to Madhuji first and then with Ruby's parents. After that, we will go to Guruji. We will follow Guruji's instructions.'

The next day, all the parents got together in Madhuji's house to discuss the matter. Vidyadhar and Anuja were surprised that Aishani's mother Madhu and Ruby's parents Badrinath and Ajita were more enlightened about their grandchildren than they had thought. In fact, they seemed to know more than they let on. Needless to say, they were also worried. In the case of Adheesh, Aishani, and their own children, they did not have to face this dilemma, as their powers appeared only after they were grown up and could be depended upon to keep their secret. These babies were not aware that they had powers and hence used them indiscriminately. Guruji was the only solution.

Kedar and Kalpesh, though not exactly in the know of these supernatural powers in their families, did know that Adheesh and Aishani had special powers and their vocation was to annihilate demons from the time of the Ramayana.

They also knew that their elder brother was fully entrenched in this. They knew that things had come to a head when Vidyadharji called everyone for a meeting, in the ground floor office of their home. They were not too surprised to see Madhuji and Ruby's parents. Vidyadhar said, 'This is a very grave discussion today regarding your children.'

He looked around. He had got everybody's attention. Each of the parents had the guilty feeling that they were not giving enough time to their children because of work pressures. They also knew that their children were very well looked after by their grandparents. They didn't have any issues on that score. Despite spending less time with the children, they had started becoming aware of the fact that the children did have some special powers, which had manifested from such a young age. There was no doubt about Adheesh and Aishani's twins. They had shown their powers a multitude of times. The others still had to show some signs of extra powers. The atmosphere was sombre. When Vidyadharji spoke, people became silent, and they listened.

Adheesh and Kedar looked at each other.

Kedar whispered, 'Have we produced freaks?'

There was an answering twinkle in Adheesh's eyes, but he kept a straight face. His father wanted their opinion before they went to Guruji and would not appreciate any levity. It was Madhuji who spoke. 'I have seen when these children play together. Darsh is the outgoing and naughty one. He keeps pulling magical pranks one after another. Once when Divya increased her height, he became extremely small just to counter her. The others clapped their hands, and I thought

I saw Nehal stretch his hands for his milk which was on the table. It was a natural gesture. By the time it crossed my mind that the table was about four feet away from him, he had finished drinking his milk and was clapping his hands in joy.'

There was a weighty silence now. Ruby's father Badrinathji said, 'We all knew that there was a possibility of such powers appearing in the children, but we had not thought that it would be so soon. When it happened to our children, they were old enough to control their powers and keep them hidden. These children are too young to understand anything.'

'Has Kalpit also shown any signs of similar powers?'

Badrinathji coughed slightly and looked a bit embarrassed. 'Not yet in the conventional manner, but which child can read and understand the Geeta and Puranas. That itself speaks of special powers.'

'We will go to Guruji tomorrow,' Vidyadharji declared.

Guruji met them in the library the next day.

'It is our great fortune that many souls with superpowers have gathered here in this one family. In the normal course of time, such powers may or may not appear for generations. This can mean one of two things. Either the number of demons is going to increase in the near future, or the demons are now going to be totally eradicated. That is why the children are showing their powers at such an early age.'

This was a new thought. Everyone was quiet as they mulled over it. Guruji continued, 'The children get along so well with each other because the Shaktis or powers have sensed that they are near their own kind. But as human children, if these Shaktis are allowed to stay together, they will do more harm than good. The children will sometimes fight with each other and sometimes play along peacefully. When they fight, it could be over a trivial matter, as is the wont of children. And when this happens, these Shaktis will rise up against each other and may even destroy each other. That will not do. These Shaktis have come into this world for a specific purpose. We have to nurture them and guide them in the right direction,' Guruji looked piercingly at each of them. He knew what he was going to say next would be a bombshell. But the others had an inkling of what Guruji would say. They had discussed this and though they might not like, they had come here for his guidance and would follow whatever he suggested.

'For this purpose, the children have to be separated and sent away to different ashrams or Gurukuls.'

Despite knowing that Guruji might suggest this, the parents were still shocked. The children were so young.

Aishani blurted out what they were all thinking. 'But Guruji, the children are too young to be sent to a boarding school. They need their parents, or at least their grandparents,' she finished lamely.

'Not so young that they cannot be sent to an ashram. You, of all the people, know how effortlessly your children use their powers, without praying and without invoking any deity. They might be having more than one power even. We cannot allow these powers to clash with one another, at least for the time being.'

Aishani desperately looked at Adheesh and her mother. Both of them looked sympathetic. Adheesh pressed her hand. Madhuji gestured her to be quiet though all her sympathy for her daughter was apparent in her look. Aishani was troubled, but Kedar and Kalpesh were shocked beyond comprehension. They were vaguely aware of Adheesh and Aishani's accomplishments, but that it would touch them in this manner they had never even imagined.

'Why our children, Guruji?' Kedar finally managed to say. 'What is our connection to all this?'

Though in their heart of hearts both Kedar and Kalpesh knew that their children too were different from them. In fact, Kedar had secretly hoped that one of his children would have some powers like Adheesh, but he had not thought that it would require such a great sacrifice. They had not interacted with Guruji at all, but they instinctively knew that his word was law here.

'You are of the same bloodline. Some dormant qualities were bound to show up in your children. A short reprieve for both of you. You will be sending your children to these ashrams after a year or so. Darsh and Divya and Kalpit will have to leave immediately for their skills to be discovered and honed. While these ashrams may look like any normal ashram, they are in fact state of the art Gurukuls, almost like ours, though in some cases more academically oriented.

No one was more surprised than Ruby. Everyone suspected that Kalpit was not only related to Ruby, but that he was her son. It was almost like an open secret. In reality, only Guruji and Aishani knew the truth. What the others could not comprehend was that Kalpit could also have some special powers. Maybe it was because of Ruby, they thought. Ruby stared at Guruji mutely and he looked at her reassuringly. She knew that Guruji would talk to her later.

'I have selected an ashram for Darsh, Divya and Kalpit. It is deep in the Himalayas and few people have even heard of it, let alone be aware of its existence. It is for special children and the teachers understand the dilemma of the parents of these kids with superpowers. They gently nurture their qualities and hone them to perfection. They train the children in such a way that they mix easily with normal kids when they come home or mix with the outside world. In a nutshell, though their powers will be enhanced, they will not be allowed to use them till the time they pass certain tests.'

Aishani, Adheesh, and Ruby looked slightly relieved though it was going to be difficult to be without the children. They also knew that they would never have been able to impart the kind of training that this Gurukul would give the children.

'What about our children, Guruji?' Kalpesh asked. 'Will they too be sent to this Gurukul?'

'Not at the moment,' Guruji replied. 'Your children are too young, and we would need to assess them further. Your son did show some powers when he effortlessly stretched his hand for the milk. After a couple of years, we will come to know about your children's latent powers. If we are still unable to see anything different, we will send them to a slightly softer and more compliant Gurukul.'

Kedar interjected, 'These Gurukuls that you talk about Guruji, will they have normal syllabus too? I mean will they teach subjects like science, history, math, etc. or will they be taught only the ancient teachings?'

'Have no doubts on that score, Kedar. Only those children

are sent to these Gurukuls who have superior intelligence. They will have more to study as they will have the traditional as well as the ancient syllabi to study.'

Kedar looked as if he had many more questions.

Guruji waited for him and the others to ask any more questions. Though they had many, somehow, they were unable to ask them. Their emotions were so entangled that they knew they wouldn't be able to ask what was in their hearts and minds.

'Right then. All of you discuss among yourselves. We will have one final meeting after a few days,' Guruji said. They folded their hands in namaste and left the Gurukul, each lost in his/her own thoughts. Ruby stayed back. She was now alone with Guruji, but she didn't say anything. She was confused. She did not know what to ask. Somehow, in the whole course of play in the present century and its social stigmas, she had begun to perceive herself and her son as inferior beings. True, no one ever said anything, but she knew that they were aware that Kalpit was her son and that she was not married to his father, nor did they know who he was. Only Aishani and Guruji knew. All this made her extra protective of him. For the time being, he was not curious about his father, but she knew that very soon he would have questions. Ruby thanked God every time she looked at her son. He was such a serious and sweet boy. His aptitude for learning had already amazed everybody. He was too mature for his age. It seemed that he saw and understood everything but didn't say much.

'Ruby don't let any inferiority complex develop in you. Your son's father is one of the greatest sages in the world. It is with great pride that I say that your son has inherited his father's great qualities. Kalpit has a great future ahead of him. He will make you proud in more ways than one.'

Ruby had tears in her eyes. She folded her hands in gratitude to Guruji. She knew that Guruji had not spoken only to reassure her. Guruji never spoke superfluously. He had seen Kalpit's calibre and assessed him. Such praise coming from Guruji acted like a balm to her soul. She was a bit surprised too at Guruji calling Swami Sivananda, Kalpit's father, one of the great sages of the world. She was never in love with him, she was just doing a job given to her by Guruji, to protect Aishani. And Kalpit was a product of that liaison. All around her, her friends were living normal lives, that is as normal as they could be under the circumstances. And here she was, saddled with a baby whose father's name she could not disclose.

Guruji answered her unspoken thoughts. 'Nobody looks down upon you though they may not understand your reasons. You are a warrior and one of the stalwarts of our Gurukul. You are the descendent of heaven's apsaras. In this birth, you have begun thinking like a human, which explains your feeling of shame. You need not look down upon yourself. You did an honourable job of protecting your leader. God has blessed you with your son. He will get the best education and the best training. He will outshine his father and all the gurus of the world, and his word will be taken as gospel everywhere.'

Ruby was openly crying now. Guruji blessed her. She bowed to him and left.

The elders and Kedar and Kalpesh had come to the Gurukul in their own cars. After seeing them off, Aishani and

Adheesh went and sat on the riverbank. Aishani took Adheesh's hand in hers and said, 'Adhee, will I be able to live without the children? We don't get much time with them in any case. Now we won't be able to see them for months on end.'

'Ash, Guruji is right. We will not be able to look after and control them all time. I have heard of this Gurukul in the Himalayas. It is so exclusive that not many in our community even know about it. Unlike our Gurukul, it is totally invisible to outsiders. A person may go near it but will not be able to see it. It is basically a school for children like ours. They have specially trained and dedicated teachers, who will look after them better than we can. And Ash....?'

'Hmm.'

'The final choice is always yours. If you decide not to send the children to this boarding school, no questions will be asked. All of us will care for our babies at home.'

'You're not being much of a help Adhee. With all our commitments, you know we cannot look and care for the babies the way they must be cared for. I cannot halt our destinies to constantly look after the kids. God knows what kind of superpower they'll spring on their grandparents or even the servants behind our backs. It's just that I'll miss them so much.' She closed her eyes and put her head on his shoulders. He held her closely and she snuggled up to him. They stayed like that for some time then got up to go home. They knew that the others too had no choice.

SARAMA, THE FEMALE DOG

Adheesh and Aishani were walking hand in hand along the outer edge of the Gurukul beside the stream. How many sessions they had conducted with their group on the banks of this stream. Sometimes the gurus and teachers took their classes here. The burbling of the stream always had a calm and soothing effect on everybody. Anyone who wanted to unwind would come and sit quietly beside the water.

Aishani always went into a contemplative mood here in this sweet and peaceful environment. Experience had taught them so much that now they could see almost everything happening in the Gurukul if they put their minds to it. Though they knew in their hearts that the only person who actually knew everything about the Gurukul was Guruji. No one else.

'Adhee!'

'Hmm?'

'One day, we must take the twins to the Gurukul's menagerie. They should be familiar with all the animals of the world.'

'You know very well, Ash, that we don't have a zoo or even an enclosure for the animals in the Gurukul. Everybody is free here including the animals and even insects.'

'Yes, Adhee, I know,' she said. 'I know that a vast part of the Gurukul has been designated for the animals along with their kind of flora and fauna. There are different places for the contemporary and for the not-so-contemporary animals. In layman's language, they can be termed as mythological creatures.'

Adheesh squeezed her shoulder and they both laughed. 'Yeah, let's go there now,' he suggested.

They walked for about half a mile and then stopped. There was no boundary wall and no enclosure, but they had reached the place where these ancient creatures and their progeny resided. Nevertheless, there was an invisible barrier which the venerable beings could not cross. This place was invisible to all, except the most experienced and senior warriors. Even some of the senior teachers were not aware of this part of the forest, and even if they ventured here, they could not see it.

'Look Adhee, the Farasi Bahari,' she said excitedly. 'What adventures we had with them!'

In return, the two Farasi Baharis or green horses, turned to look at them. Memory stirred in them too, it appeared, as they trotted up to Adheesh and Aishani and nuzzled them. Aishani patted them affectionately and gave them some sweets to eat. The horses played with them for some time, then trotted away to graze.

Adheesh and Aishani walked further. Suddenly, two dogs rushed at them and jumped all over them. There were four or five of them. Aishani was startled. They loved dogs but had never got around to keeping one. One of them, probably the oldest, a bitch, had a thick, brown coat. The other two had thick white fur. They all looked like fox terriers but were not of that breed. This was the primordial abode of the divine animals. Adheesh and Aishani knew that these canine creatures had a story to tell. Their curiosity was aroused. Maybe, when they had the time, they would look them up in the library. Though they did not look to be hungry, the dogs seemed to be baring their teeth. Aishani was a bit scared. There were four or five dogs of different colours and shapes.

'Adhee, I have a niggling feeling that we are seeing only what we are allowed to see. I think there are many more animals and birds and hybrids here. Till now we have seen only horses, some birds and now these dogs. Do you think the twins will be able to see more animals and birds?'

'As far as the Gurukul's qualifications are concerned, the twins are nowhere, but they're our children and they've already shown some powers. They might be able to see more than us.'

'Adhee,' she sighed, interlinking her fingers with his, 'Sometimes I think we would have been better off without our powers.'

'And sometimes?' he teased.

She smiled, both of them knowing that they wouldn't

want their lives any different.

A couple of dogs began to follow them, wagging their tails. One was brown and the other was black. They looked like a cross between a Labrador and a Fox Terrier, but they could not really make out their breed. The black one was a bitch. She was long and was about two and a half feet in height. She had a broad head, and her eyes were limpid pools with irises as dark as chocolate. They reflected a sense of humour. She looked at them as if she wanted to say something. Aishani tentatively patted her head. The dog responded by licking her hand. Both the dogs walked with them to the end of their habitat. Adheesh and Aishani walked back to the main Gurukul.

'Ash let's go and take Guruji's permission to show the menagerie to the kids. We can take Ruby and her son too.'

'Good idea! Let's go and ask Guruji,' she answered enthusiastically. They went towards his cottage. Guruji was in consultation with a couple of other gurus from the nearby states. This was a bit surprising. Normally Guruji held these meetings in the libraries or in the annexure of the museum. They were happy to wait outside. Guruji's cottage. As usual, they stood and appreciated the surroundings that were so well kept and natural. They felt that all their questions and stress vanished as soon as they entered this place. They went to a corner of the garden and waited. Soon they saw two distinguished looking sages come out of the cottage. The sages spotted them and nodded to them. Adheesh and Aishani folded their hands in namaste.

After a few minutes, Guruji called them inside. They touched his feet and sat down. Guruji did not ask them the purpose of their visit. He was engrossed in his own thoughts. They waited. After some time Guruji spoke, 'The female dog you saw was Sarama, a descendent of the dogs of the gods and devatas. You could see her because she felt that both of you could help her. You know that there are other gurukuls like ours across the country and across the world too.'

They nodded. They were not surprised that Guruji knew that they had met a couple of dogs in the menagerie of the Gurukul. Guruji knew everything.

'The people you saw going out of here just now are the heads of other Gurukuls though they are relatively smaller than ours. They are facing the same problem. You know all these ashrams are self-sustaining. We have our farms with cows to provide us with milk and its by-products. We have our own apiaries too that give us enough honey to satisfy our needs. And we have our watchdogs. The story goes back a long time when civilization was new. There were Asuras or demons, devatas, human beings and other living things like quadrupeds, birds, and water beings. The Asuras were the wicked ones, and all the others were graded in varying degrees of goodness.'

'Cows in our culture have always been regarded as the nurturers of humanity, even more so in ancient times. Milk was in any case used to nurture new-borns, and butter was used for consumption and for oblation during a havan. In earlier times, cows and horses were used as payments to the priest for performing the Yagna. Cows have been equated with the rays of the sun. Here comes the role of the Panis who were very strong demons. They stole all the cows and hid them in rocky terrain. Nobody could find the cows. It was only

Sarama, the divine hound, who could sniff out the Panis and lead her masters to them. Sarama is also known as the seeker of dawn, of truth. The symbolic meaning here is that Sarama the dawn finds the cows who are rays of the sun, and then they are followed by Indra, the God of light. In the present context, Sarama is known as any female dog.'

They knew that there was more to the story. They waited patiently. After a pause, Guruji resumed his tale. 'History has repeated itself innumerable times, but it has not diluted the gravity of the situation. Maybe the threat is more acute now in Kaliyuga.'

'Does this mean that the cows from these ashrams have been stolen and have to be retrieved?' Adheesh enquired.

Aishani volunteered the answer. 'We will have to follow the female dog Sarama to find the cows, right, Guruji?'

'Yes, Aishani, these descendants of Sarama have a heightened sense of smell and very high intuition. Only they can lead you to the stolen cows.'

'Guruji, I think it's because of their intuition that these dogs came to us. I did feel as if they wanted to say something,' she added.

'Sarama is nimble footed and has other great powers. She will lead you to the enclosures where the cows have been hidden. Even I don't know the exact location of the place, but I do know that they are hidden behind some rocky paddocks near the Western tributary of the Indus River.'

'That is near Ladakh?' Adheesh said.

'That's right, Adheesh. Going there with Sarama is the easy part, but retrieving the cows is of utmost importance.'

'Guruji, first we find the cows; then we destroy the Panis and then we liberate the cows,' Adheesh said.

Guruji nodded.

'Two important questions, Guruji,' said Adheesh again, 'The first one is how to destroy the Panis. They are supposed to be one of the strongest demons in the world, almost invincible. The second is, after we free the cows, where will they go and how?'

'The answer to the first question requires more work. The Panis, though the fiercest and the strongest of demons, do not have magic, which we have in plenty. Rather, they do not have the magic of words. Our ancient Mahabali warriors and our sages had the power of words. This means that they could invoke the gods and their divine weapons through special incantations. Once the deities bestowed their weapons to a particular being, their Astras would come to that person and pledge their allegiance. The Astra would remain with that person for the stipulated time. Till that time, it would remain hidden and invisible, but would be at the beck and call of that person. Aishani will have to prepare herself for this divine astra, while you, Uday and Jayant will assist her in retrieving the cows. Jayant is required for his vision in case of any hidden places.'

'Once you destroy the demons and liberate the cows, your part will be over. There will be another group of workers from other Gurukuls, who will take the cows to their respective homes.'

Guruji gave them some more instructions, after which they left. One week later, they were in Manali. With them was Sarama and her male pup, Sabala. They had hired a four-wheeler Safari for this long journey. Travelling with the dogs by train or air was not very practical. They stayed overnight at a hotel in Manali. The next morning, they started early for Ladakh. It was getting colder, and the scenery was beautiful. Their vehicle went through the Rohtang Pass, the long corridor of snow and ice. They were in the Himalayas now. Manali to Ladakh was a journey of about ten hours. They reached around four in the evening. They had already made their reservations at a small hotel. The behaviour of Sarama and Sabala surprised them. They were almost like humans in their behaviour. They communicated with them with their eyes. Their demeanour radiated love and positivity. It was a beautiful journey. Aishani was torn between enjoying the landscape and being ready for the job ahead. Finally, she decided to soak in the beauty of the white snow, the landscape and the mountains which were now becoming taller. Their caps were covered with snow.

She was fully prepared for her task. Guruji had initiated her into using the Parvatastra. Parvat means mountain. When this divine weapon was activated, it would send a hail of huge rocks the size of small mountains at the enemies and crush them. It was almost like a thunderstorm of rocks falling on the ground. This would continue till every single enemy was destroyed. Along with Guruji's guidance, it had taken her almost a week to invoke the Parvatastra. Parvatastra belonged to Indra, the ruler of heaven. Hence, she had to invoke Indra devata so that he could bestow the Astra on her.

The next morning, they left early. Uday drove while Jayant and Aishani sat at the back with the dogs, each immersed in his and her own thoughts. The dogs instinctively knew where to go, and Jayant was looking at every nook and cranny for any signs of the hidden Panis or the cows. Adheesh was sitting in the front with Uday, both fully alert. Aishani barely saw the stark beauty of the place; she was so abstracted. In some places there were bare mountains down which the river flowed. In other places there were bits of ice floating on the water. Everywhere it was flowing by the mountains. In some places they could see some men and women working, but they could not make out what they were doing. When they reached nearer, they were surprised to see that these men and women were larger and taller than the average human beings. Were they the Panis, Aishani wondered. She knew that the Panis could not hide nor become invisible. She thought back to the sages and deities who could perform so many things which could be termed as magic, but was actually, an advanced form of science. If the Panis had magic, then it would have been a herculean task to retrieve the cows.

Suddenly Sarama barked. It began as a growl coming from deep inside her stomach and then came out as an excited bark. She and Sabala began wagging their tails and barking excitedly. Uday slowed down the car and they all looked around. There were miles and miles of bare mountains, occasionally interspersed with clumps of shrubs and wildflowers. Through this stark beauty, flowed the Indus river.

Adheesh spoke to Sarama, 'There is nothing here Devshuni.' Sarama was called Devshuni in ancient times. It meant the dog of the devatas. Sarama looked at him with her warm, limpid, brown eyes, wagged her tail and gave a low growl. All of them examined the place very carefully, but there was nothing but a barren landscape of breath-taking beauty. There was no movement and no sound, apart from the soft ripple of the flowing river. Uday looked at Adheesh, who nodded and Uday started the car. Instantly, both the dogs began barking fiercely. Uday stopped. The dogs became quiet.

'Well, something is here, we just don't know where,' Adheesh commented wryly. 'We'll have to find out.'

They got down from the car and started examining every nook and cranny. But they saw only the bare mountains and a few shrubs here and there. Sarama and Sabala had begun to bark again. Puzzled, they turned to Jayant for help and were surprised to see him in a trance. This meant that there was something or someone there whom they could not see.

'Adheesh, I can see something!' Jayant's eyes were closed, and his head was moving from left to right. 'They're here! The Panis are here! And the cows are here too. My God! I've never seen so many cows together in one place in my life. And the Panis are huge, they are so fierce looking,' Jayant was mumbling. He always talked like this when he was in a trance and was seeing hidden things that were not visible to anyone else. The team did not have any problem with his incoherent statements, they were used to it and could understand him very well.

'Where, Jayant, where?' cried Aishani. 'We cannot see anything. There's only this bare, stark mountain in front of us. The Panis don't have any magic to hide inside the mountain or make the cows invisible. Tell us exactly where they are!'

'They are behind the mountain,' Jayant answered softly.

'I cannot see the way to the enclosure, but there are thousands of cows there and the Panis are guarding them.'

Sarama and Sabala's excited barking were louder, and they were running here and there as if asking Adheesh and the others to follow them.

'We'll wait for Jayant to show the way. If not, then we'll follow Devshuni and her son,' Adheesh declared.

They could see that Jayant was trying his level best to see the hideaway of the cows, but it was taking a lot of time. Maybe it was because of the solid wall of mountains that he could not penetrate. They waited for some time.

'Leave it now, Jayant,' Adheesh said softly. 'It's still early noon and it's a bit clearer in afternoon. Jayant nodded and got up. They followed the Devshuni. She, along with her son Sabala, ran back the way from where they had come. There were moss- and lichen-covered boulders across the ground. There were no signs of any living beings there, but they were all on high alert. They knew that the Panis were somewhere here though their logic could not locate the demons. After five hundred metres or so, Sarama stopped. Her bark was now more insistent. She would bark and disappear into a crack in mountain wall. Sarama was quite thin and could wriggle through the crack but nobody else could follow her. They were puzzled. Even Sabala was hesitant to follow her inside.

Jayant said, 'There is something here. I can again see the Panis and the cows. This crack in the mountain is an optical illusion, not magic. We can all go inside.'

Adheesh peered at the crack, put his hands inside the crack. It disappeared. Emboldened, he tried to enter the fissure while the others watched. He disappeared. Surprised but not shocked, they all followed Adheesh into the mountain. As it turned out, the crack was not a fissure. It just looked like one. They could easily walk inside. The passage was a worn out blanket of grass and mud, flanked by the mountain on both sides. The sunlight came in through the chinks in the ridges and fell on the path forming a design, like a mural. They continued further down the path. Somewhere along the mud and grass trail, the vegetation started. There wasn't much of sunlight. The vegetation was covered with dew and moving lazily like thousands of white fireflies all moving in one direction. Gradually the path faded and there was just a silvery mist and a few broken patches of vegetation. They followed Sarama and Sabala. A whole new vista opened up before them. Jayant urged them to go on. However, he was unable to gauge the exact distance to the camp of the Panis and where the herds of cows were kept.

Suddenly Sarama ran away from them at lightning speed. Sabala followed his mother. They all ran after the dogs. Adheesh looked at Aishani. Her eyes were half closed and she seemed to be concentrating on something. He knew what she was doing. She was calling for her divine weapon. He held her hand and said, 'You close your eyes and meditate, sweetheart. I'll guide you down the path.' He picked her up in his arms and ran forward. She felt light in his arms. Adheesh was a strong warrior, and it was easy for him to run even on such difficult terrain with Aishani in his arms. Uday glanced at them for a fraction of a second and then ran ahead of them so that he would encounter the Panis first, and thus shield them.

Suddenly swift, sharp arrows rained on them. They ducked and took refuge among the shrubs. The rising fog was enveloping everything. Of course, there were only the bare mountain walls and a few shrubs here and there. All of a sudden, a couple of Panis appeared before them. They were huge and looked scary with bulging eyes and protruding sharp teeth. They were clad in heavy armour and were obviously fully prepared to fight. They looked like mountains themselves. They had the cunningness and cruelty of all demons, but they did not possess any superpowers. Aishani asked to be put down from Adheesh's arms. He knew that she was relieved that the Panis had come out to confront them. Now she could attack them. He also knew that she did not like to assault anybody unless it was absolutely necessary.

From far away they could hear the faint sounds of the bellowing of the cows. That meant that the cows were not very far off. Suddenly a large number of Panis jumped on Adheesh and the others. The attack shook the earth. Or rather, the mountains shook under the onslaught of the Panis. What the Panis did not have by way of magic, they more than made up with their aggression and fierceness. Adheesh and Uday were putting up a good fight. There was an almost equal show of strength, but the Panis outnumbered them. Jayant also fought, but he was no match for the Panis. It was just the situation where Aishani would have to use her weapon. She stood in a corner, identified all the Panis there, closed her eyes, whispered to her Astra, and shot four arrows into the air, one in each direction. The arrows went up high in the sky and burst into a huge ball of fire. Out of this huge fiery ball came out mountains that shuddered in the air for a moment and then came hurtling down on the Panis. It was such a majestic and imposing sight that even Adheesh and Uday paused for a moment to view it. The Panis did not stand a chance. They knew that Devshuni Sarama had knowledge of their hideout, but they had thought that nothing would happen to them in Kaliyuga.

The mountains produced by Aishani's arrows zeroed in on the Panis, fell on them, their own force magnified by the earth's gravitational pull and crushed all the Panis to death. It took about thirty minutes to crush every single demon, after which the arrows came back to Aishani. She was dazed and exhausted by now. Adheesh knew that she was spent. He picked her up in his arms again and they all ran towards the enclosure where the cows were kept. There were hundreds of thousands of cows there, all healthy and in good condition, thankfully. They took deep breaths and tried to slow down the flow of adrenaline. Aishani was sitting on Adheesh's lap. She was almost in a coma, totally oblivious of the situation around her.

They heard footsteps approaching. Adheesh looked up. Two devatas were approaching them. They stood up and folded their hands in greeting. The devatas responded in the same manner.

'We are the Ashwins. It is our job to rescue lost and kidnapped beings. All of you have performed a praiseworthy job. Your work here is over now. We will take over and herd these cows to their respective ashrams.'

All of them folded their hands in a gesture of respect to

the Ashwins. Surprisingly, as they were leaving, the Ashwins bowed deeply to Aishani.

PEY AND PEYMAKILIR

'This war has brought the country to its knees,' said Vashishtji, the librarian. There was a lull in the activities of the Gurukul, a vacation almost. The hibernating demons had yet to wake up. This was conveyed to Guruji and Adheesh and Uday. Since it was a Gurukul, the downtime was used constructively. Some of the shishyas were allowed to go home, while others chose to stay back to either complete their backlog of studies and training or simply because they enjoyed themselves here. Many of the serious ones went to the library to catch up on research or study. Even Vashishtji was relatively free. Most of the students came here to increase their knowledge slowly and steadily. But then during emergencies, warriors like Adheesh and Uday came and demanded some particular books. As they had done yesterday.

"It's not only our soldiers who are dying on the battlefield. The soldiers on the other side are also dying. Killing and dying are the norms during a battle. What we are concerned about is that many soldiers are dying for reasons other than war," Vashishtji waited for effect and for his words to sink in.

The seniors smiled with their eyes, while the juniors were all agog with curiosity and anticipation. They knew that a demon was going to enter the picture and if they were lucky, there would be more than one demon. They were right. Vashishtji was talking about demons in the battlefield.

'These are the demons who eat and drink the flesh and blood of the dead soldiers. Some soldiers are so badly maimed or mutilated that it becomes impossible to pick them up in one piece, forget about transporting their bodies to their homes. It is easier and kinder for these corpses to be buried in the battlefield itself than try to pick them up and take to the nearest medical centre.'

One of the junior warriors piped up, 'This must be the cue for these demons to come and devour the flesh and blood of the dead soldiers. But, though gory and sickening, isn't it kinder to let them do so?'

It was time for Vashishtji to wind up the discussion. He said, 'No doubt, you will be summoned by Guruji to go to the front and find the demons who are killing and eating the injured soldiers, who would have survived otherwise.'

'I always wanted to join the army,' Uday said wistfully.

'Bhaiya, you can demolish any army single-handedly,' Tejas said, looking at Uday adoringly.

Uday swiped his head good-naturedly. The others laughed.

Sure enough, they were summoned by Guruji in the evening and were promptly sent back to the library to find out more about these demons.

They reported to Guruji the next morning. Guruji had summoned Devnath too. As he was Adheesh's bodyguard, Devnath never went inside Guruji's cottage unless called. Today, Guruji had specifically asked for him. They knew that it must be for a special reason. He shuffled inside. He was clearly uncomfortable in these hallowed surroundings, even if Guruji's cottage was sparsely furnished.

It was always Adheesh's prerogative to begin any presentation.

He began, 'These demons are known as Pey and Peymakilir. Pey is the male demon, and its female form is Peymakilir. Their original habitat is in southern India, but they have been found in Tibet and China too.

'They are popular demons in South Indian folklore. It is said that when soldiers fall down on the battlefield, these two demons swoop down on the hapless and dying souls and eat their flesh and drink their blood. They look like human beings but are very pale. The female is the more vicious of the two. She devours the flesh of the dying soldiers and performs a macabre dance while doing so. The male drinks the blood of the dying soldiers. They are sometimes called the angels of mercy because the injured soldiers who might die an agonizing death are put out of their misery by Pey and Peymakilir, thus reducing their agony.'

Adheesh stopped and looked around for their reactions.

Jayant asked, 'If indeed they are devouring the bodies of

the dying in this manner, then why stop them? It seems they are doing a good thing.'

It was Guruji who answered this question. 'Till this point it was almost alright, but this is the Kaliyuga where no rules are followed. Pey and Peymakilir may be devouring only dying bodies in earlier eras, but now they haunt the battlegrounds and wolf down soldiers who are only slightly hurt and might be unconscious. They intercept these soldiers before they are taken to the hospital. In a nutshell, they eat the healthy soldiers too. The only condition is that the soldiers should be in or near the battlefield,' he said.

'It is imperative that Devnath goes with you,' Guruji continued. He looked toward Devnath and said, 'You have a vast knowledge of dead, undead and nearly dying people. You can also make out who will surely die an agonizing and painful death. You will have to segregate the living from the dead. The others will take the living and the barely living to safety and provide them succour on the way. Beware, the Pey and the Peymakilir have now begun eating healthy soldiers too. All of you will need to protect yourselves and others too.'

Devnath was overwhelmed by Guruji's directive. Humbly he folded his hands and bowed his head. All of them nodded in agreement too.

'Guruji, is there any special way by which we can destroy these demons?' Adheesh asked.

'I am coming to that, Adheesh. You stay back. The rest of you, go back and plan your strategy and choose your roles for this mission.'

After touching Guruji's feet and taking his blessing, the

others left.

Guruji turned to Adheesh. 'Which Astra do you think will eliminate these battlefield demons?'

Adheesh knew that despite his faith in them, Guruji still tested their knowledge and intuition from time to time. Guruji knew what weapon was to be used, he just wanted Adheesh's reasoning and opinion.

'These demons are very cruel and cunning. They know the battlefields like the back of their hands. They will change their shapes, become invisible, and dance on top of the dying souls. They are hardened felons. The way I see it, the only way they can be controlled is by using the Agni Astra or Agneyastra on them.'

Guruji nodded approvingly. 'I was also thinking the same thing, but it will take some time to invoke the Agni Devata. God knows how many soldiers will be killed in this period by the enemies and by the demons.'

'Guruji, please give me this diksha immediately. We want to save as many lives as possible.'

Guruji took him to the chamber which was known as the museum. It was a museum per se. One feature of the museum was that it housed the likeness of the entire ancient divine weapons which had once been used by the gods and their avatars. The second-year student warriors were brought here and taught the history and the input and output of the power of weapons. Kept in their velvet-lined cases, they looked like any other antique weapon. The students and even their teachers would have been astounded had they known that these were the real Astras, which had been deactivated. The

Gurukul worked strictly on a need-to-know basis.

To graduate to the level of using the divine weapons, one had to perform centuries of Tapa and continue with it in their succeeding births. Adheesh and Aishani were two such warriors who were qualified to handle a few of the divine weapons.

They entered a small room in one of the annexures of the museum. The Agneyastra was kept on a red velvet cloth inside a rectangular glass enclosure. These divine weapons were always at the beck and call of their deities, in this case the Agni Devata. But nonetheless, a human being would always have to chant the Agneyastra mantra to invoke the Agni Devata and his divine weapon. This weapon was the size of a normal trident, except that instead of three prongs there were six, which, after activation, threw fire and electricity at the enemy, scorching them immediately and turning them into cinders. Once the powerful weapon was locked onto a target, it would return to its master after demolishing the enemy. No being could escape the weapon – not man nor demons nor devatas. Hence it was reiterated that the Agneyastra should never be used for frivolous purposes or to settle personal scores. It should be invoked only in case of a dire emergency and mankind was in danger of becoming extinct. In the case of the demons Pey and Peymakilir, they had crossed all boundaries and were devouring live soldiers now. There was no stopping them now that they had tasted healthy soldiers.

Both Guruji and Adheesh sat in front of the Agneyastra. Guruji transferred the Agneyastra mantra to Adheesh and gave him a black agate mala with 108 beads. They sat there chanting the mantra. They chanted day and night without a break for three days. On the fourth day there was a slight movement in the weapon. It began imbibing a sort of a reddish lustre. Some electrical sparks also started coming out of it. It was lying in a horizontal position. It began straightening and was almost vertical now as if raring to go.

'Good work, Adheesh! It usually takes eleven days to invoke the Agneyasatra and another forty-three days to fully activate it. It is your strong power that shortened this process. Now you must prepare to go to the border with your team. May God be with you!' Adheesh touched Guruji's feet, received his blessing and left.

He went to the usual place behind the Gurukul to find everybody waiting for him under the neem tree. They had already decided on their actions and roles. Devnath was going to find the living and dead soldiers, that is fathom who was going to survive. Any soldier who had an iota of life left in him would be whisked away by Aishani and Ruby to safety. Uday would lead the assault along with Jayant and Tejas, who would use their special abilities as usual. They did not ask Adheesh about his role as they knew that he was going to use a divine weapon. They did not ask as it was forbidden to divulge any information about the weapons.

It took them a day to reach the border. It was evening by the time they arrived at their destination. They went straight to the battlefield. It was now almost night, and everything was a greyish shade of black since there was no electricity and no source of light. The ground was littered with dead and dying soldiers. There seemed to be a temporary ceasefire. They could hear the roar of the guns from far afar, but here there was complete silence. There was a sinister and malignant atmosphere about the whole place. They did not see anything apart from the dead bodies on the ground. Some seemed asleep, while others were mangled beyond recognition with their blood, flesh and bones strewn around. All of them had seen grotesque dead bodies in the course of their missions, but every time they were horrified and filled with despair. Adheesh looked at Devnath who went to work immediately. He began from the outer periphery.

Without any revulsion, Devnath began touching the fallen soldiers. He looked at Aishani. After their experiences on Mount Kailash, Devnath had more faith in Aishani than anyone else.

'Bhabhi, this one is alive,' he was holding the head of a torn and broken corpse. 'He will survive and recover too.'

Aishani and Ruby rushed to that soldier, who appeared dead. But if Devnath said he was alive, then it was so. It was too dark to see anything clearly. Jayant and Tejas were by their side. Guruji had given Tejas a special torch, the light of which wasn't too bright. Too bright a light would have affected their already heightened sense of revulsion and despair. There were broken and burnt trees. Tejas jumped onto the higher branches and flashed the torchlight on the ground so that the others could make out the dead bodies and not step on them. Whenever the light shone on the ground, it glistened as if the rain had fallen, but the liquid wasn't water, it was blood. Devnath was working feverishly, trying to save as many of the soldiers as possible.

They had brought two makeshift stretchers with them. They put the soldiers on stretchers and took them away from the battleground. Adheesh and Uday were on the alert for any signs of Pey and Peymakilir. Suddenly there was an urgent whisper from Jayant, 'Adheesh! They are here!'

Immediately, their weapons ready, Adheesh and Uday looked around. They could not see anything or anyone.

'Where?' Uday asked. He had his weapons, the Pash and the Gram which Einar had given him, ready. Adheesh's divyastra was with him. Uday directed the others to take away as many of the still alive soldiers as possible.

They squinted their eyes to see more clearly. Gradually they could make out some shimmering and slim creatures. Looking closely, they realized that they looked like humans though very pale in colour and they were naked. They were swaying over the dead and the dying, utterly oblivious of Adheesh and Uday. Their eyes were neon, sometimes appearing red and sometimes yellow. They were bounding from one body to another emitting short and soft hysterical shrieks in their excitement. They could not decide from where to begin. Then ear-splitting sounds reverberated all over the battlefield. After their gory, outrageous, and vulgar dancing over the dead and dying soldiers, the Pey and Peymakilir began to feed on them. Loud yelps and masticating sounds could be heard along with guzzling and squelching of blood. In between Adheesh and Uday could hear shrill screams. Puzzled they tried to pinpoint the source of the screams. They could not though now the screams were more regular.

'Adheesh,' Uday whispered, 'The screams are the Pey and the Peymakilir celebrating. They have not seen this much food and drink for a long time. Look, they are dancing too.'

Sometimes they would hear the cries and groans of a fallen soldier. They were immediately taken away by Aishani, Ruby, Tejas and a few other warriors who Adheesh had selected for their team.

Jayant had been giving them a commentary on the movement of the demons as they were visible only now and then. Pey was drinking the blood of a dead soldier and his partner demon was waiting for her turn to feed on the flesh. Sometimes they shone as silvery ghouls and sometimes only their skeletons were seen. Suddenly, Jayant stopped his commentary and gasped. The others looked at him questioningly.

'Oh!' Jayant drew in his breath sharply. 'They are not just one pair. I can also see more than five pairs of demons. They seem to be merging in the darkness.'

This was news indeed, though it made Adheesh's work easier. He could now make full use of the Agneyastra. Somehow, they had to come together at the same time. His eyes met Devnath's who nodded his head imperceptibly.

In their excitement, the demons danced on top of the corpses. It was a chilling sight. The Pey and the Peymakilir and their pale silvery skeletons, with the blood dribbling from their mouths and their bodies smeared with torn pieces of flesh, they looked like ghouls from a horror movie.

Devnath was swiftly identifying the alive and the barely alive soldiers and Aishani and Ruby were treating them with the herbs and medicines that they had brought.

A dense fog had started to roll in. There wasn't much time, Adheesh knew. He could use his Astra only if the demons were eating living soldiers. After feeding on a couple of corpses, a group of Peys and Peymakilirs glided to where Aishani and Ruby were tending to the injured soldiers. Aishani was up in an instant, her sword held aloft, but Ruby and Tejas stopped her. 'No, Ash, don't! These are supernatural creatures. They will do more harm to us if we attack them now. Remember, Adheesh has his divine weapon. We don't know what it is, but it is sure to destroy these bloodsucking demons.'

Aishani stopped. She knew that by confronting these demons, she might interfere with Adheesh's task. On a subconscious level, she knew that the Pey and Peymakilir had to attack living soldiers before Adheesh could attack them.

Soon the Pey and Peymakilir smelt the half-dead soldiers being tended to by Aishani and Ruby. They became excited and shimmered towards the place. They danced and screeched in anticipation.

Adheesh instructed Uday to take their team as far away as he could and not look back. The Astra was so potent that just by being there people could be hurt. He then summoned the Agneyastra. Closing his eyes, he reiterated the mantra, spoke the name of the enemies, and shot the arrow towards the demons.

There were huge lightning flashes from the six prongs of the Agneyastra, then from each bolt of fire came out other sparks of fire which fell on the demons and burnt them up immediately. Adheesh thought he had seen about four pairs of Pey and Peymakilir, but because of their jiggling shimmer, he could not be sure.

The demons were caught unawares. Their limited self-centred brains could not assimilate the fact that a weapon of Satyug could be available in Kaliyuga. Nor could they have thought that such warriors as Adheesh and his team could exist in Kaliyuga. The whole operation was over in a matter of minutes. The Agneyastra returned to the Agni Devata.

Adheesh sat down on the ground. Aishani was immediately by his side. She knew the repercussions of using divine weapons.

'I'm all right, Ash,' he said with a smile. Her heart melted with love for him. 'My hero,' she whispered, looking at him adoringly.

'I'll go and see how to reach the nearest military post and hospital safely,' he said.

With the help of Devnath, they picked up as many of the injured soldiers as possible and carried them to where Aishani and Ruby tended to them. This went on till mid-morning the next day when the ambulances and the medical staff of the Indian army reached them and took over.

DAHURASURAN

Aishani was playing with the children. It was early morning. She had habituated the twins to be early risers. After all, they would be soon going to their boarding school in the Himalayas. She enjoyed this private time with her children. Their tutor would come to teach them from nine in the morning, and after that everyone would become busy. She and Adheesh would get ready for the Gurukul. Ruby's son Kalpit was also being tutored along with Darsh and Divya. Though Kalpit had not yet shown signs of any supernatural powers, still it could not to be ruled out as his mother Ruby was an apsara, and his father was an outstanding and illustrious sage. Nobody knew who his father was or where he was at the moment. Ruby had an inkling that he had gone to the mountains for penance. He wasn't aware that he had a child nor was Ruby going to tell him if she met him ever.

'Ash, Guruji has called me. He did not mention you. I'll go; you follow me at the usual time.'

'Ok, Adhee. Any idea why Guruji has called you now?'

'Not really. But there are some demons that have escaped from the other warriors. Maybe it's about them.'

'Okay, I'll get the children ready for their classes. I'll follow you in the car. Devnath will drop me and then come back to guard the children.'

Adheesh kissed her and the children and left.

Guruji was in his cottage. He had just finished his meditation and was waiting for Adheesh. He touched Guruji's feet and was blessed in return. Without waiting, Guruji began, 'There was a giant demon, Dahurasuran, in the bygone era. Rakshasas are evil as everyone is aware. But this rakshasa was the epitome of evil. He did barbaric deeds, even by the demon standards. His crimes kept increasing, as he had extracted a boon from God that made him invincible. When he asked God for this boon, he was told that he could not become immortal. He would have to ask for another boon. So, the next boon which he asked for was that only a woman would be able to kill him. In his arrogance because of his might and strength, he knew that no woman would be able to touch him, let alone kill him. God granted him his wish. Since then, his tortures and cruelties knew no bounds. Even devatas could not touch him, let alone humans. News of his depraved and cruel deeds reached far and wide. There was nobody to stop him as he was protected by the boon. As we have seen, a minuscule fraction of these demons has somehow survived till the present time. The present Dahurasuran may not be as active but is nevertheless no less dangerous than the ancient one.'

Guruji continued, 'I had sent very senior and experienced warriors to tackle him, but to no avail. Our warriors have returned empty-handed; some of them injured and mutilated too.'

'It's because of the boon,' Adheesh said. He knew what was happening. Aishani was recouping after one of her assignments. She wasn't in a fit condition to kill a demon. Guruji, in wanting to protect Aishani, had sent male warriors to defeat Dahurasuran. But they could not overpower him because they were men. In ancient times, Dahurasuran was a demon, who prayed and performed penance to God for thousands of years. Though eons had passed, the basic nature of humans and demons has remained the same. In fact, things had turned worse in that humans have become more demon-like in their conduct. Demons carried out their shenanigans under the guise of benefaction. Earlier, everyone knew that demons were wicked and cruel, and humans were simple and generally good. Now the line dividing both is getting blurred. It is almost impossible to differentiate the demon from human beings. Ultimately it was the angry Ma Durga in her human form who killed him. Sometimes great anger is required to destroy great evil. The present descendent of the demon Dahurasuran is the great industrialist, Dasra Kumar. In the eyes of the world, he is a great man, but insiders and those near to him know what he is like. They are either too scared to speak up or are demons themselves.'

Adheesh nodded grimly. 'I will find out more details, Guruji, and apprise Aishani of the situation too. Like Ma

Durga, she too will have to be in her most belligerent form, full of rage, to annihilate this, Dasra Kumar.'

'You do that, Adheesh, then both of you come to me.'

Adheesh touched Guruji's feet and left.

It seemed to Aishani that she was slowly dying inside.

'Adhee, this cannot be happening! This Dasra Kumar is the epitome of all the evil that I have come across. Even demons have their credo and principles. They kill, maim, torture, are greedy, vain, and many other things. But this man – wait – he is not a man. We know that he is a demon, in the literal sense. He does all these evil things so naturally. It comes to him so easily, as if he has been honing these cruel and manipulative skills for ages. He has made a fine art of the whole thing. Look at the way the world reveres him. He is hailed as a messiah, but he exploits everyone. He will even use a baby, even if it is to his benefit. Forget about factory workers and other such people.' Her shoulders were heaving with anger, her nose had flared up, her eyes were spewing fire.

Adheesh put his arms around her. This is what was required of her, this building up anger, slowly and gradually, till it rose to a crescendo and the fury itself turned into an entity.

'Shh, baby, control yourself,' he said softly.

'I can't, Adheesh,' she cried, pushing away his arms. 'He has exploited, killed, maimed, stolen from the poorest of the poor, and of course, he must have eaten so many. Nobody has heard of his sexual exploits. He is cunning enough to conceal it. He has bought over the media with his money. If that has not worked, he has found their weakness and exploited them mercilessly. He has no mercy.'

'Yes, Ash,' Adheesh responded grimly. 'His exploits are not the cruelty of a human being. They are the machinations of a demonic brain, which has become craftier and more honed through the ages. He cannot be caught and put in a prison cell, like a human being. He has to be killed and destroyed or mother earth will be swarming with demons again. Guruji has from time to time sent his warriors to annihilate him, but either they are killed, or they come back mutilated.

'And this happens because of the boon that God granted to him?' Aishani was perplexed. She vaguely knew the story of Dahurasuran. She knew that ultimately Goddess Durga had killed him.

'What's the problem here, Adheesh? Why did Guruji waste so many warriors to kill him? If it is destined that I have to execute him, then so be it. He has tortured innumerable numbers of people. If humans catch him, he is capable of extricating himself. Besides he has the boon too.'

'Yes, Ash, you are fully capable of destroying him. He is not an abnormal human being. He is a demon. Guruji must have had his own reasons for sending the other warriors to confront him. As for me, I can think of a few points. One is that Guruji may have thought that, after mixing with humans through the ages may have weakened his powers. Secondly, during that period you had lost your memory, I was already in the south. Uday was with Guruji to assist in your cure. The third and the most important point is that, Mahakali, the most violent form of Maa Durga, has to be in a terrible rage to kill such a demon. This is not the anger of a human, rather it is the furious rage of the goddess, which gives her the incentive, the strength to kill such a strong demon.'

'And being a human, and now a mother, I cannot muster that kind of rage,' she whispered, completing his sentence.

Adheesh looked at her but kept quiet.

'Ash, before we go to Guruji for his directive, let us think of what we can do to resolve this situation.'

'Adheesh?'

He looked at her.

'When I had lost my memory, I believe the only person who could help in reviving my memory was someone who loved me unconditionally and who would perform all the rituals with Guruji with full commitment and faith. You were not there, so how did I regain my memory?'

'I too have thought about it, baby. It seems, I am not the only one who loves you with all his heart and soul and keeps it all bottled up inside his heart.'

'Uday,' she whispered.

He nodded sadly, 'Yes.'

'But, but, how, when?' she was genuinely confused, 'He never gave any indication. No, it's not possible! If I am not aware of it, then who else would know?'

'Somebody knew, Ash, and warned him,' Adheesh said.

'Who, Adhee? Who can read our thoughts and who would dare warn him?'

'Only one person, Ash. Only one person understands and has the right to warn him and protect all of us,' he stated.

'Who?' she began, then stopped short. 'Do you mean Guruji? Guruji knew and he warned Uday?'

'There is no other explanation, Ash. Guruji and Uday will

not talk to us about it. Let us leave it there. Thinking about it will bring more heartbreak.'

'How do you know about it, Adhee? Did his secret slip out from him?'

'No, sweetheart, but I have sometimes seen him glancing at you casually, but with different eyes. Uday is probably not aware of this, nor will he ever cross the boundary he has set for himself. My suspicions proved correct, when I had to go south, and Guruji asked Uday to give you drink the memory potion.'

'Oh, Adhee, what a mess,' she went into his arms. They stayed like that for some time, taking strength from each other.

After some time, Aishani shook off her feelings and said, 'Now for our latest assignment, Adhee.'

'Yes,' he said. 'When you hear about the exploits of this demon, a murderous rage will develop in you which will help you destroy it.'

She nodded and smiled involuntarily, 'Everywhere you see and hear that anger is one of the most harmful emotions. One must get rid of it, to attain Nirvana. Here we are going to think of ways, to increase my anger, to superhuman levels.'

Adheesh smiled back, though there was no humour in his eyes. They were humans. Every time they performed their superhuman duties, they had to pay a heavy price for it. Their bodies and emotions were human, though their brains may be bordering on superhuman. They had periodically used the divine weapons too. They had enough strength, vitality, and magic to destroy the demons with the divine weapons, and sometimes with the traditional human weapons. It was as if, while using the divine weapons, they would take over the role of the deity, whose weapons they were using temporarily. Later when they returned to their human bodies, their bodies could not comprehend the changes that had taken place and would remain sick for a long period. Now in order to kill a rakshasa, a deity's anger had to be imposed on her. He shuddered when he thought of it and the consequences. Will his sweet Ash be able to come out of it normally?

Guruji and Adheesh and the core team, knew that Aishani had a fraction of Maa Durga's power. Some called it Maa Durga's blessing, while others looked up to her as Maa Durga herself. Adheesh knew that she had some powers of Mahakali too. Mahakali is one of the ten mahavidyas of Maa Durga.

She is the ferocious form of Maa Durga. She is also known as the devourer of time. Her complexion is black, and she has three eyes, which represent the past, present, and future. She has shiny, white fang-like teeth, and she has a gaping mouth from which her red bloody tongue hangs out. She has dishevelled hair and wears a short sari of tiger skins. She wears a long garland of skulls and severed arms and bones hanging from her neck. Along with this garland, she also wears one of red flowers. Her bangles are made up of bones. She has four hands. She carries a blood-dripping demon head in one hand. In her other hand, she holds a sword, while the other two hands are empty. Her eyes spew rage and ferociousness. The earth trembles with every step of hers.

This rage would enter Aishani's body, making her a killing machine. His heart trembled. He knew that his thinking was incorrect. Mahakali's rage and her sword were used only to demolish the most vicious demons. Her sword symbolises intellect and wisdom. Mahakali who carries it, has the sense of responsibility, and the wisdom to discern right from wrong. In any case his Aishani would never kill anybody only for the sake of killing. This was a matter for Guruji. Guruji had called all of them the next day in the library. They were there five minutes, before Guruji entered the annexure of the library, where they generally had their meetings with Guruji.

'I want all of you to sit here and find out everything about a demon called Dahurasuran. Apparently, he or his descendants have been creating havoc in today's world, with the same cruel and negative actions. He has taken the form of a human and is one of the foremost businessmen in the world. On top of that, he is a Godman. He has the goodwill of almost everybody and he is unstoppable. Reportedly, if he is not stopped now, he will take over the world, and the demons will rule the Earth.'

'Yes, Guruji,' they almost said in unison, 'What is his name in his human avatar?' asked Uday.

'His name is Dasra Kumar,' they nodded and went to the other parts of the library. Only Adheesh, Aishani and Uday stayed. They were the senior most warriors of the Gurukul, and Guruji depended on them to a large extent.

'Uday, you will guide the others in their research, Aishani you will go to a quiet spot and meditate on Maa Durga. Adheesh, I will give you instructions in a minute.'

Both Aishani and Uday knew what Guruji meant by it. Guruji wanted to give some more confidential instructions to Adheesh, which was normal and regular. Adheesh was Guruji's chief warrior. Guruji gave him separate instructions from time to time. They understood this and respected it. Adheesh had most of the responsibilities both in and outside Gurukul. There was no duty specifically delegated to him, for he was Guruji's number two, and he had many private discussions with Guruji. Uday was next in line, but sometimes even he was excluded from these conversations.

Guruji turned to Adheesh, 'Adheesh, I know that you are very worried about Aishani and the after-effects of the rage that she will use to get rid of the Dahurasuran. That Dahurasuran will be eliminated is not in doubt. Aishani will have that much power and incitement to demolish him. You are worried, that she may not be able to survive her own rage.'

Adheesh kept quiet. There was no point in hiding his discomfort from Guruji. Who knows, how long her convalescence, would last?

'We will not let any demon get the better of us. Aishani will recover and fully recover,' Guruji assured him, 'Though it might take more time.'

Adheesh was a bit reassured, but he was her partner in more ways than one. If he couldn't do anything about it, then he was going to sit with her and share her pain and the turmoil later on. He knew that Aishani would not have it any other way. They had pledged to themselves and Guruji and to Lord Hanuman, to rid the Earth of all the demons. That is what they had been doing all these years, in their past births, and that is what they will continue to do in the future too.

The next day they all met in the same place in the library. Guruji looked at their sober faces and knew that they had arrived at their own conclusions. Aishani was not there. As

Guruji had instructed, she was in deep meditation, under one of her chosen trees. They were worried. They were right too, Guruji knew. They were warriors and Aishani's protectors.

'What have you read and discovered?' Guruji enquired.

Slowly they told him about the demon Dahurasuran, about his boon, and about his cruel exploits which were fanned by his knowledge that no male person could kill him. They also told Guruji, how he was finally killed by Mahakali. Nobody knew whether the present Rakshasas was an extraction of the original Dahurasuran or his descendent. Dasra Kumar was one of the world's leading industrialists, with a hand in almost everything. And further, he was a Godman. His fan following was in millions. He had an excellent media damage control system in all parts of the world, that not only gave him excellent publicity, but kept any negative news, from leaking out.

Guruji heard out their reports. Guruji knew everything. When they sat here and gave their information gleaned from the library, the information was also heard by the others, and they too learned about their assignments.

It took them a couple of hours to recount everything about the demon Dahurasuran and Dasra Kumar. Most probably he knew about his ancestry, which encouraged him to perform such cruel acts.

'If he is not annihilated now, very soon the time will come, when he will rule the Earth along with his cohorts. There is no other solution but to evoke Mahakali's anger through Aishani,' said Jayant.

It was a very solemn group that kept their heads down and waited for Guruji's instructions. They didn't want to engage in this activity, but dissent to Guruji was not in their blood. All they wanted was to protect Aishani, as was their wont.

'Every morning after Aishani takes a break from her meditation, one of you will sit with her and recount the horrors and havoc which Dasra Kumar is inflicting on the people and children of this world. Uday will make the itinerary of the time and place for such meetings.'

Uday nodded. His eyes had turned black, a sure sign that he wanted to kill the demon himself, and spare Aishani the pain. He would have gladly done it too, had it not been for the boon, that the demon had. Aishani was the only choice. He chose Ruby to recount the horror of the crimes which Dasra Kumar aka Dahurasuran, had unleashed on humanity.

The next day Ruby met Aishani after she had completed her morning meditations. They smiled at each other, though Ruby's smile was a trifle sad. Aishani understood, 'Come Ruby, don't be so sad. We'll overpower this demon, as we have done so many times. Granted some of them have been easier to eliminate and some were difficult. But then, that is life. Each of us has chosen this life willingly and now we must adhere to it.'

'Yes Ash,' there were tears in Ruby's eyes, then she blurted out, 'I love you so much Ash, it's our job to protect you, not to push you towards carnage and devastation. This is what we have to do now.'

'Shush Ruby, I'm all prepared for it, we know what the asuras, rakshasas, danavs and other demons do. This one might have created more havoc than the others. It's a matter of degree only. Come on, out with his atrocities.'

Ruby kept quiet. And then she began, 'Dahurasuran has factories all over the world. He exploits and employs the cheapest labour. Even then, he does not pay them their full wages, but makes them slog for hours without breaks. When they are unable to work anymore, his cohorts, who are a legion, inflict third-degree torture, and more on them.'

Aishani was paying full attention. But that was Aishani, always focused on the task ahead. Ruby sighed.

'He has quite a number of favourite torture methods. We don't know all of them, but what we do know makes up for all the rest. Obviously, his favourite is boiling the victims in water and oil. Though they still prefer to eat raw flesh, they have modified their tastes through the ages and have now started eating cooked flesh, especially human flesh. It's the tortured screams that turn them on.'

Aishani had become very still, 'Go on,' she said grimly.

Ruby looked at her apprehensively, but Aishani was still intent on listening.

'Mutilating the human or even animal body is also one of their sports. They mutilate a body and then just leave it there to die slowly, the victim, howling in pain and agony.'

Ruby left after some time, leaving Aishani to ruminate.

The next day, the same exercise was repeated, with another member of the team. This time it was her brother Jayant. Jayant told Aishani stories about how Dasra Kumar or Dahurasuran was involved in illegal organ harvesting and trading. In many places, it was his main business. Organs were taken out and sold without the consent of the donor, and later, if the donor survived, it was good, if not, he or she was just left to die a painful death. Dasra Kumar was also involved in converting small children as frontline soldiers. Both boys and girls were sexually exploited. Aishani flinched, as if her own children would be subjected to this horror, if Dahurasuran was not stopped or destroyed. Her face had turned hot and flushed with anger. She would have killed him had he been in front of her. Jayant's heart cried, on observing her reaction. They were all inciting her rage. That, coupled with her meditations on Mahakali and Ma Durga, would make her rage as incandescent as Mahakali's, and kill Dahurasuran.

From then on, every day after her meditation, a member of their team would be allotted by Uday, to come to her and recount the atrocities of Dasra Kumar or Dahurasuran. Sometimes they would be horrified themselves, as they recounted the gruesome and heinous activities of Dahurasuran, and his legion of accomplices. Their blood would boil at the very thought of these abominable activities. They would have killed the demon themselves, except for the boon.

The stories, coupled with Aishani's growing anger and power, had begun showing their effect. There were visible changes in her persona. Her body had become darker, it was becoming black. She was angry and restless. She could not sleep. Restlessly, she kept on perambulating, near the huge Bunyan tree. Her eyes had become blood-shot and she was panting with every step. They were wary of her now. She did not maintain eye contact with them, but just kept muttering to herself. The entire team of the warriors stayed there with her, but at some distance from her. They did not want to interfere with her growing anger.

Jayant could clearly see the changes that were taking place in her, which the others could not.

'She has now begun to resemble Mahakali. When I stare hard enough, it seems that I can see the garland of skulls around her neck and accessories made of bones. I am yet to see a sword in her hand.'

'That is because the sword is yet to materialise. Her fury has reached its pinnacle, but still, that point has to be reached, where Mahakali's sword will come to her of its own volition,' Adheesh informed them grimly.

'But how will she kill Dahurasuran? He is not here. In this state, Aishani cannot go anywhere.'

'Guruji is negotiating this part. The average person do not know about our Gurukul, but everyone knows Guruji and the talks which he gives in our country and all over the world. Dasra Kumar was in Europe recently. Guruji too was there. The two Godmen met amidst full media glare. They hit it off straight away, and why not. Their relationship goes back hundreds of years, if not more. Guruji invited him to our ashram which he has enthusiastically accepted. They will be coming here day after tomorrow.'

There was no need to tell Aishani anything now. Even the rest of the team could now see her changed appearance. The average human being would have been petrified, on seeing such a frightful and ghastly persona. But they also knew that Mahakali had entered Aishani's body and would annihilate anybody who opposed her in destroying the demon Dahurasuran.

When Dasra Kumar or Dahurasuran came to the Gurukul he was surrounded by bodyguards. It took a few minutes for Guruji to convince him that so many guards were not required. His security staff did not agree, but ultimately conceded, as they realised that their esteemed client was not in a dangerous place. In any case, Dahurasuran was quite capable of looking after himself. He was reborn with all his powers intact with the knowledge that he was invincible. That made him the most dreaded person on the planet, though hardly any humans knew it. Ultimately, only two of his security guards accompanied him. They could not compromise on that. Guruji had expected that.

Guruji personally took him around the ashram and showed him the salient features of the ashram. Nobody else could have done it. Being such a great and powerful demon, he too had his share of magic and intuition. He would have seen through every guide of the Gurukul and all its glory. Certain things were almost always hidden from the visitors; like the seniors' library, the armoury museum, and other places such as the real geography of the Gurukul. Areal demon like Dasra Kumar, with a normal guide, would have seen everything and would have been overwhelmed by the treasures of the Gurukul. The next step would have been to overpower everybody and loot the Gurukul. But since Guruji was the guide, Dasra could only see what Guruji wanted him to see, which in any case was still too much. The plan was to entice and distract him with the riches and glory of the Gurukul, so much that he would not pay much attention, to where they were going.

'I am overwhelmed with the abundance of the resources of your Ashram, I have never seen any place like this,' he exclaimed delightedly. There was a gleam in his eyes. Guruji knew that he had begun scheming to plunder the Gurukul. Seemingly oblivious to his thoughts, Guruji responded blithely, 'I am delighted by your appreciation. You have seen only a fraction of the riches of the Gurukul. It will take you more than a week to see all resources of the Gurukul. I shall gradually show you all the treasures of the ashram.'

Guruji could make out that Dasra Kumar was genuinely excited and was now more than willing to follow him without any queries. After some time, Guruji noticed that Dasra Kumar was becoming a tad restless. He was wiping his sweat.

'You are feeling hot, let us sit here and cool ourselves with a cold drink,' Guruji waved his fingers in the air. Immediately there appeared two girls in immaculate dresses with tall glasses of the most delicious drink. He eyed the girls lasciviously, then asked Guruji, 'I become hot whenever I sense any presence around. I'm sure this is because of the immaculate and pristine environs of this place. Everything is so pure, that a sinner like me becomes uncomfortable,' he laughed at his own joke.

Guruji laughed along with him, 'Yes, that too or maybe you have really sinned. Come, let me take you to the Northern side of the Gurukul.'

Dasra Kumar laughed along with Guruji, but he was slightly flustered now. On one side were his greed, cruelty, and arrogance and on the other, was an unknown and barely recognizable discomfort. There was an imperceptible glimmer of a long-forgotten memory. He brushed it aside, but nevertheless glanced at his guards. They were faithfully following them with their guns at the ready. Suddenly, there were tremors on the ground which stopped in a moment. The tremor commenced again and then repeated at intervals. It seemed as if, somebody huge was walking towards them. The heat too had increased. Dasra Kumar looked at Guruji, 'What is this? A trap?' he smiled fiendishly, 'You obviously don't know me, I cannot be trapped or killed by anyone,' he growled, ready to jump at whoever was plodding towards them.

Before he could go any farther, a ferocious female jumped in front of them. The colour of her body was darker than midnight black. Her eyes were smouldering and red. She was wearing a sari-like dress, made out of animal skins. Her hair was long and black, and she was wearing a garland of skulls around her neck. In her left hand, she was holding a demon's severed head and in her other hand, she was holding a huge sword. Her bangles and anklets were made up of bones. It was her footsteps that were making the Earth tremble.

Dasra Kumar or Dahurasuran guffawed, 'You have brought me here to face this? She is no match for me!'

Guruji said soberly, 'If you truly ask for forgiveness even now, after all your savagery and inhumanity, Mahakali may spare you.'

'Hah! I will finish her off in less than a minute,' he declared. He himself began changing. He grew as tall and broad as a giant. His body became hairy, and his eye teeth protruded out of his mouth. Weapons materialised in his hands. He looked every bit the rakshasa that he was. His security guards were used to his metamorphoses and the dangers surrounding him. They rushed to his side and charged at the apparition in front of them. She brushed them away like flies. They were flung hundreds of feet away.

Adheesh and the rest of the team were standing behind some bushes and watching the whole scenario. Tejas had wound up around a tree in excitement. Adheesh and Uday were in full readiness to go to Aishani, should the need arise. Aishani was not Aishani anymore. Mahakali had entered her and nobody in the universe could overcome her now.

Dahurasuran lunged at Mahakali. She deflected him and he fell on the ground behind her. A full-blown battle erupted between them. This went on for half an hour, both of them striking at each other, Dahurasuran laughing loudly secure at the thought of his boon. Mahakali was spewing smoke and rage whenever she struck him. Mahakali then swung her sword forcefully in a wide arc and slew his head from his body. Blood spurted from his neck and his head was thrown at a distance away from his body. Mahakali stood over his body panting in anger. Adrenaline was still flowing strongly in her veins. They all went near her but stayed a safe distance. Slowly and very slowly another miracle began unfolding before their eyes. The rancour and the rage left her body. It was as if, a live entity came out of her body, which they knew was her extreme rage. The rage which came out of her body turned into a child and began crying. Till now Mahakali or the restored Aishani was oblivious of her surroundings. She just stood over the body of the rakshasas and kept on breathing noisily. It was only when she heard the cries of a baby that she turned around. Tears welled in her eyes. She took the baby in her arms and tried to soothe it. But the baby did not stop crying. Then finding that she had no choice, she sat down and began feeding the baby. They waited. There was total silence except for the sound of the feeding baby. They knew that the wrath of Kali had killed the demon. After killing the demon, her wrath metamorphosed into a child. Kali or Aishani fed the child with her breast milk.

After some time, Guruji gestured to Adheesh. Adheesh went near her and touched her softly. She looked up, and slowly comprehension dawned. She looked at the baby, but it was fading away and finally vanished. Bhagwan Shiva made both Kali and the child merge with him. From this had merged a form of Shiva, which was Bhairava. Since Bhairava was thus created by Shiva, he is said to be one of the sons of Shiva.

Aishani's eyes rolled up and she fainted. Guruji knew that Mahakali had gone up and joined Mahadev.

Guruji folded his hands, 'Jai ho Devi.' On Guruji's cue, they all folded their hands in homage to Mahakali. Now only Aishani was left there lying in a dead faint. Her body was black and burnt. Adheesh picked her up. They all knew that it would take her months to recoup from Mahakali's rage and power that had entered her body.

FIRE AND VARUNASTRA

There was a lull in the activities of the Gurukul. They all knew that it was a fleeting phase, but a feeling of well-being had set in. So much of rest or inactivity was making them restless too. Even Aishani was bored. The children were in their respective schools; her mother-in-law ran their home smoothly on well-oiled hinges.

They were sitting on the river front. Adheesh was throwing pebbles into the river. They fell without a splash. The pebbles would skip three to four times over the water before sliding smoothly in. Aishani smiled. This was Adheesh's favourite sport. Both of them respected the elements. In Adheesh's case, it was more so with water. Ever since their initiation with knowledge of their past births, water had played a vital role in their lives. It was the flow and sound of water that was instrumental in reviving a greater part of their memory. In the initial days of their courtship Guruji had sent them to a secluded and secret hideout in the forest to meditate and interact with nature. This knowledge would have come much earlier to them had the tragedy of her father's death not come upon them. Aishani had held herself responsible for her father's death for a long time. Adheesh had stood like a rock beside her.

Sitting here beside the river, they reminisced about their earlier days.

'Adhee, I don't know whether I want to go back and destroy more demons or go forward and destroy more demons,' she said.

He smiled and sat down beside her. Putting an arm around her, he said, 'Ever my fighter princess, even in the past and the future, she wants to annihilate demons.'

She snuggled into his arms and sighed, 'What else is there to do, Adhee? You cannot fight with your destiny.'

'Nor do we want to, baby. Doing what we do gives us such a big high. Getting rid of such menaces is a great aphrodisiac. We couldn't have asked for a greater destiny.'

'Do you think our children will follow in our footsteps?'

'They're too young to do so now. They may or may not want to do what we are doing, or they may want to do it in a different way. Maybe their destiny will take them somewhere else. It's better not to think too much about these things.' He turned her towards himself and looked into her eyes. 'Ash, we didn't have children in our past births. We don't know why. We won't question now. In this birth, we have been blessed to have our twins. Let us enjoy our babies as long as we can. God has given us children; God will decide what they will do later in life.'

'I understand, Adhee. That's why I want to give them everything in the world.'

He smiled. 'That's a sure-shot way to spoil the kids. We must make sure we impart the proper sanskars to them; we must ensure that they understand the difference between right and wrong. Life is a struggle, baby, and we have learnt it the hard way. Nothing is easy here in this Mrityulok. Darsh and Divya are our children. They have already demonstrated their supernatural powers, though they are not aware that they have any powers. They will have to work hard. They will have it easier than us, but with the world rushing to God knows where, they will not have it easy to combine the past with the present and the future.'

Aishani sighed. 'I know all that, Adhee. I miss them so much. I just want to hold them and hug them.'

'Same here, sweetheart. I too want to spend time with them. When they come home, we will be with them all the time.'

'Adhee, I have a feeling that something big is going to happen. The demons have not made any moves for a long time. Even Guruji is unusually quiet. There is something brewing somewhere. I can feel it in my bones.'

'I hope you're wrong, Ash, but it's been quiet for quite a long time. And yes, why is Guruji quiet? Is he preparing for a huge onslaught? I think he'll summon us in a couple of days.'

Guruji did call them two days later. Uday was also present.

This time they met not in the library but in one of the small annexures of the armoury. It was a small stuffy room and there were no weapons or armour there. There were just four asanas. It was rather strange for Guruji to hold a meeting here. Guruji sprinkled Gangajal over them and whispered some mantras over their heads. They now knew that things were serious, perhaps more serious than they could have imagined. As if reading their thoughts, Guruji said, 'Yes, it is more serious and hazardous than ever before. That we will be facing danger is a forgone conclusion. But this is by far the most dangerous demon that we are going to face. He is fiery and unstoppable.'

Guruji paused. There was no particular reaction from the three warriors, though they were reverentially paying full attention to him. They had undergone too many altercations to be actually scared of yet another demon. Guruji looked at the warriors. They were the best in the whole world.

'When you face an unbeatable enemy, sometimes it is better to change the turf and fool the enemy instead of jeopardising everyone.'

They looked a bit more interested now. What did Guruji mean by changing the turf? Would they have to go somewhere else to fight this demon? Wouldn't they be allowed to use the divine weapons?

'Even with a divine weapon, it's going to be a very close call.'

'Which demon is this, Guruji?'

'This demon is from the time when Bhagwan Vishnu came to the Earth in his Krishna avatar. The name of the demon was Pralambasura. He was known as the fiery demon.

He was a huge, colossal demon, his body full of fire and anger. It was not the normal kind of fire. It would ignite anybody or anything that came within a radius of a mile. Once anybody got burnt or singed by his fire there was no way the person could be saved.'

'So how was he vanquished, Guruji?' Aishani asked.

'That was the time of the child Krishna,' Guruji said. 'The avatar himself. Who could counter Him? He just sucked up all the fire and wrath into his own body and saved his friends and the jungle where they were grazing their cows.'

They waited, knowing there was more to come.

'We have successfully destroyed innumerable demons through the ages. Most of the time we have won, but there are times when we have lost too. That has always been a waste of time. A full life is gone and then we had to wait for the next life, recall and educate and train again for everything.'

They waited. Sometimes Guruji lengthened a story quite a lot.

'I have not yet come to the point. Now the demon of today is a direct descendant of Pralambasura. The demon Pralambasura's descendants had disappeared when Krishna absorbed him into his own body. He has surfaced now, obviously angrier, and as fiery as ever. There is no Krishna now to vanquish Pralambasura. We have to face him ourselves,' Guruji declared.

'Guruji, while it's true that Krishna Bhagwan is not here to contain this demon, but we can certainly improvise with whatever weapons we do have, with whatever powers we possess. I think we must be having a few divine weapons to counter the demon Pralambasura.'

'Yes, Adheesh, we do have a couple of divine weapons to counter the deadly fire of this most dangerous demon, but even that will not be enough. Our fall is imminent if he decides to pay us a visit, which our intelligence tells us, will be very soon in the future.'

They stared at Guruji in incredulous amazement. Guruji had just said that their fall was imminent.

'His fire is so deadly that whatever it touches dies immediately and never comes back. Hence, he has to be killed before he kills us.'

'I can think of one divine weapon, Guruji,' Adheesh said thoughtfully.

'Yes, Adheesh, the Varunastra or the divine weapon of Varun Dev, the God of rain. Nobody and nothing can stand against the Varunastra, not even the demon Pralambasura.'

'Then why the hesitation, Guruji, in facing this demon?' Uday asked. He himself was not qualified to use the divine weapons, but he was aware that were used by Aishani and sometimes by Adheesh too. In matters of utmost gravity, Guruji kept Uday in the loop. Many a time, Uday had behaved in a more mature manner than either Adheesh or Aishani. Another plus point was that Uday could keep his emotions in check, to the extent that he was almost emotionless.

'Because Uday, we don't have enough time to invoke Varun Dev, without whose acquiescence his Astra cannot be activated. Invoking Varun Dev may take anything between ten and twelve days and Pralambasura may be here in two or three days.'

Aishani gave a gasp. This was horrifying. They would perish in the fire because they did not have enough time. This could not be allowed. Adheesh looked at Guruji, who gave him a look in return. And Adheesh heaved a sigh of relief.

'It's not going to be easy,' Guruji continued. 'Aishani will not be with you for these few days.'

Aishani stared at Guruji. He was certainly talking in riddles.

'This is an exercise which even I have performed only a couple of times. Till now there has not been much time or need for it.'

Everyone looked puzzled or confused.

'I am going to shrink our Gurukul to almost one-hundredth of its size and hide it somewhere safely, without anybody being the wiser. Adheesh, you and Uday round up everybody immediately and make sure they stay here in the Gurukul. Aishani, I will initiate you to the Varunastra and its corresponding invocation and mantra.'

'Guruji, I have a few questions,' Uday blurted out.

'Yes, Uday? But hurry up. There is hardly any time.'

'I'll be quick. Guruji, you said the demon Pralambasura is coming here to burn down our Gurukul. Won't he create more havoc when he doesn't find the Gurukul here?'

'The Gurukul will be here. Pralambasura will burn down the whole place in a matter of days, except that it will only be an illusion of our Gurukul. Only Aishani will be in hiding somewhere, where she should not be disturbed at all. As for me, I will be in both places, ensuring that no untoward incidents take place.'

'Where will I be, Guruji?' Aishani asked. They were not new to demons or invoking the devatas and their divine weapons. But the whole Gurukul becoming microscopic was certainly new. And they were running out of time.

'We have to find a place for both you and our Gurukul.'

'Guruji, I know where the miniature Gurukul can be hidden,' Aishani said excitedly. Guruji smiled at her. Of course, he knew what she was thinking. Even Adheesh could sense her thoughts.

'The huge Parijat tree in our backyard. It's just a matter of a few days. And before anybody becomes suspicious, the Gurukul will be back in its former place in full glory,' Aishani said.

Uday looked most puzzled. He was aware of the Parijat tree in Aishani's house, but he wasn't aware of its importance. For Aishani and Adheesh, it was significant as they had been married under a Parijat tree in Barabanki when they had gone into the past. The Parijat tree is also known as the wish-fulfilling tree, and it has magical and miraculous properties. Uday was a seasoned warrior from the ancient ages. He did not remember much from his past births, but he remembered enough to know that magic existed, and that Aishani and Adheesh were his leaders.

'That's an excellent idea, Aishani! I too was thinking more or less on the same lines,' Guruji agreed.

'Where will Aishani meditate, Guruji?' Adheesh was naturally extremely concerned about Aishani's safety.

'We cannot afford to have any distractions as far as Aishani is concerned. I think her mother's house will be the safest as Madhuji knows the importance of peace and solitude during meditation. Additionally, you can designate a worthy and knowledgeable guard to ensure that nobody disturbs her.' Adheesh knew that Guruji was hinting at Devnath, but was gracious enough not to say so, as Devnath was Adheesh's personal guard. But Adheesh would do anything to keep Aishani safe.

'Yes, Guruji, I'll post Devnath in front of her room. I too will be there whenever I get a chance.'

'Right, off you go then,' Guruji was all business-like now. 'Aishani, go to your mother's house and prepare yourself for your meditation. Include your mother too in whichever way you think best.' Turning to Adheesh and Uday, he added, 'Round up all the inhabitants of the Gurukul. We will be leaving tonight itself.'

'Yes, Guruji.' They touched his feet and hurried off.

'Ash!' Madhuji was ecstatic. 'What a pleasant surprise! Ever since the babies left for their boarding schools, you've become busier. I see you less frequently now. At least when the babies were here, I saw you every day when you dropped them off or picked them up.'

'Amma, stop!' Aishani said with a laugh. She embraced her mother.

Madhuji sensed that all was not fine. 'What's the matter? Why are you all tensed up?'

'Amma, let's go to your room. There's not much of time and there is plenty of explaining to do.'

Madhuji was enough of a warrior to guess that something was drastically wrong. Once in her mother's bedroom,

Aishani shut the door and quickly explained everything to her. Madhuji immediately grasped the urgency and asked only a few probing questions. Aishani looked at her mother suspiciously. 'Amma, you seem to be aware of such things. Has such a thing happened earlier too? Amma! Answer me!' she gently shook her mother.

'Once, when your father was here. He, along with Guruji, hid a number of people and things here.'

'Oh Amma, you can really hide things, I wonder how many more secrets you have!'

'That even I don't know.' Mother and daughter shared a laugh. Then her mother became serious and said, 'Ash, go to your room and adjust it to suit your meditation requirements. In your Baba's almirah, there are several extra asanas. You'll need them for Adheesh and Guruji. I'll quickly go and clean up the backyard of weeds and shrubs.'

'But not around the Parijat tree, Amma.'

'No, no, not there, they become life-giving plants under the tree.'

'Amma, I think Baba's study will be best suited for my invocations under Guruji's guidance. What do you think?'

'That's good, you go on and prepare the study the way Guruji would want it.'

It was dusk now. Devnath turned up and stood there quietly. He had been briefed by Adheesh. In any case, he wouldn't have asked any questions.

At around seven in the evening, Guruji arrived along with Adheesh and Uday. Aishani and Adheesh looked at each other. Love and reassurance was abundant in the look that passed between them. Adheesh and Uday were carrying two huge boxes. Aishani's eyes widened. So, this was the entire Gurukul! It was magic! She had encountered microscopic demons, but a microscopic Gurukul was new to her. How were the people, flora and fauna reacting there? Were they even aware that they had been shrunk? The questions flashed in Aishani's mind, but she did not have time to waste thinking about them. That was for later. Her mother led them to the backyard, to the Parijat tree. Aishani followed. Once when she was quite young, she had seen her father going inside the tree. But when she went there, the tree was solid, and her father was not to be seen. Later when she asked him, he had laughed and said that he had gone behind the tree to clear the grass. Of course, now she knew better.

Adheesh and Uday carefully put down the two boxes in front of the tree. Guruji sat before the tree, spread out a mat and put various herbs and talismans on it. None of them had seen these things earlier. But then there had never been a need like today. Guruji was using them because of the dire emergency. They all sat around Guruji, waiting for him to complete his rituals. They could make out Guruji too was under some pressure. His beloved Gurukul was there in front of him in its miniature form. They all knew that the Gurukul was Guruji's life. He had nurtured it with his flesh and blood. And he would go to any lengths to save his beloved Gurukul. They sat around Guruji, but at a distance from him so that he had enough space to perform his rituals. These rituals were totally different from those they had seen earlier. After some time, Guruji opened his eyes and gestured to Madhuji. She handed him something she had been holding in her hands. Aishani stared at her mother in surprise. But her mother was a seasoned and experienced warrior. After her father's death, maybe Guruji relied on her mother for many things that might have belonged to her father.

Aishani suddenly remembered something. Amma had given leave to the two servants, but the house must be getting curious about the comings and goings, and it might get irritated and begin banging its doors and windows. She quickly got up and went to the main lobby where she knew the house paid attention the most. She knew that the house was always happy to see her and that it missed her terribly. She stood in the lobby and concentrated on one of the doors. After a couple of minutes, she understood that the house was ready for her. She spoke to it mentally. Though she did not tell it what was happening, she told it about the utmost need to be absolutely silent for the next ten days or so. Aishani was the daughter of the house. When she demanded something, the house listened. It had been quite excited, seeing so many people. Since they were familiar people, it merely sighed softly and had maybe banged a door or two quietly. But after the conversation with Aishani, it went completely quiet, and Aishani knew there would be no disturbance from the house. In fact, now it would keep even outside noises at bay. She quietly went back towards the Parijat tree. The boxes with the Gurukul were not there. Adheesh and Uday were touching Guruji's feet. Then they all walked into the tree. She knew that their Gurukul was now inside the tree.

There was nothing in front of the Parijat tree now. Guruji

looked at Aishani., who bowed and led him to Baba's study. Devnath was already on guard outside the study. He came to attention the moment he saw Guruji.

The next seven days were spent in rigorous meditation and chanting by Guruji and Aishani. They prayed to Varun Devata, the God of water and sky and the celestial oceans.

On the seventh day, Aishani thought she heard the tinkling of water coming from the western side. She was too experienced to think that it was only in her imagination. She knew that Varun Devata had heard them and was now coming to them. Gradually the soft sound of running water turned into an angry roar and it seemed as if they were being submerged in an ocean of angry water. Slowly she opened her eyes. There was complete silence and there was nothing different about the study. Guruji was sitting in front of her, his eyes closed and his lips silently chanting mantras. She too closed her eyes and prepared for another round of mantras. She knew that Guruji was meditating on Bhagwan Shiva, the proponent of the Varunastra. Guruji had directed her to chant the Varunastra mantra along with some other mantras. But the moment she closed her eyes, the sound and smell of the ocean came to her again. This time she folded her hands too. She knew that Varun Devata was with them. She kept on chanting his mantra and waited for Guruji to come out of his meditation. After a few minutes Guruji slowly opened his eyes and looked towards the West. He bowed and folded his hands in respect. There was nobody there but there was a strong smell of water and the sound of powerful waves. She could not see Varun Devata but could sense his presence.

Guruji was paying obeisance to the invisible deity. There was a proper dialogue going on between Guruji and the Varun Devata. Gradually she realized that the sound of the waves had become louder and angrier. Aishani guessed that Guruji must have explained the grave emergency to Varun Devata and the god was infuriated now.

Aishani stood there with her hands folded in supplication to Varun Devata. For a moment she was confused. If Varun Devata was himself here, would he not destroy the demon Pralambasura? But it could be against the laws of the gods or nature itself. But the demons were killing humans again and again. In any case, demons never followed any rules. Would the devatas too go against the rules?

Apparently not. The devatas would always follow rules, although they would lend their weapons to deserving humans from time to time. By now Aishani was finely attuned to the atmosphere around her. Though she could not see Varun Devata, she could now feel him standing opposite her. Was it her imagination or had Varun Devata's demeanour changed? Did he incline his head to her? She could not be sure, nor did she want to analyse it too much. There were much more pressing requirements to be dealt with. Suddenly she felt something heavy in her hands. She looked down. In her hands was a weapon with rounded blades on both ends. The weapon was dripping with water. She was startled to hear a deep voice.

'I am giving you my weapon to conquer this creature who is spewing fire all over your Gurukul. Go and destroy it with my Astra. Just like water, it will take the shape of any Astra that you desire. Now go and save your Gurukul.' Aishani knew that it was Varun Devata speaking to her. There was just an inflection of respect and deference in his tone. Aishani looked at Guruji, who nodded imperceptibly. It answered many asked and unasked questions. She was relieved. From the corner of her eye, she spied Adheesh entering the study. Even more relieved now, she bowed to the invisible Varun Devata and with his weapon in her hands, began marching towards her beloved Gurukul. Adheesh was with her. He came up to her and whispered, 'Ash, there is no time to waste. I'm going to pick you up and we'll be there in a matter of minutes.'

Aishani nodded, her mind and thoughts totally focused on her adversary now. Adheesh picked her up in his arms and almost flew to where the Gurukul was. Despite knowing what to expect, they still gasped. More than half of the Gurukul was burnt to cinder. Whatever was left was singed beyond repair. They scoured the landscape for the perpetrator of this massive destruction. After some time, they could make out a moving roaring fire dancing on the treetops or whatever was left of the trees. There were raucous, ear-splitting guffaws coming out from that huge figure of fire. Aishani's blood boiled. She aimed the Varunastra at the figure and pulled its strings. There were more than two transparent strings in it. As soon as she set it off, the arrows became hundreds of water cannons and hit the demon Pralambasura. With a strangled cry he broke into small balls of fire and fell to the ground. But Pralambasura had not survived the ages without a few tricks of his own. The small balls of fire rushed to each other and joined up. In a flash, he had come together and flown away but not before he had seen who his opponents were. The huge ball of fire went up in the air and vanished. The Gurukul was gone.

'Ash,' Adheesh said urgently. 'There is no time. If this demon completes his destruction here, he may go elsewhere and start destroying again. That cannot be allowed. I will somehow try to divert its attention, even if it's for a minute. That should be enough for you to destroy it.'

Aishani nodded. She was wary of this kind of tactic. That was how her father had died and she had still not fully forgiven herself. Now it was Adheesh, her Adheesh, the reason for her living. But she was much more seasoned and powerful warrior now, not a novice anymore.

Adheesh looked around, made some rapid calculations. He fired his arrows in the eastern side of the Gurukul. Sure enough, Pralambasura was trying to burn some left-over buildings there. These were not visible earlier, but with everything so badly burnt the defences or the Kavach over these buildings had weakened and they could now be seen. Pralambasura was igniting the buildings by jumping on them and blowing fire from his hands and sometimes from his eyes and mouth too. Their beautiful Gurukul was being burned by this devil, and only for fun. Though it did not need any provocation, nevertheless Adheesh was provoking it. Aishani was not going to take any chances now. She had to be incredibly careful as the Varunastra could touch Adheesh too. Now she was going to work from top to bottom. If she fired the tumultuous water arrows to the top, to escape them, Pralambasura would jump down, where she would be already waiting with her weapon turned into water scythes. This time when she fired her Varunastra, it seemed as if they were innumerable number of water hoses sending out water at high pressure. The fires were immediately doused, though they didn't entirely decimate the demon Pralambasura. But now he was too gravely injured and had no option than to jump down from the building to the ground and somehow try to escape. Bits of him lay scattered on the ground, fiery embers moving in a desperate bid to join to become whole again. Aishani was waiting with her deadly water scythes. And she used them mercilessly. The remnants of the demon were destroyed completely.

Both of them scoured the Gurukul for even the smallest ember of fire. After an hour or so, they were satisfied that the demon Pralambasura had been totally obliterated.

'I think we should call the cleaners now,' Adheesh said.

'No need, they are already here.' Guruji was standing there with them. 'Let's go to the Parijat tree, thank it, and restore the Gurukul to its original site. By the time we return, the cleaners would have removed all the soot and muck.'

'Yes, Guruji,' they said together, bowing with folded hands. Guruji disappeared. Adheesh picked up Aishani in his arms as he knew she was exhausted and this way they could reach her mother's house faster. She put her arms around his neck. Surprised, he looked down at her. At other times, after using a divine weapon, she would return to her normal human form with every ounce of her energy drained out. This time, it was not so. She was still fine. Probably because she still had to return the Varunastra to Varun Devata. But for the moment, he was happy that his Ash was happy and that she was in his arms.

Uday and Madhuji were waiting for them along with

Devnath. The house was quiet, though it did open a window softly when it saw Aishani. Guruji and Aishani first went to the study where they reiterated their gratitude to the Varun Devata and returned the Varunastra to him. The astra vanished from its place and the study was as dry as before. Guruji hurried to the Parijat tree and began his rituals. They sat around, fully alert, and ready to help if needed. After half an hour, Guruji opened his eyes. He gestured to Uday and Adheesh, who went into the Parijat tree and came out with the two boxes holding the Gurukul. Guruji gestured to them. The Gurukul transport was waiting for them outside Madhuji's house. Carefully placing the huge boxes on board, they drove towards the Gurukul's location. Guruji had already left. Another set of rituals had to be performed at the site to restore the Gurukul to its former glory.

Aishani turned towards her mother and said, 'Amma, I have to go to the Gurukul now. Later, I won't have the strength to witness such a great miracle.'

Mother and daughter embraced each other. Madhuji's eyes were moist. 'Amma, don't worry, nothing will happen to me, as long as I have Baba's and your blessings.'

'Yes, beta, I know. How can it be otherwise?' Madhuji wiped her tears. Aishani and now her family were her reasons for living and she wanted it no other way. Aishani went inside and silently thanked the house. The house sighed. It too missed her. It was happiest when the children were there, playing all around and banging the doors and windows. She then went to the Parijat tree, folded her hands in gratitude, and then left for the Gurukul. Devnath followed at a discreet distance.

They reached the Gurukul in approximately fifteen minutes. The invisible entrances were back in position. Her eyes widened in amazement. She could not believe this was the same place where she and Adheesh had destroyed the demon Pralambasura. Adheesh and Ruby came up to Aishani. She hugged Ruby tightly. Ruby looked at her closely. 'Ash, is anything the matter? Why do you look so relieved to see me? We met only yesterday.'

'Nothing, Ruby. Sometimes it takes a catastrophe to make you realise how much you love your friends.' Ruby's eyes narrowed, but she let it go at that. She knew that is she was supposed to know anything, then Aishani would tell her.

Tejas butted in and said, 'I have been roaming here and there as usual, nothing special. I don't know why, but it seems as if I was sitting in a very cramped place. But now I can breathe easily. You think the Gurukul shrank or something?' Aishani laughed. He had hit the nail on the head unwittingly. She was feeling weaker now. 'As long as you are comfortable and can breathe now,' she added.

Jayant guessed that something was amiss. But they were all too mature to ask or show any curiosity.

Adheesh said, 'Ash, you're not looking good. Come, let us go to the infirmary where Vaidyaji will look after you.' And he led her away.

ANOTHER WORLD

Guruji was worried. But only Adheesh and Aishani could see the worry lines on his face. And it made them anxious. Guruji was never worried, but whenever he was perturbed, they got scared. It meant that great upheavals were about to take place, generally of the most alarming kind. Nothing fazed them, except Guruji's furrowed forehead. They were alarmed but curious too. They decided to wait it out. Finally, after a week or so, Guruji summoned them. Hurriedly, they went to his cottage.

'A demon has been troubling the people in the northern part of our country. We have sent other warriors to dispose of this demon and they have been successful too.'

They were puzzled. Then what was worrying Guruji? From the look on Guruji's face, they could make out that he was far from satisfied. There must be more to this story. Did Guruji want to send them on a mission? They waited for more information.

'This demon seems to be resurrecting himself again and again.'

They were not surprised. In their world, such things did happen occasionally.

'Does he have a boon that he will not die at the hands of a human being?' Adheesh asked.

'That could be also one of the reasons. But there is more to it than that. Whenever he has been killed, the warriors have not really seen his body. It just seems to disappear into thin air and then he reappears after a fortnight or so.'

'Could it be that seconds before his death, he has the power to vanish. Then after recouping, he returns?' Adheesh asked.

'Yes, that is an explanation and a convincing one at that,' Guruji replied. 'But there is more to it than this simple explanation.'

They waited for Guruji to continue.

'There are minute differences when this demon reappears after his destruction. It seems that he does not fully come back as the same demon, though he looks and acts the same way. The warriors who have fought with him have not been able to pinpoint the differences, but they swear that the returning demon was not the same one that they had killed.'

'Maybe there are two or more demons, Guruji,' Aishani said. 'Or maybe his body vanishes somewhere, and his lookalike comes back to this world.'

Guruji looked sharply at Aishani. 'What did you say just now? Repeat it!'

Both Aishani and Adheesh were surprised. Guruji could read even their thoughts and here he was asking her to repeat her words.

'I said that maybe another demon who is his lookalike replaces him for some time.'

'No, repeat what you said after that.'

Adheesh said, 'Guruji, may I repeat what she said?'

Guruji nodded.

'The last part of her sentence was 'and his lookalike comes to this world.'

Aishani turned to Guruji, 'Yes Guruji, that is what I had said. Is it wrong?'

'On the contrary, Aishani beta, it is one the best guesses or the only right explanation,' Guruji declared.

Stupefied, Aishani asked, 'What did I say, Guruji?'

'Beta, you said that his lookalike comes to this world.'

Aishani thought it was better to keep quiet and wait. She turned to look at Adheesh. He wore a stunned, disbelieving look.

'You have almost guessed it, Adheesh. Even I had not thought that such a happening would take place in this century, though I had an inkling of it.'

Adheesh and Aishani were becoming more curious by the minute. But they knew that Guruji would take his time.

'Aishani, your sentence means that after being killed in battle, the demon dematerialises to another world and in his place another demon comes to this world. Both these demons are lookalikes. We have to join the dots together to get a clearer picture.'

'Another world? We know of three worlds, Guruji – Swarga lok, Prithvi lok and Pataal lok. These demons must be from Pataal lok then,' Aishani said.

Guruji kept quiet for a minute, apparently deciding from where to begin. 'Among the innumerable planets, our planet is smaller than a pinprick. There are many planets like ours, each with its own sun and solar system.'

They nodded. They knew this. All this had been taught to them in school. But Guruji reiterating this fact set their antennae buzzing. They knew that there were innumerable number of planets in the universe, but what did that have to do with them? Was this demon from another planet? Did he have a different set of powers unlike in their planet. Adheesh and Aishani were clearly out of their depth here.

'Your thoughts are going in the right direction, but much research has to be undertaken before we can arrive at any conclusion. You will have to go to a particular bookshelf in the seniors' library which is invisible to Vashishtji too. I am going to give you the mantra and the code to this part of the library. Go there and find out as much as you can about alternate worlds and these creatures who keep shuttling between worlds.'

'Will our other team members be there too?' Adheesh enquired.

'Not just now. This is too mindboggling a concept for everyone to grasp. I might inform them gradually if the need arises. For all we know, there could be only one or two demons travelling between the worlds. If required, the others too will be made familiar to this reality.'

'Yes, Guruji,' they replied in chorus. After taking his blessings, they left. They went to the library straightaway. They chanted the mantras which Guruji had given them. In a corner of the library, a room shimmered and materialised. They went to it, but it remained closed. They softly whispered the code. It slid open. They went inside and stared in awe. It seemed as if they were floating in a glass room high up in the clouds. They looked down at the floor and their eyes widened in surprise. The floor too was transparent and seemed to be made of glass. They were floating in space!

'This is so dramatic, Adhee,' Aishani said with a nervous giggle. 'It seems as if we are in space.'

'For all you know we might be in space. Maybe this part of the library is in space. Whatever it is, let's get down to work.'

'Yes, let's do that.' They went to different bookshelves and took out a few books. Some books came to them willingly and some just stuck to the bookshelves and would not come out. Aishani rolled her eyes. Either a code was needed to pick up these books, or they had to pass a few tests to reach the higher level of access to these books which were recorded by the gods themselves. The literature they came across here was mindboggling to say the least. To begin with, there was the grading of the worlds which they had not really thought of. They began reading.

There were innumerable worlds in the universe, according to the books. They found from one Purana that there are seven higher worlds or lokas and seven lower worlds. The higher ones are Bhuloka, Bhuvar Loka, Swarga loka, Mahar Loka, Jana

Loka, Tapa Loka, and Satya Loka. The lower ones are Atala, Vitala, Sutala, Rasaataala, Talatala, Mahataala and Patala or Naraka. In between these worlds there are a number of worlds where people go to or are sent to according to their Karmas.

After some time, they discussed their findings. They were overwhelmed by all the information. More so with the thought that Guruji might send them to one of these alternate worlds.

'Do these parallel worlds really exist, Adhee? I had read about them in one of the science fiction books, though I have never believed in them. If such worlds do exist, why do they if everyone and everything is the same? Of course, if our great books say so, then it must be so.'

'They are not exact replicas of our world, Ash. Look, all this is very new to us. All the answers seem to be vague. The demons here have an added advantage over us, especially those who come here to torment and kill our people. First, they are twins and second, they have routinely been travelling from one world to another. We will have to comprehend that fact first, then go to the other world and see how we can get rid of the demons there.'

'How do you know that they are twins?'

'There is a hint in one of the books that there are twin demons who roam from one world to another. It's not clear. Perhaps Guruji will give us more information.'

'Adhee, we don't know anything about this other world, its rules and regulations, and the kind of people there. If it's a parallel world, then would people like us be there too?'

'I don't know, Ash,' he said. 'I guess we'll just have to go there and find out.'

Aishani's eyes were shining with excitement. She felt like a child. She caught his hand and sparks flew, bursts of blue, white and pink electricity. They looked at each other in wonder. So much water had flown under the bridge. Their love through the years had only deepened and strengthened but it had mellowed down too. Now the sparks appeared when they were together and excited about something. The sparks had almost petered out in the last couple of years.

'There are two ways of reaching these parallel worlds. One is obviously with the help of the Garuda Devata,' Adheesh said.

'And the other?'

'It has to be through a portal. At present, we do not know about any portal that will take us to another parallel world. What if there are more than two parallel worlds, what if....' He was at a loss for words.

Aishani pressed his hand. 'This is an unchartered territory for us. We have still to annihilate all the demons on this earth. And now we find out that there are more demons in these parallel worlds too that we might have to vanquish.'

'While we are quite experienced in destroying demons on our earth, I don't think we should interfere in the workings of other universes. They are not exactly mirror copies of our galaxy. There are bound to be minor differences.'

'You mean that in these parallel universes, the people and living beings are the same, but their roles could be different?'

'I suppose I meant that, but I am not sure. I have to go and live there for some time to discover these differences,' Adheesh said.

'What do you mean you will go and live there? You think I will let you go alone? I will go with you and that's that,' Aishani stated flatly.

Adheesh let it go. He knew better than to argue with her.

'We cannot even share it with our team. It's too sensitive a matter. Disclosing it would be volatile at the moment.'

'I don't think we can share it with anybody, Adhee. Let us go to Guruji and see if he can divulge any more information.'

In the evening, they went to meet Guruji. He heard them out.

'Guruji, we understand now that there may be a few demons who come from a parallel world, create chaos in our world, then flee back to their world. But to destroy them, we must know something about them and their history.' Aishani queried.

Guruji answered, 'These two demons are from our world. In ancient times, they were very learned and distinguished brothers. They had impressed so many devatas and sages with their knowledge, service, and loyalty that they bestowed many boons on them. One of the boons was the ability to travel from one world to another.'

'Guruji, they must have other superpowers apart from travelling between parallel worlds. Our warriors have killed them so many times, but they still come back. Either they are too many or they resurrect and return. We have to know more about them.'

'Well, Ash, you know what they say. A rose by any other name, etc. In the same way, a demon is a demon by any other name. These two demons whose names are Atapi and Vatapi are the same, they are just demons. The only difference is that there are two of them working together and in tandem. They are brothers. Vatapi was a king and he ruled over his kingdom called Badami. They were very fond of hosting the great sages of that time in the hope of extracting boons from them. In some instances, they succeeded too. Vatapi knows the art of transformation and he can change into any life form that he desires. In the same way, Atapi managed to learn the Mritsanjeevni mantra from one of the sages. This can bring a person back from the dead. Armed with these two boons, the two brothers used their powers to kill, loot and eat people. They would call people on the pretext of feeding them. Using his powers, Vatapi would turn himself into a goat which Atapi would kill and cook. After the guests had eaten their full, Atapi would call out and Vatapi would burst forth from the person's stomach. The guest would die, and the demons would feed on the guest. This went on for an extremely long time till they invited the great sage Agastya for a feast. Sage Agastya knew about these demons. He not only digested the demon Vatapi but also burnt down Atapi, turning him to cinder. From that time onwards, any descendant of theirs has been mortally scared of fire. They would rather eat raw food than use fire to cook it. They also keep huge amounts of water with them, as they would be the first ones to be affected by a fire.'

'What about their teleporting abilities, Guruji?' Adheesh asked.

'Even I'm not truly clear on this point, Adheesh. I think they had extracted this boon from Narad Muni, who travels all over the universe. Nobody can trick Narad Muni, but I think in this case, the demons were successful in doing that.'

'So now what do we do, Guruji?' Aishani asked. She was quite thrilled at the thought of discovering a new world where everything would be the same but different too. Their job would be the same, to exterminate demons. In a way it would be a continuation of their work but in a parallel world. Not so with Adheesh. Though he was also proactive about such adventures, this was unknown and uncharted territory, where people would be the same but different too. Plus, Aishani had to be protected at all costs. Then there were the children. They would have to ensure that they returned after a short while. He kept his thoughts to himself, however. He did not want to dent Aishani's enthusiasm. In any case, she had all the worries of the world on her slender shoulders. Let her have her moments of carefree thoughts.

Guruji looked at him impassively as if reading his thoughts. But the pressing matter was the destruction of the two demons, Atapi and Vatapi, who were creating havoc in this world.

'It will be Amavasya after five days when the demons can be expected to attack again. This gives us some time to prepare. Aishani will meditate to invoke her divine Astra, while you, Adheesh, will prepare your weapons and whatever gadgets you need. We will meet here on Amavasya, that is on Friday, at 11 p.m.'

They nodded in agreement, touched Guruji's feet, and left. They went to the far corner of the Gurukul behind the classrooms and sat under their favourite Banyan tree, a place where they were hidden from view but from where they could see everything.

Aishani leaned against Adheesh and let out a worried sigh. 'Oh Adhee, we've crossed so many bridges and now this. God knows which other places we'll have to go to.'

'Our destiny is to destroy the demons, wherever they are, whoever they are. If we go to an interesting and exciting place, that'll be just a bonus, baby.'

'I know, Adhee, but this is so different than what we are used to. I think in all our births we have stayed only on this planet. Adhee, you think we are being promoted?'

'Or maybe demoted!' They laughed together which released some of their tension. 'Let's go home, freshen up, then we'll come back and discuss what we should do next.'

Hand in hand they went home.

They were standing in front of a huge cave, barely camouflaged with some shrubs and plants and twigs. It was as if no efforts had been made to hide this overwhelming and extraordinary entrance. Had they come to the wrong place? But Guruji never made any mistakes in his calculations.

'You will go into the tunnel inside this cave. After walking for a mile approximately, the scenario will change somewhat. The place will turn into a tunnel with doors on both the sides. After mentally chanting the given mantra for a few minutes, both of you will count the number of entrances and enter the third door on your right. I don't have to repeat anything to both of you, but this is a monumental moment. There will be many doors on both sides, not doors in the traditional sense, but different kinds of entrances and thresholds. Each separate entrance represents a different world. In any case, you will not be able to enter these worlds unless you are spiritually positively or negatively inclined. There are innumerable worlds in the universe. Both of you have enough powers to enter or at least visit a few of these worlds. Entering a portal is easy but returning to your base may not be all that easy. So do take care and work with extreme caution and care,' Guruji said.

'Today is Amavasya (dark phase of the moon). At exactly 04:05 hours, you will enter the third entrance. Memorise this place exactly as it is. When it is time for you to return, you will come to the same place on the other side and do the same things, but instead of turning to the third on your right, you will be turning to the third door from your left. I have made an invisible swastika on either side of the door of this portal. This can be seen only by the two of you. It will gradually fade away. So, you must complete your mission as fast as you can and return. If the symbol fades, then returning could be a problem as the portals keep shifting their positions. Our researchers do not have much experience in this field as these portals are not frequently used. Have you understood everything?'

They smiled inwardly as he was treating them like school children. 'Yes, Guruji,' they chorused. Guruji nodded, satisfied for the moment. They knew that Guruji was worried for them. They had been to many dangerous places, but this was the first time that they were going to a parallel world to destroy a demon.

Soon it was time for them to leave. They touched Guruji's feet and took his blessings. Guruji softly chanted a few mantras over them, blew on their foreheads and sprinkled holy water on them. They went inside the cave and entered the tunnel after a mile or so. Then at the time they were told, they entered the third door from the right.

They looked around. They were in some kind of a forest. Hand in hand they walked around, feeling lightheaded and intrusive too.

'Adhee,' Aishani whispered. He looked at her questioningly. 'This looks like our forest.' He nodded grimly and held her hand tightly.

'But it is not exactly our forest,' he said.

'Yes.' She didn't know why she was whispering, even when everything was the same. There was a feeling of not belonging. They had been to plenty of places where they did not belong and were not welcome either. But the sombre atmosphere around her gave her the heebie-jeebies. Adheesh understood her feelings. 'Ash, we are not here to explore this world. We are here to find and finish off the demons Atapi and Vatapi.'

'Adhee, do you think these two demons also use the same portals?'

'Could be, Ash.'

She shuddered. 'I hope not, Adhee. Imagine rubbing shoulders with a demon while crossing through the worlds.'

Adheesh laughed. They both enjoyed a joke or two even when in dire danger.

Adheesh pressed her hand. 'The last time we killed the demon Vatapi, it was just outside our Gurukul. Maybe there is a portal outside the Gurukul too.'

'Adhee, it's natural to be curious. In fact, I am shocked at the similarities, and we have yet to discover the differences. Are the people here the same? Everything cannot be the same, otherwise what would be the purpose of there being a parallel world. My gut feeling says that this world has more negativity than ours.'

'That's a negative thought,' he said with a smile.

'Shall we go outside this Gurukul? In our world, the demons were found outside the Gurukul. Maybe they are doing the same thing here.'

'Yes, let's do that,' he concurred.

They went towards the entrance of the Gurukul, but it was not there. Puzzled they looked around. After five minutes they saw it. There it was, but it wasn't as they had thought it would be. It was not invisible to the naked human eye. Anybody could see from inside and outside. That was a revelation. Either the humans here were too emancipated to accept the Gurukul for what it stood for, or... What? Adheesh couldn't think of a proper explanation.

They were tired. They had searched for the demons Atapi and Vatapi, without any success. Going around the Ashram had drained them of their energy. Everything was so topsy-turvy. They deliberately avoided meeting any people in this Ashram. The strange thing was when they did chance upon a familiar figure, that person would just give them a perfunctory look and continue on his or her way. Both Adheesh and Aishani were humble people, though fully aware of their powers and capabilities. They kept to themselves and were always occupied with their missions and their family. Nevertheless, there was such an awe-inspiring aura around them, that not only the students but teachers and gurus gave them respect whenever they met. Not so here. They were almost ignored here.

They sat under a tree outside the Gurukul, slightly puzzled, but not very worried. They were totally focussed on the task ahead with no guidance as to how the demons Atapi and Vatapi looked or any other related intelligence.

'Adheesh, tell me the story of these two demons. I have a general idea, but I did not go into details, as I had to wind up so many things. There was no time because I had to meditate to invoke the Agneyastra. I knew that you know about them in detail and that you would fill in the blanks for me at our convenience.'

Adheesh understood. Aishani's life was full to the hilt. No matter how much he shared, it remained mostly her responsibility and she took it very seriously and did it sincerely. He told her the story of Atapi and Vatapi again. She listened attentively with a slight frown on her forehead, which meant that she was totally engrossed in the story.

'So, you see, from the time when Sage Agastya ate and digested one and burnt the other one to cinders, their direct descendants have become wary of fire. They always keep water near them. It seems they have a natural fear of fire and unnecessarily try to douse any flames.'

'Yes, but the Agneyastra which Guruji has given us does not get extinguished by water. It is a divine weapon; it will abate and recede only after its target is destroyed. Now it's time for me to meditate on the Agneyastra. I'll go and sit under that tree there. You be the lookout.'

'Okay, I hope you don't get disturbed.'

'Don't worry, love. I can concentrate in the middle of a storm.'

They smiled at each other. Aishani made a place for herself under the huge tree, sat down and closed her eyes. Adheesh hovered nearby, trying to give her as much privacy as possible. He just hoped that Atapi and Vatapi would pass by soon. It took Aishani an hour to complete her meditation. The Agneyastra was with her. It had to be acknowledged and strengthened and prayed to every day. Though it was invisible, it was with her, and would take its original form when invoked by her. It was like a spear with branches. When invoked all the arms of the spear would burn with a reddish and yellow fire, the unnatural heat of which would instantly burn or melt its target. It was a divine weapon and it never failed.

This went on for another four days. The only thing they knew was that Atapi and Vatapi liked to get hold of their guests or victims from the entrance of the Gurukul because that was where they got the maximum number of erudite people. Their hatred for sages or educated Brahmins had its root in the beginning when the original Atapi and Vatapi used to entertain great sages in the hope of extracting boons from them. Once after a powerful sage, incredibly happy with their hospitality urged them to ask for a boon, Atapi asked for a son as illustrious as Indra. Even though the sage could grant him the boon he did not do so. From then on, both the demon brothers began hating sages and later, the Brahmins, who were supposed to be representatives of God on earth. They did not change their names as they reminded them of their hate.

Adheesh and Aishani roamed about the Gurukul in the hope of catching the demons. They found the atmosphere of this Gurukul stifling. They kept an extremely low profile.

They did not want anybody to think that anything was amiss. Once they thought they saw Uday. Quickly they went behind a broad tree and peeped from there. What they saw shocked them. Uday was climbing trees and hanging from its branches and roaring with amusement and laughter. There was another slim boy with Uday and horror of horrors; it was Tejas, a totally sober Tejas, though he had stretched himself a bit. It was as if they had exchanged their nature and personalities. Adheesh and Aishani stared at them unbelievingly, then they went and sat outside the ashram. Uday was laughing loudly. He said, 'Yo bro, you don't know how to enjoy life. Stop being so serious. The world will not be wiped out if you stop worrying about it for a minute. I am your elder brother. We'll go to the club in the evening and enjoy ourselves.'

'Not today, Uday bhaiya, I have to complete my assignment. It's a difficult one. You go, I'll come some other time,' Tejas said.

'Okay, suit yourself,' Uday said nonchalantly. 'Toodle-doo then.' Uday left, whistling under his breath. Aishani and Adheesh were shocked. Never in their wildest imagination could they have thought that Uday would behave in this carefree manner.

'I think this travel between the worlds is most misleading and confusing. We are neither in the evil world nor the good world. We are somewhere in between,' Adheesh said thoughtfully.

'I wonder if the other members of our team or even our parents are the same,' Aishani said wonderingly.

'All this could become very disturbing for us, Ash.

Curiosity kills the cat. We are here in this world for a specific task. We will complete it and leave this place,' he said firmly.

'You're right, Adhee. We should not become too interested in the people of this world, specially of this Gurukul. We have been here for almost five days, doing nothing, just twiddling our thumbs. The demons have not showed up. We don't even know whether they are here or somewhere totally different. But I have this nagging feeling that if we communicate with some of our so-called team mates here, we might glean some information about Atapi and Vatapi.'

Adheesh was quiet for some time, as if weighing her intuition and judgment. He never took her suggestions lightly. What she was suggesting had merit. Till now they had been unable to find the demons. They could not keep the divine Astra with them indefinitely, it was only a loan from the gods. Though no time limit had been given to them, he knew that the Astra could become impatient and then it might not work at its optimum strength. The Agneyastra which Guruji had entrusted to Aishani was only a part of the main Astra since they had to destroy only two demons or maybe a couple more if they accompanied their targets. It was small but equally deadly against a small group of demons. It would have been a waste of energy and power to use the full Agneyastra in all its glory on just two demons.

'You think the Guruji here would be the same or different from our Guruji?' he almost acquiesced to her idea.

Aishani heaved a sigh of relief. His question was a loaded one. If Guruji here was not the same, then would he really like to help them? Wouldn't he like to use the team here to kill the demons? Well, that was a risk they had to take.

The next morning, they went to Guruji's cottage. They stood rooted in shock as they reached the cottage. There was a teacher, a junior guru, tending to the garden. The teacher had his back towards them, but they had caught a glimpse of his face. Now he turned towards them. It was Swami Sivananda, Ruby's paramour in their world. Adheesh and Aishani stood rooted to the spot. Swami Sivananda smiled and greeted them. 'Adheesh and Aishani! What are you two doing here? I thought you two had gone on a mission.' Suddenly he turned towards some shrubs and called out, 'Kalpit, how many times have I told you not to hide in the bushes. The insects there can bite you.'

They watched in awe as a child of about four came out of the bushes, laughing. He went to Swami Sivananda and held his hand. Sivananda looked at them and said, 'Ruby is busy, she is taking a class. Kalpit doesn't stay still, so he's here with me. You two must have come to meet Guruji. He must have finished his meditation. I'll go and check.' He went inside, leaving them open-mouthed. Adheesh turned to Aishani and with one finger put her chin up. Aishani was too shaken up to notice the humour of the gesture.

'Swami Sivananda had gone to the Himalayas to do penance. You think he came back and married Ruby? In some fields, he is Guruji's equal. Here he is acting like an average administrator of the Gurukul, like Manoharji.'

'Ash, this is not our world. This is a parallel world where things and people are the same, but not really. There has to be some difference between two worlds.'

Aishani swallowed and nodded but didn't look convinced. Sivananda returned and said, 'Guruji is free now. He will see you for fifteen minutes.'

They nodded. Since when had Guruji given them allotted times? Quietly they went in. The inside of the cottage was, more or less the same, except that there were two more bookshelves and chairs instead of asanas. It was looking slightly more modern than their Guruji's cottage, though it was still quite spartan.

There was a twinkle in Guruji's eyes as if he were laughing at his own joke or at their discomfiture.

'It seems that both of you have not really settled down. You are here for a specific job,' Guruji said blandly.

They touched Guruji's feet. He blessed them. They kept quiet, wondering whether he was their Guruji or from this world. As if reading their thoughts, Guruji replied enigmatically, 'For people like me, it doesn't matter which world we come from. I am in all the worlds. I just have to adjust myself to the fine nuances of the world in which I am present.'

Aishani said tentatively, 'Guruji, is it really you? You had bid goodbye to us at the border of our Gurukul. You did not tell us that you would be here too. Not that we don't like it. In fact, I am very much relieved, and I am sure Adheesh is too,' she said hastily.

Guruji's eyes twinkled again, then he became serious. 'I am from this world and your Guruji is from your world. But we have to be the same. These alternate or parallel worlds are the same, but they have their differences. There are many theories about these planets. One theory is that when a desire is very strong and a person cannot fulfil it on his or her planet, they are sent to these parallel worlds to realise their dreams. Another theory is that these planets have a proper hierarchy, from good to bad or bad to good. We fulfil our destinies on our own planets. If we don't, then we are sent to such planets. But enough of this. I have some idea of the reason for your visit here.'

'Yes Guruji,' Aishani said. Both Adheesh and Aishani were now slightly relieved that at least the Guruji of this world did not seem so unfamiliar.

ALTERNATE WORLD

'Aishani beta, you don't have to explain anything. Go about the work for which you have come here. I will designate Tejas to give you any information on the demons Atapi and Vatapi. Everybody in this Gurukul knows both of you, but not in this manner. That is why I had to send this Gurukul's Adheesh and Aishani for another mission so that nobody gets confused. Just remember your Tejas and this Tejas are different and so are many people here. You will have to conduct yourself with great tact, so that they don't get unnecessarily suspicious.'

The conversation seemed to be over. Adheesh and Aishani were again at a loss. Things were so strange and puzzling. Hesitatingly Aishani asked, 'Guruji, the person attending your garden....'

'He is Sivananda. He is one of the teachers here. He attends to me personally and he is Ruby's husband too,' Guruji said with a smile.

Aishani could not stop herself. 'But, but... in our Gurukul, he is the great Swami Sivananda, the owner of an equally great Gurukul. He is your assistant here. And Ruby's husband!'

'Aishani don't look so shocked,' Guruji said in a soothing tone. 'Beta there are many parallel worlds in this universe. You have come to one of the nearest ones, and only because a couple of demons have been troubling your world and then escaping here. Things are slightly different here or you can say just a bit askew. It could be your world or this world, depends on who is watching whom. Take things as they are,' so saying Guruji gestured to Sivananda who had already summoned Tejas.

Tejas came into the cottage. He was smartly dressed and looked much taller than their Tejas. He bowed to Guruji and then looked startled when he saw Aishani and Adheesh.

'Adheesh and Aishani had to postpone their mission as something more important has come up here. Are you ready for your test, Tejas?'

Tejas nodded. 'Yes, Guruji,' he said.

'Good! Your examiners will be Adheesh and Aishani. There is no one here more qualified than them to take your examination.'

Adheesh and Aishani kept quiet. This world was opening in front of them like a kaleidoscope and it was better to go with the flow. Besides Guruji had said that Tejas would be able to help them with the whereabouts of Atapi and Vatapi. All three of them went out together.

Once outside, Tejas turned towards them and touched their feet.

'You don't have to touch our feet, Tejas,' Aishani said as she laughingly pushed him away. 'We are friends, and you are my younger brother.'

Tejas answered seriously, 'But I've always touched your feet since I can remember. And I must say it's a surprise to me that you are going to take my exam. I thought both of you had gone on a long mission.'

'Even we are surprised. We know you so well that we can already predict your result,' Adheesh said. 'By the way, we are not very used to taking anybody's test, so you'll have to guide us in certain areas.'

'Of course, Adheesh, but you do conduct classes so many times and take exams too.' Tejas seemed just a bit surprised though not suspicious. Adheesh and Aishani looked at each other.

Two days passed in which they learned quite a lot about Tejas' new personality. In this world, Tejas was as quiet as Uday in their world, but his powers were the same, that is he could stretch and elongate himself to extreme lengths. They tested him as much as they could devise. Most of the time, Adheesh ended up talking to him. Tejas was a warrior in both the worlds. He had intuition too. They could make out that this new Tejas was slightly puzzled by their behaviour.

'Can I ask you something, Adheesh?' Adheesh nodded and waited.

'When you had gone on your mission, did something

happen? Did both of you get hurt? Or did you get hurt in the head? Both of you treat me like a child, almost like a baby brother. I have never had this kind of bias from you. Not that I don't like it,' he added hurriedly.

Adheesh looked at Aishani. She nodded. He took a deep breath, then began, 'You are right, Tejas. There is a difference in our behaviour, not because something has happened to us, but because we are different.'

They could make out that Tejas was surprised, but not alarmed. He waited for more information. Adheesh carried on, 'We have come from another world, a parallel world where everything is seemingly the same except for a few differences here and there. The Adheesh and Aishani of this world have indeed gone on a mission and are still there. We too have come here on a mission. We are chasing two demons Atapi and Vatapi, who have created havoc in both these worlds. Guruji felt that you would be able to help us in locating these villains, as they are here at present.'

'I? How can I know about these demons? I haven't even heard of them, leave alone know them.'

Tejas was still reeling under the impact of the revelation about the alternate worlds. Of course, as an ancient warrior, he did have an idea of the concept of various worlds in the universe, but he knew them as graded Swarg Lokas or heavens or graded Narak Lokas or hells of which there were seven each. This was such a vast conundrum that he could not begin to comprehend it. He looked at them closely. They looked exactly like his Adheesh and Aishani, but there were minuscule differences which he had noticed subconsciously. His brain was still unable to assimilate the information. Adheesh waited for the information to sink in before he proceeded.

'Look Tejas, initially we were as bewildered as you, but these two demons have done a much smarter act than us. We were fully content with fighting the demons in our own world. There was no time left for anything else. Apparently, these demons learnt the art of travelling from one world to another. We don't know whether they can travel only through these two worlds or other worlds too. The fact is that they will create chaos and mayhem wherever they go. They are so powerful that we have to stop them before they do any major damage to the worlds.'

Tejas as well as Adheesh and Aishani were finding it difficult to easily accept each other. But they had no choice.

'Think, Tejas,' Aishani appealed to him. 'When Guruji chose you to assist us, he must have known that you are privy to some information of which even you are not aware. Maybe you noticed these demons as a very casual thing. You'll have to think hard, Tejas.'

Tejas nodded weakly. This was information overload. They sat down under a tree. At least that was common to both the worlds.

'Tell me,' Tejas queried. 'Are you two married?'

Shocked, they stared at him. But Tejas was getting the hang of it now. 'Wait, let me inform you, the Adheesh and Aishani of this world are not married, at least not as yet.' He grinned as he saw their discomfiture.

'Yes, we are married,' Aishani answered. 'But that is hardly the point.'

'I know, I know. I just need some time to think. Look, guys, can I share this information with some other people? It'll be easier for me to digest it.' Tejas was clearly still extremely uncomfortable.

'I don't think that this will be the right time to share the information. From what I could deduce, Uday could spread this secret information swiftly. Even the demons may get a whiff of it and the game will be over even before it starts. Let Guruji decide who to share this information with.'

Tejas nodded. He did not need any more convincing.

'Give me some time to think about the demons. Say, I don't think you have a place to stay here. Come with me. I know exactly the place where you'll be hidden as well as be comfortable too. Follow me.'

He led them to a secluded part of the Gurukul. There was a cottage in a clearing. Adheesh and Aishani started. This was the same cottage where Kamadeva and Rati had left them after their marriage in the past. There was an emotional burst of memories. Both of them looked at their hands. Their hands were shining, the sparks literally bursting to come out. Somehow, they willed the sparks to stop, but not before Tejas had noticed it. His eyes widened but he kept quiet. Had it been the Tejas of their world, he would have hooted, wound himself around trees and teased them mercilessly.

'I'll come back tomorrow. In the meantime, I'll go through every incident which I have witnessed in the past one year or so. Let's see if I can come up with something. I think there are some provisions there for cooking too.'

'Don't worry, we can manage. We're familiar with the

Gurukul too, you know,' Aishani reminded him dryly.

Tejas nodded and left them alone. Bemused, they sat down on a tree stump.

'Oh Adhee, it's just like going into the past. Everything is the same, but so different.'

'Interesting too,' he commented.

She looked at him, stupefied. Then they both burst out laughing.

'Let's finish our work and go home. I'm missing the children,' she said with a sigh.

'We're not even married in this world!'

'This too is so strange. Are we in a different time here?'

They spent half the night talking, then drifted off to sleep.

The next day, Tejas was there early in the morning, giving them a surprise again.

'I think there was a minor strange incident sometime back. It's about two rich merchants who supply a few things to the Gurukul. You know, just a few mundane things. Our Gurukul is self-sufficient, but a few things are required from outside. These two merchants are very fond of hosting parties and their menu is out of this world. They have all kinds of cuisine on offer and people really vie for their barbeque evenings. But twice, I sort of noticed subconsciously that whenever they hosted their gala shindig, a couple of invitees disappeared. Since the guests were from far off places everyone assumed that they must have left after informing the hosts. The hosts certainly acted that way. But now I think back, there could be some other reason.'

'Good boy,' Aishani patted him on the back. Tejas

flinched. Aishani realised her mistake and hastily drew back her hand.

'You could be right, Tejas,' Adheesh said. 'Any chance of these two merchants coming this way in the near future?'

'I haven't paid much attention to their comings and goings, though I have attended one of their lavish parties. Their vulgar display repelled me, so I did not attend any other party. I think they host one party every month, which is attended by a large number of our Gurukul residents. I think they will visit us again in a week's time.'

'That's good.' Aishani was relieved. Besides wanting to complete their work fast, she was getting worried about the Agneyastra too. These were living and breathing divine Astras. She knew that they had physical forms too. Aishani wanted to finish their task before the potency of the Astra diminished.

'Tejas, I think it'll be better if you find out more about this. We might make a few faux pas and make people uncomfortable or even suspicious. People might mistake us for shape-shifting demons or something,' Adheesh said.

Tejas nodded. 'You're right. You know how Uday is. Before you know, he will have tom-tommed the whole thing to the world.'

Adheesh and Aishani looked at each other. This was such a reversal of roles in this world between Tejas and Uday. Thankfully, their powers were the same.

'I'll come back in the evening, hopefully with the relevant information,' Tejas said. As an afterthought, he stopped and asked, 'Is it possible for me to visit your world?'

'I don't see why not,' Aishani said carefully. 'But we are

not the deciding entities here. Guruji will be the best judge of that, but we will definitely put in a word for you to see our world.'

Tejas had to be content with that. After he left, Adheesh and Aishani sat down on the tree stump lying outside their cottage.

'You think Guruji will allow him to go to the other world?' Aishani asked Adheesh.

'It all depends on one's karma, baby, and destiny. We were destined to come here chasing the demons.'

'And the demons? How did they reach this world? This is literally expanding their hunting base to the power of n. What have they done to deserve this reward?'

'I don't know, Ash. Probably to realise the full potential of good, evil has to be there to show the way.' He added thoughtfully, 'We are warriors, baby, not thinkers. Let's leave all that to Guruji. We will lose our focus if we dwell too much on these philosophical matters.'

Aishani sighed, not really paying too much attention to Adheesh. 'I think it will be catastrophic if people start visiting parallel worlds. The criminals will hide in some world, the good people will keep on getting confused and there will be chaos everywhere.'

Adheesh nodded. 'You are right as usual.'

She took his hand in hers and they smiled at each other. 'Let's not waste our time, let's do something worthwhile.'

They spent their time in the cottage. As much as they wanted to explore this new Gurukul, they did not do so, for fear of their real identity being discovered.

Tejas returned in the evening. After the initial awkward pause, he began, 'These two merchants will come here after four days. Their names are Atapi and Vatapi. I wonder why they haven't changed their names. Probably they have become so emboldened because they haven't been caught in so many centuries.'

'And in the meantime, they have killed so many people and created mayhem without anybody being the wiser,' Adheesh said grimly, 'This Kaliyuga is the best time for them. They have shone in these times with their vilest deeds and cruelty. Humans too have become greedy. Their greed has grown to gigantic proportions. In this aspect they have become demons themselves.'

He looked at Aishani. Though she looked calm, he knew she was seething from inside. He checked himself. From past experience, he knew that in order to control Aishani and her righteousness, he had to be cool and collected himself. Her feelings knew no bounds when she was with him. It was as if she instinctively knew that he would be there to control her whenever she crossed the limit.

Four days later, they were at the banquet hosted by Atapi and Vatapi. The banquet was in full swing. This was a much awaited event. People vied for an invitation to this feast. Of course, the main attraction of the feast was that one could desire any food item and it would be produced. The more adventurous guests, who were a bit familiar with such banquets, brought their own exotic menus. Each and everything on these menus would be served. Many people came to witness the magic of the feast. One had to merely utter the rarest of the rare dish and it would be offered. The server would take their order and repeat it to Atapi and Vatapi, who were taking a personal interest in looking after their guests. It was almost like a carnival. Adheesh and Aishani were there too. Had they not known about the nefariousness of these two demons, they too would have been extremely impressed by their hospitality.

There was a huge vegetarian section and a smaller non-vegetarian section at the other end of the hall. Both Adheesh and Aishani were keeping a sharp eye on this corner. Tejas was alert on the vegetarian side. Adheesh had taken some food and was eating it. It was not their habit to eat before a task, but there had to be a semblance of being a normal erudite guest.

It was a huge venue with loud music and flashing neon lights everywhere. It was all jovial but there was an eerie feeling too. People had begun to dance. But the real star was the food. The tables were groaning under gourmet delicacies. Different kinds of kormas and biryanis lined the tables along with all sorts of pickles and chutneys. There were mountains of salads placed at regular intervals. The uniformed waiters moved soundlessly and efficiently, making sure that every glass and plate was full.

Despite such a fun-filled and magical atmosphere with happy guests, Adheesh and Aishani felt lonely. When your mission is different, the cheerfulness doesn't touch you, it leaves you high and dry and, in their case, angry too. There was so much of bonhomie in the air that the crowd seemed like one colossal happy behemoth.

Finally, they were able to penetrate the haze of sound and colour and see what was happening behind the dense curtain of high shrubs. Through the centuries the demons' culinary skills had reached the pinnacle of their cooking profession. Vatapi could transform himself into a delicious and succulent dish and was presented to the guest in a matter of seconds. Again, in a matter of seconds, Atapi with his Mritsanjeevni mantra would bring his brother back to life. The demon brothers were very particular that their victims would be only the most erudite Brahmins. Tonight, they had found two Brahmin scholars. One was from the Gurukul itself and one a pandit from outside the Gurukul. The Pandit from outside the Gurukul was lying on the ground with his guts blown away with the undigested food and intestines strewn around. It was a sickly, gory sight. The demon Atapi was chanting a mantra. After five minutes, he called out, 'Vatapi, come now my brother, you have collected our food.' Immediately the undigested parts of the food from the pandit's stomach gathered and turned into the demon Vatapi. This was very conveniently done behind the thick shrubs so that nobody could see what was happening.

Adheesh could not stop himself now. Seething with anger, he jumped in front of Atapi and slashed him with his khukhri. Though the khukhri was not a match for the demon's strength and power, still the element of surprise worked in his favour. These demons could not be killed with traditional weapons.

'God knows how many human beings both of you have killed tonight,' Adheesh said angrily.

'And we will kill you too today,' Atapi said with a loud laugh. It was a guttural laugh coming from his Adam's apple. Aishani could see it moving. He swung his fist and struck Adheesh on his chest. Adheesh staggered and fell back a bit.

Vatapi, who had come to life, also lunged towards Adheesh.

By now Aishani was ready with the Agneyastra. She closed her eyes and invoked the divine Astra. In an instant the weapon was in her hand. The huge fork with long and sharp prongs seemed to be forged from several metals and shone with a coppery glow. Aishani's anger had transferred into it, and it was burning bright. Small red and yellow flames were spurting out of it.

One look at the Agneyastra and the demons knew that their end was near. They had never seen the Agneyastra before, but a dim, blurry memory now came to the fore. These were the same memories that granted them the ability to change their forms. This same memory was responsible for the extreme hatred that they had towards Brahmins. This same consciousness told them that the divine Astra in front of them and the woman holding it was ringing their death knell and that there would be no escape.

Adheesh was watching the whole affair as if in a dream. He was slightly hurt by Atapi lunging at him. He knew the drill, but even he could not make out whose anger was stronger, Aishani's or the Astra's. The demons knew that they were going to die, and as is the case with any living being, the cunning duo did not wish to die. In the vast course of time, they had garnered some more outstanding tricks. They already had two boons. The third was to escape into a parallel world in times of danger.

With one swipe of her Astra, Aishani swiped at Vatapi who was near her. He burst into flames and turned into ash within seconds. Vatapi was caught unawares and paid for it, but Atapi had his wits fully around him. He ran to the opposite side with Aishani in hot pursuit. The thick shrubs hid them from any guests, who were anyway too far gone to notice these minor scuffles. Adheesh knew that Atapi was speeding towards the entrance to the parallel world. He almost heaved a sigh of relief. One gone, one to go. At least after this mess they'll be in their own world with their own people.

The Agneyastra seemed to have an impetus of its own. It had identified its victim. The Astra would rest only after destroying its target. Though Aishani was controlling it, it was also manipulating Aishani, giving her extra strength to run after Atapi. Adheesh too was running with her and covering her making sure that her path was clear from all sides and that no other demon was there to block her way. Now there was no other thought in Aishani's mind. She was totally focused on killing the demon. But the demon had done this exercise innumerable number of times. Here he was one up on Adheesh and Aishani. Most of their lives they had chased demons and killed them. Atapi could think even in these dire circumstances. He ran headlong through the door which led to Adheesh and Aishani's original world. Adheesh could now see the swastika on the entrance to their world. It had almost faded. He was grateful that Guruji had made the sign as now there were clusters of entrances in the same place. They all looked the same. Without the sign they might have made a mistake and entered the wrong portal. Aishani followed the demon with the Agneyastra in her hand, poised to strike him. She jumped through the portal at breakneck speed, with Adheesh jumping in after her.

The interval between Aishani jumping through the portal after the demon and Adheesh jumping after her must have been mere seconds, but when he crossed the entrance into his own world, Aishani and Atapi were nowhere in sight. Adheesh was worried but not too much. Both the demon and Aishani with the Agneyastra were running as fast as lightning. Adheesh was faster than both, but he had positioned himself behind Aishani so that he could protect her from any untoward menace. He knew that Aishani was perfectly capable of looking after herself. But now he had to fly in different directions to find them. Taking a quick decision, he decided to go towards the south first. He was so fast that he was almost flying. He searched for them within a radius of five kilometres but did not see them. He then flew towards the West with no luck. Slightly worried now, he went in the other two directions. Nothing. By now she must have killed the demon Atapi, he surmised. But if the demon was burnt by the Agneyastra, then where was Aishani. A thought came to him. She had kept the Agneyastra for a slightly longer time because they could not find the demons. Hence after disposing off the demon, she must be in a hurry to restore the Agneyastra to its proper place in the Gurukul's museum, where it would again become an artifact.

Adheesh rushed to Guruji's cottage. 'How beautiful,' he thought. And what a relief that Swami Sivananda was not there to greet him and grant him a time for an appointment with Guruji. He felt a rush of elation. Nothing like home to make you happy. Now, to take Ash and go home. The children were not there, but at least they would meet their own people. He stood outside Guruji's cottage and waited. He knew that

Guruji would sense his presence and call him inside.

Guruji beckoned him after five minutes. He went inside and touched Guruji's feet. What a satisfying feeling to sit on an aasan in front of Guruji, instead of on a chair. Guruji kept quiet and waited for Adheesh to speak and give him a report of their adventures. Adheesh began slowly, then picked up momentum and recounted their whole experience.

'Aishani must have come to the museum to return the Agneyastra to its place. This will take some time,' he said.

'Adheesh,' Guruji said softly. 'Aishani has not come here. I was just going to ask you where she is.'

Adheesh looked at Guruji stupefied. He was dazed.

'The last I saw; Aishani was chasing Atapi and both of them jumped through the portal into our world. I searched for her but couldn't find her. So, I thought she must have come here to return the Agneyastra.' The blood drained from his face. 'I'll take a few more people and go in search of her. She may have hurt herself in the process.' He got up to leave.

'Adheesh, wait,' Guruji said. Adheesh turned back questioningly. Every moment counted now.

'You have searched for her everywhere. Wait for a few more minutes. I am going to see where she is or in which direction.'

Guruji closed his eyes and went into a trance. Adheesh sat down. Guruji was right. He knew Guruji would find out where Aishani was. After that, it would be just a matter of minutes before they reached her. Reconciling himself with the thought, he waited, though fretfully. Normally Guruji would come out with the answers after about fifteen minutes of meditation. It was half an hour now. Adheesh was getting extremely worried now. This was very unlike Guruji. Adheesh began praying. He now knew that Aishani's disappearance was not natural. But where could she have gone. The Agneyastra was not conditioned to fail. It was fool proof, and it was a divine weapon. So where did Aishani go after killing the demon, Atapi. Impatiently he waited for Guruji to open his eyes.

After ages, it seemed to him, Guruji opened his eyes, though it was only half an hour. Adheesh looked at Guruji impatiently. Guruji looked at him seriously and said, 'Adheesh, Aishani is not here in this world.'

For a moment, the words did not register. Then when realisation dawned, he reeled under the impact of those words.

'Is she…,' he whispered hoarsely but could not articulate the words. They were not immortal. Their destiny was such that anything could happen anytime. They lived on a sword's edge. He froze.

'Adheesh, control yourself,' Guruji said, sternly. Then Guruji lowered his voice and said softly, that is as softly as Guruji could. In their line of work, there was no space for emotions. Emotions made a person weak and hesitant which resulted in defeat and death.

'No, Aishani is not dead,' Guruji said emphatically. 'She is just not in this world.'

By this time, Adheesh had composed himself. 'Did she go back to that alternate world? How did that happen? I was right behind her.'

'She did not go back to that alternate world. The demon Atapi, besides being cunning, had one more skill up his sleeve.

He obviously could jump to more than two worlds. The portals keep shifting in various directions. They are sometimes bunched up together and sometimes at a distance from each other. At that moment when Aishani was chasing Atapi, the doors were together in a sort of a cluster. He cunningly jumped into another portal with Aishani in hot pursuit. You had your wits about you, but even you were not aware that they had jumped through a different portal. Nor was Aishani.'

'What about the Agneyastra? Aishani was carrying it. Would it have functioned there in this third world?'

'The Agneyastra is a divine weapon. It will work everywhere, but it has to be returned here, in this world.'

'So how do we find Aishani, Guruji?' he asked desperately. He looked at Guruji.

'There is no one way to these portals. Like I explained to you earlier, they keep shifting their position, sometimes they are at a distance from each other and sometimes they almost overlap. These overlapping positions are the most confusing and risky. You don't know which world you have entered where most of the things are same but different too. Disorientation sets in and people become directionless. That is why it is so important to be grounded in your world.'

'Guruji, we have to get Aishani back,' Adheesh stated simply.

'Yes, we will bring her back, even if it means visiting more than one parallel world. We don't know which parallel world she is in.'

'I have to do it, Guruji. There is no alternative,' he said quietly.

Guruji nodded solemnly. 'Tomorrow I will call a meeting of our researchers. I am going to call researchers from other Gurukuls too. That may take a couple of days. You will, of course, be there for all the meetings.'

Adheesh nodded, touched Guruji's feet and slowly walked away.

Acknowledgements

There have been many people who have been directly or indirectly involved in the formation of this book. It is difficult for me to pinpoint.

My publisher Renu Kaul Verma who has been so instrumental in ensuring that my manuscripts become books. Without her continual support and vision, my books would not have seen the light of day. My editor Shailaja Nair, who not only is an excellent editor but now a good friend too. The hard working and sweet Alisha who worked on this book with great warmth, precision, and skill. Prateek, Somesh Kumar Mishra, Faiza, Saraswathi and the rest of team Vitasta. My humble thanks to each of you for helping me so much.

My sons, Saurabh and Sarvesh, along with their wives Shubhra and Deepika, who gave me loads of moral support. My grandchildren Aaroh, Myra and Avitraya, who know what their dadi is doing and who sometimes surprised me with their ideas. My husband and best friend, Arun who supported me every step of the way and without whose encouragement it would have been very difficult to write these books.

About The Author

Shubira is an avid follower of the Indian epics. She has always found a new and extra interpretation whenever she has reread the epics like the Ramayan, Mahabharata or Gita. She believes that we all have some demonic qualities in us which have to be crushed in order to bring out the best in us. She feels that mythological stories are true happenings which occurred such a long time ago that we are unable to substantiate them.

Shubira began her career as an educationist and has worked in educational institutions all over the country. She has a keen interest in the human psyche. She did her Honours in Psychology and then her masters in English literature. Along with being a teacher she is an astrologer too. She has been writing articles on astrology and social issues. She is married to an Air Force officer and now lives in the National Capital Region.

Prequels To The Book